W9-DFB-000

LITTLE,
BROWN

L B

LARGE
PRINT

HAVEN

A Novel

EMMA DONOGHUE

LITTLE, BROWN AND COMPANY

LARGE PRINT EDITION

Little, Brown and Company
Hachette Book Group
1290 Avenue of the Americas, New York, NY 10104
littlebrown.com

First Edition: August 2022

Little, Brown and Company is a division of Hachette Book Group, Inc. The Little, Brown name and logo are trademarks of Hachette Book Group, Inc.

The publisher is not responsible for websites (or their content) that are not owned by the publisher.

The Hachette Speakers Bureau provides a wide range of authors for speaking events. To find out more, go to hachettespeakersbureau.com or call (866) 376-6591.

ISBN 9780316413930 (hardcover) / 9780316445917 (large print)
LCCN 2021950803

Printing 1, 2022

LSC-C

Printed in the United States of America

For Anne Schuurman and Zoë Sinel

What, then, consoles us
in this human society full of calamities,
but the unfeigned faith and mutual love
of true and good friends?

—Augustine, *City of God*, AD 426

CONTENTS

HAVEN

MONASTERY

TRIAN'S STOMACH GROWLS. He's not twenty yet, still growing, and always hungry.

The first fast-day after Easter, and the hall is crammed with more than thirty monks and their Abbot, as well as the families who serve them and work the land. Even the Abbess is here, though not her nuns, who dine in their quarters at the other end of the double monastery. Also half a dozen strangers, come to Cluain Mhic Nóis to study with one of the celebrated teachers, or for a few months or weeks of respite from the grasping world.

The Abbot's led the congregation in saying grace in Latin, and is eating already. Trian gestures to his neighbour to help himself to roast swan and onions from their platter. Then Trian spoons what's left onto his own trencher. He makes himself chew slowly, and rations out his ale in sips. The rich meat's gone down all too soon, and then he lets himself eat half the round of three-day-old bread, saturated with savoury juice.

His red-faced neighbour downs another cup of ale, belches, and looks sideways at Trian's remaining bread.

Trian pushes it towards him. Sits still and tells himself that he's had enough, *Deo gratias*, thank God.

Chatter, argument, laughter; the hubbub of Gaelic rises and fills the hall like smoke. Out of the corner of his eye Trian catches a shape looming in the doorway: the stranger called Artt, who walks along the wall now, away from the Abbot's table, and lowers himself onto a bench at the back of the hall.

Trian's fascinated. This Artt has the bearing of a warrior king, but he behaves like a scrupulous monk working out a long penance. It's been a fortnight since Trian took the boat across the river to ferry this man over to the monastery, carried Artt's meagre possessions to the guest hut, washed his broad feet (cracked nails, a sign of hard travels), and brought him food, and Trian hasn't dared address a word to him yet.

Of course the monks have shared every scrap of information and hearsay. Scholar, priest, hermit, Artt is the most famous visitor to

Cluain Mhic Nóis in the six years Trian's been here, and possibly in the half century since its founding. From a clan of judges in the West, fostered out to a holy man at the age of seven—as soon as Artt knew more than his master, he sought out another, and another, but outshone them all. Now in his prime, familiar with many tongues, the sage is said to have read every book written, and has copied out dozens. Artt can work complex sums in his mind and chart the tracks of the stars. One of the band of solitaries who've been carrying the light of the Gospel from Ireland across a pagan-gripped continent, this soldier for Christ has converted whole tribes among the Picts, the Franks, even the Lombards.

Still, Artt looks to Trian as fresh as if he's just returned from the Land of Youth. Brown-haired, grey-eyed, the man is as brawny as some hero who can toss with one hand a boulder twice the size of his head. Artt's single blemish—the blackened stump of the little finger on his massive right hand—is rumoured to be a mark of God's favour: proof that he's done the impossible by surviving the plague.

Now Artt is sitting with his trencher dry in front of him, shaking his head no matter what he's offered. As Trian watches, Artt breaks off a piece of the bread and chews it. He ignores the ale flasks and fills his beaker with water.

At the top of the hall, a monk is speaking into the Abbot's right ear, their eyes on the honoured guest as the boy refills their cups with wine.

The Abbot smacks the table. When the noise quietens, he calls out, 'Brother Artt, are none of our dishes to your taste?'

Artt answers in his deep, melodious voice. 'Thank you, Father. I keep the fast.'

'As do we all, every week, to mark the day our Lord Christ was put to death.' The Abbot smiles stiffly at the heaped remains on his platter. 'Don't waterfowl count as fish, since they feed only on fish and weeds?'

Artt's sharply incised lips press together. 'By custom more than by logic.'

Too little air in this stifling hall. Trian feels sick, thinking of how greedily he gulped down his own portion of swan, and still longs for more.

The Abbot's flushed now. 'Will you take eggs or cheese, then?'

Artt sips his water while the whole community waits. 'No thank you.' The silence stretches. 'Nor butter, milk, nor whey. Whatever comes out of an animal is of the same nature as its flesh.'

The Abbot's jowly face shuts tight.

If one of Trian's brother monks said such a thing, it would be insubordination and earn a beating. But this Artt is a living saint, and can't be wrong, can he?

Then is the Abbot wrong about the rules of fasting?

But for Trian to judge his own master would be disobedience, so he'd better turn his thoughts aside this minute.

Maybe Artt's come among them to stir up their souls, he tells himself; to inspire them to live more cleanly.

The Abbot gestures almost violently to Cormac, a few places away from Trian: 'Entertain us, Brothers.'

The humped old monk is on his feet at once, lyre in hand, and nodding to the other musicians. Trian's already pulling his pipe out of the narrow bag that hangs from his belt. They all hasten around the tables into the middle of the hall, blocking the Abbot's view of his guest. They wait for Cormac to pick a tune—something familiar and cheerful—then hurry to find their unison.

Hours later, Artt lurches out of sleep. He finds himself on his feet, one hand pressed against the wattle wall. The other visitors are still snoring, but his heart is going so hard he feels he'll never sleep again. His dream, so close he can taste the salt on his lips.

He throws on his sheepskin cloak over his nightshirt. He remembers to get the little roll of painted linen out of his satchel before he leaves the hut.

Halfway between Nocturns and Vigil, Artt would say by the way the fat moon sits on the tips of the yews guarding the church. He turns the other way, seeking out the Abbot's quarters. It's the most handsome building after the church—all in wood, with a carved lintel. When Artt bangs on the door, a yawning servant comes to turn him away.

'I'm aware it's the middle of the night. Rouse your master.'

The groggy whimper of a child, several rooms back; a light voice, protesting. Artt steps to one side, for fear of laying eyes on the woman in her nightclothes. It's not strictly against the laws of the Church for an Abbot to have a wife—*Better to marry than burn in lust,* the apostle Paul conceded—but it disgusts Artt. Like most abbots, this one comes from the clan that gave these lands, so clearly his concern is to maintain his kin's grazing rights as much as to govern his monastery. Artt believes monks should be ruled by one committed to the way of Christ, who spends his days praying, fasting, and working, and his nights alone.

Wrapped up in furs, rubbing his swollen lids with a hand that's never done manual labour, the Abbot appears in the doorway, holding up a taper.

Artt cuts off the tetchy greeting. 'Father, I have had a dream.'

'Couldn't you tell me about it in the morning?'

'A vision,' he clarifies. 'An island in the sea. I saw myself there. As if I were a bird or an angel, looking down on the three of us.'

'Three?'

'I was with an old monk, and a young one.' The Abbot shows no sign of understanding him. 'The dream is an instruction to withdraw from the world. To set out on pilgrimage with two companions, find this island, and found a monastic retreat.'

The Abbot's mouth opens and shuts, a fish gasping. 'Artt, Brother—'

Through his teeth: 'I saw it. I was *there*.'

'On this, ah, island? Which is…where, do you believe?'

'Far away, in the western ocean. Away from everything.' Artt holds up the map in his hand,

and lets the linen unroll. The letters HIBERNIA float beside the jagged silhouette that resembles an oak leaf or a wolfskin.

The Abbot peers at it, bringing his flame close. 'Where's our abbey of Cluain Mhic Nóis?'

Is he ignorant, or are his eyes weak? 'Here, in the very middle of the country, halfway down the Sionan, our greatest river.' Artt points to the heartland. 'Our men of God who go into the wild places—since there are no deserts in our Hibernia, of course, many establish houses in forests or glens, or on lake islands.'

'Indeed, isn't Ireland a byword for such holy hermitages?'

His host's smug tone sticks in Artt's craw. Standing there swaddled in embroidered linen, reeking of Gaulish wine. How many times the Abbot must have recited Christ's call—*Sell all you have, give it to the poor and follow me*—without ever hearing it.

But Artt hasn't come here in the middle of the night to preach to the Abbot, only to get his permission. He pushes on. 'Those who hate the world most have to go even farther to escape its seductions, right out to sea.' He moves his finger to the right. 'See, in the waters between us and Albion? Blessed Nessán and Colm Cille each landed on his allotted rock there.'

The Abbot nods at the familiar names.

'Then this large island off our north coast,' touching a dot on the map, 'sainted Comgall's claimed that one for God. But it is in the great ocean on our western side that the water's most richly seeded with refuges.' Artt taps to the left of Hibernia with one nail. 'The blessed Ríoch discovered his here, for instance, and Macdara to the south of him. Farther south again, holy Éanna, Brecan, Senán and Caomhán—they set up their monasteries among the isles of Aran, like beacons on the frontier of Christendom, manned only by the best fighters, keeping the devil out by the power of prayer.' Artt's finger slides down that coast. 'For all my researches, I haven't yet learned of any monks south of there,' he admits. 'But there must be more islands that way. Empty ones, even less tainted by the world's breath. That's where I'm to go, with one old monk and one young one, and the message of my dream tonight is that I must waste no time.'

The plump lips purse. 'Three men—that's few, Brother. Twelve would be more usual, like the apostles. When holy Ciarán settled on the site of what would become this blessed foundation'—the Abbot gestures grandly at church, hall, library, scriptorium, dormitories, workshops, shelters for livestock—'he had eight with him.'

Stone-faced, Artt quotes the Lord: '*Where two or three gather in my name, I am there.*'

A small sigh. 'In your dream—did you recognise this pair of monks?'

He nods. 'The first was the hunched fellow with the dented head, who played the lyre tonight.' Artt's seen him all over Cluain Mhic Nóis, doing repairs, tending the plots, slow-moving but dogged.

The Abbot's mouth turns down in surprise. 'Cormac? He was a late convert. Nobody knows his years.'

'A pious man?'

'For all I know.'

But the Abbott should know; a master is supposed to look into the naked hearts of his men.

'He can certainly turn his hand to anything. I suppose he'd be useful to you.'

Artt wonders cynically if the Abbot will be less willing to spare him a monk with a life's worth of work left in him. 'Also the gangly, red-haired one, the piper.'

'Oh, Trian? He's a strange boy all right.'

In the guest hut, Artt has watched this Trian rush to meet needs before they're mentioned. Earnest-looking, not one of those messers with their shoves and jokes. A *ciotóg*, of course, an awkward left-hander; some call that trait the devil's mark, but Artt doesn't blame the young man for his misfortune. He noticed that Trian ate only half his trencher tonight, giving the rest to the fat fellow beside him. '*Strange how?*'

'Hard to say. Nothing bad,' the Abbot assures him. 'A bit of a daydreamer.'

But Artt has to trust his heaven-sent vision.

The Abbot puts his head on one side. 'For such an uncertain voyage, wouldn't you be better off choosing strong, seasoned men of middle years?'

His anxiety sounds genuine. But would he really be ready to give up such men? Besides, the decision is not Artt's. 'It's God who's chosen these two.'

'And if they refuse? I must tell you, I won't compel any of my sworn monks to leave.'

They won't refuse. Artt knows it in his bones.

As the monks in the church sing Vigil, later that night, Cormac sways. Vigil's the hardest of the six holy hours, for him; the rags of sleep cling to his legs, his tongue, his mind. He takes a big breath of the rich beeswax scent and straightens up.

His shoulder twitches; he glances down at the seam and picks out a louse. When Cormac first came to Cluain Mhic Nóis he found himself scratching all the time, and tried various preventives to keep the pests out of his bedding and clothes. Gradually he came to understand it as part of monastic life, like the bells. *God's messengers,* some of the brethren call the lice; once you make your peace with them, the bites hardly itch.

Cormac feels watched, somehow.

Across the golden pool of light from the candelabra, their famous guest has a hawk's gaze fixed on Cormac.

He drops his eyes. What awful error could he have made, to draw down on himself the attention of this extraordinary man? Maybe it's just his almost-bald, bockedy skull; strangers often stare. He buries himself in the prayer.

When Vigil's over, they all file out, yawning, under a sky still diamonded with stars. Cormac heads towards the cell he shares with just one other old-timer, looking forward to the luxury of his straw-and-chaff pallet, sheets and blanket and pillow, a few more hours of sleep before dawn.

A heavy hand grasps his shoulder. The holy man.

There's no doubt in Artt's bass, sonorous

tones, only authority, and an urgency that speeds Cormac's pulse. He begins as if taking up a previous conversation. 'In our country, Brother, lovers of Christ have been called not to the red martyrdom of violent death so many on the Continent of Europe have endured, but to the pale martyrdom of world-renouncing.'

Cormac nods helplessly. Why is the visitor preaching arcanely, to him alone, in the middle of the night?

'The fact is, Cluain Mhic Nóis has lost its way.'

He flinches, to hear that put so baldly.

Artt's wave takes in the starlit grounds all the way to the palisade that rings them. 'This monastery has sat on rich land so long, safe from starvation and raiders, that its brethren have lowered the shield of perpetual prayer. Greed has crept in, and laziness, and spite, and lust.'

Cormac can't deny a word of that. He's seen monks come to blows, and suspected some of fornicating with the women or each other. But the thing is, he has lived so many years that the varieties of human weakness have lost their power to shock him.

'Will you leave this place behind and come with me, Brother?'

The question makes Cormac stare.

'Sail to the west in search of a far haven where we can live purely,' Artt asks, 'working and giving glory to our Maker?'

Picked for such a mission, at Cormac's age?

Then again, he remembers, the most celebrated of travellers, holy Breandán, lived past ninety, and voyaged till the very end.

Cormac hasn't felt discontented at Cluain Mhic Nóis, only bored, on occasion. He's assumed this is the effect of a routine, undemanding life. Or of old age itself; a certain slackness in the rope. Suddenly to be invited to join a brave band venturing into unknown waters...He tries to speak, but finds his throat too dry.

Artt's voice goes deeper: 'What I must know is, are you strong enough in faith?'

He hasn't asked if Cormac wants this. More a command, then, like that of Jesus to the fishermen: *Come, follow me.*

Cormac swallows. It doesn't occur to him to refuse. 'I think so.' Then, more firmly: 'I believe so. I'm tough old meat.'

A rare smile lights Artt's face like the moon through cloud.

Excitement prickles in Cormac's soles.

'Your Abbot tells me you were baptised only fifteen years back.'

He nods, sheepish; he was a wizened apple

among the harvest offerings. 'Before that I worked our kin's land.' He gives himself a moment to find the words. 'I had a wife and three children by her. The next time the plague came, I lost them all.' He glimpses the tangle of those small limbs, creamy skin spotted blue-black. Their daughter had just taken her first steps.

'But you survived.'

'It so happened the infection never touched me.' After that he hung around as an uncle to his brothers' children, a ghost at the feast.

'Don't credit happenstance,' Artt rebukes him. 'God in his wisdom saw fit to spare you, so you could come to Christ.'

'That happened only many years later,' Cormac admits, 'and by accident.'

One thick eyebrow jumps.

Cormac's fingers go up to the little crater above his left ear. 'A slingstone stove my head in.'

'In battle?'

That seems too grand a word for it. 'Well, we were disputing with another clan. The blow sent me out of my senses. But my brother's wife had heard the Christians had strong medicine'—he almost said *magic*—'so my people brought me to Cluain Mhic Nóis. A monk called Fiach, he saved me.' Gone now, along with most of the folk Cormac's ever known, all his elders and many far younger.

'How?' Artt asks.

'Cut the scalp and peeled me like an apple. With a hand drill he bored holes until the smashed piece came right off. Then he sewed the skin back over the hole, and poulticed me with herbs, and prayed till my fever broke.'

'You were quite well again?'

'Better than before, in fact, *Deo gratias*.' Cormac makes a cross on his forehead. 'Wits a bit sharper and memory roomier.'

'See what the Lord can accomplish? *I was a stone lying in the deep mud,*' Artt intones, '*and he who is mighty came and in his mercy lifted me up.*'

Cormac nods. 'I told this Fiach I owed him my life, but he said he was Christ's bondman, so now I too belonged to Christ. I was baptised and taught to read, and took vows.' He remembers sending word to his kin to divide up his fields and cattle.

'You were preserved so you could join my pilgrimage,' Artt insists.

Might all that's happened to Cormac have been leading to this? 'May I ask...why would you want me?' He glances down at his gnarled knuckles, the pearl swellings around his fingernails. 'I had skills and powers in my prime, but these days—'

Artt cuts him off. 'I care nothing for your skills or powers.'

Cormac looks away, embarrassed.

'God put you in my dream.'

That disconcerts him. 'And how many of us do you mean to bring?'

'Two.'

It hits Cormac then, the full honour of it. In the twilight of his days, he has heard the call to arms; his Lord has need of him.

The rising sun's sharp in Trian's eyes as he stands outside the hut he shares with three other young monks. He's still in his nightshirt; the knock at the door has roused them early. Pulse pounding, so he can hardly make out the holy man's words. 'I was...in your dream?'

Artt nods, impatient. 'Ours will be a sacred wandering.'

A chance for Trian to trade his mundane existence for an adventure, like a heroic deed out of a song.

'Then, once we find the island,' Artt warns, 'it will be a hard life.'

'That'll suit me,' Trian manages to get out.

Artt squeezes his shoulder till it almost hurts. 'A small brotherhood—you and I and Brother Cormac—but mighty in faith.'

Cormac? Trian's startled only because of the monk's age. They've played music together for years, rarely exchanging a word. Cormac is a fount of lore, of course, and skilled at gardening and building, whereas Trian is unaware of possessing any special talents. Ungainly and odd, and he knows it; knowing doesn't help it.

'Did you grow up on the river?' Artt asks.

'At the sea'—he gestures east—'many days from here.'

'You've no family, I understand.'

'My parents gave me to Cluain Mhic Nóis when I was thirteen.'

'In payment of a debt?'

Trian shrugs; no one ever said so.

'Jesus told his followers to hate their own fathers and mothers, wives and children,' Artt remarks. 'You are already free and clear of those ties.'

Trian frowns, trying to call up the faces of his father, mother, brothers, sisters. Need he go so far as to hate them, since he's almost forgotten them? There was a time he did miss them sorely, but over six years they've receded to the far back of his mind. He imagines it is the same for them. He tries to remember the words his mother said at the gate, before handing him over. 'They thought I'd be safe here. *My soul,* I suppose they meant.'

Artt puffs his breath. 'A safety of the body only. This place is riddled with sin, as a book with worm tunnels.'

Trian looks down, mortified.

'I've caught a whiff of the same rot in even more-celebrated abbeys,' Artt tells him. 'Monkish life is one long war against the devil. And when dozens of men live together... well, where better for wolves to hide than in a great flock of sheep?'

Trian broods over the times he's seen the rules broken but turned a blind eye. He's never felt it his place to cast blame; just kept his head down and worked harder.

'Well, I mean to pull you out of this mire,' Artt says. 'A couple of brethren, that's all the fellowship a man needs. Besides, three is the most sacred number.' Putting his thumb to the third finger of his left hand so the other three are left standing: Father, Son, and Holy Spirit, threefold God.

Trian stares at the dark stub on Artt's other hand, living proof that this man can survive all trials. A confessional impulse opens his throat.

'Thank you. A thousand thanks. But I must warn you, I am not worthy.'

Those bright grey eyes narrow. 'Brother, which of us is *worthy*? We all stink of sin.'

Trian blinks.

'What matters is, we three have been chosen.'

Four days later, on a cloudy spring morning, Artt carries an ironbound wooden chest down to the riverbank where the narrow boat waits.

Curled up at bow and stern, this craft—the larger of the monastery's two—is the length of two men. Like a frail tent inverted in the water, it strikes him; nothing more solid than a dozen oxhides bark-tanned, puzzled together over an ash-wood skeleton and pulled drum-tight with leather thongs. The vessel has been freshly curried with wool grease to keep out the water, the joins pasted with pine pitch one last time. Artt takes it as a sign that the single mast in its socket and the flat yard with its sail furled make the shape of the cross on which Jesus was nailed. *Christus,* he murmurs silently, *Christus, Christus.*

Their cowled, unbleached robes hitched up to their knees, Cormac and Trian are packing the boat. Artt takes off his shoes and wades into the cool water to help. He glimpses the whole party as if from a vertiginous height. Himself, brown hair still unsilvered; one bent man with only strings of grey hair; one bony redhead. Beards freshly cropped; long hair tied back at the nape and tonsured at the crown in a triangle (strongest of forms, sign of the Holy Trinity).

Right where the mast meets the hull sits the grooved anchor stone, wrapped about with thorny branches for added traction and attached to the gunnel by coils of nettle rope. Beside it the old monk and the young one are putting the heaviest things: three yew buckets; a stack of earthenware crocks set into an iron cooking pot; a wicker creel crammed with griddle, tripod and hook, chisels and hammers. But the grassy bank is still covered in baggage.

'Brothers,' Artt objects, 'if we bring all this, we'll founder at the first hard wind.' *And deserve it, for their greed.* 'We don't need half of it. Here, let's start by putting the holy chest in the very middle.' He makes room and sets it against the base of the mast. 'It holds all I'll require to celebrate Mass, as well as two codices—my own work—with supplies to make more.'

The figure stuns them: two whole books, out of the dozen or so that hang in satchels on the library's pegs. 'The Abbot has been generous,' Cormac murmurs.

Artt juts out his chin. 'Ah, but when we set up our outpost of prayer in the ocean, the copies we produce will increase the honour of this monastery and the whole Church, as saplings glorify the tree from which their seeds blew.' He passes Trian a tiny leather flask. 'Holy water, blessed by the Pope in Rome—this will guard our boat from danger.'

Trian kisses it and tucks it under the bow.

Artt scans the litter of goods. 'Now, what's that great roll?'

'Hides for mending the hull if it were to get holed,' Cormac says.

'One will do, surely?'

Trian hesitates. 'In case of spreading rot . . .'

'Hold on, here's more.' Artt points at another roll.

'That's our spare sail, in case the wind were to rip the first.'

'Then we'll bring the spare instead of the three hides,' Artt decides, 'and cut patches from its edge if needed. If our hull moulders *and* our sail tears, it'll be a sign to halt our journey and settle there.'

Without a word, Trian heaves the other skins back onto the bank.

Artt unrolls the spare sail and folds it into a great square to lay flat over the laths at the bow end. Behind the mast he stacks charcoal, candles, oats, and wheat flour for Communion bread, all in linen sacks waxed to keep out water. 'Now, absolute necessities only.'

'Food for the journey, and water.' Trian holds up a basket and three goatskin flasks.

'Seeds and herbs.' Cormac shows a small wooden box.

'Of course. But what can we do without?'

The old man discards their whetstones, and also the scrapers for defleshing skins, as the monks can fashion stones as they go. But he argues for a spade (ash, tipped with iron) and a mason's dividers and L-shaped square.

Artt throws a crowbar back onto the bank. Cormac points out that if they lever rocks with the spade, it could crack in two. Artt can't know what conditions they'll face on their island, so he allows the crowbar. But he says no to the rest of the ironmongery: billhook for brush-clearing, pitchfork, trowel, spring shears. He tosses half a dozen pegs back, then decides they may be needed for attaching pulleys for heavy lifting, and wades around to pick them up again. He rejects a fishing spear—*can't the monks sharpen branches, as required?*—but allows nets.

'We could leave this big axe,' Trian offers.

Cormac grimaces. 'For felling trees, though—'

'Won't the small hatchet do us?'

True, if the arm's strong enough and works long enough. Artt nods approval. He challenges the older monk: 'Brother Cormac, what else?'

Cormac squints around. 'We could share one spare set of clothes, maybe—not likely we'll all get soiled or soaked at the same time?'

'Excellent.' Artt casts the other robes and shoes onto the bank.

Similarly, he decides that one set of fire-starting gear will do.

'The blankets?' Trian suggests. 'Our cloaks could serve to cover us.'

'That's the spirit.'

The young monk is jettisoning items as if they burn his fingers now: a flask of whey, a skin of ale, three leather mugs, a chopping board.

Artt finds a jar of honey to put back, and another of pickled cabbage. But the pile around the mast still seems too high. 'What's in this bag?'

'My lyre.' Cormac corrects himself, 'I mean, the Abbot's entrusted it to me.'

Artt weighs up the matter. 'I'm not one of those zealots who believes the sound of instruments to be sensual or barbaric. But what I would say is, we'll need nothing but our own mouths to make music. Plainchant is so pure, it flies directly to God's ears.'

He notices Trian bite his lip, and readies for the first hint of insubordination. But no, the young man's stepping over to lay a slim pipe with the other discards.

Here comes the Abbot in his vestments of white striped vertically with purple, flanked by his favourite advisers. With every second step he leans on a crozier with a hook of riddled ivory—more like a king's mace, it strikes Artt, than the humble crook of a shepherd of souls.

Artt steps up onto the bank with the two monks behind him. He guesses the Abbot's relieved at the prospect of seeing the back of this troublesome guest, for all it's costing the monastery.

'Still barely half-packed, I see,' the Abbot calls.

'No, it's done. The rest you may take back, with my thanks.'

He's gratified by the Abbot's surprise.

'Your austerity puts us to shame.' Doubtfully: 'You're still fixed in your purpose?'

'Quite fixed.'

'And you, Brothers?'

Artt's eyes move between the two monks, who nod.

'There can be no turning back,' the Abbot warns them.

Is that true concern for their welfare, Artt wonders? *Or does this man not understand that no one turns back from a sacred mission?*

'Amen,' Cormac says gruffly.

'Amen,' Trian echoes.

'Well, then. I release you from your vows.'

Despite his muddy feet and his wet-edged robe, Artt matches the Abbot's formality: 'Brothers, will you now pledge yourselves to me?'

The two drop to their knees on the soft ground, Cormac more heavily.

'For the second time in your lives, do you vow poverty?'

They say it in unison: 'I vow, Father.'

'Again, do you vow chastity?'

'I vow.'

'And will you swear fealty and obedience to me?'

'I vow.'

The men sound out that new promise with as much conviction as the familiar ones, even though five days ago Artt hadn't yet spoken to either. He lifts them up. He kisses the

old monk's whiskery mouth, the youth's soft
one.

'Monks should be steady as rock, and humble
as slaves,' the Abbot intones sanctimoniously.
'Cleave to your new Superior, your Father and
soul-friend, your Abbot for the rest of your
days.'

Artt finds he balks at the title of *Abbot;* it
smacks of land-deeds, somehow, fur robes and
roast swan. 'I believe I'll be their *Prior* instead.
First among equals.'

Cormac and Trian exchange an uncertain
glance. The younger asks, 'May we call you
Father, though?'

An odd shiver of delight. 'Of course.'

'Thank you, Father.'

'Thank you, Father.'

It's the first time Artt's ever been addressed
that way.

Other monks have trickled down to the
Sionan now, in ones and twos. He notices
some fond smiles and bows of farewell. Cormac's embracing many of the monks. 'Brother
Conall, Brother Lugaid! Brother Ercc, would
you give me your blessing?' Several of them
are weeping to see him go. Trian hangs back,
but does bow to several.

Among this crowd, Artt supposes some must
be gripped by envy, wondering what can have

marked out the concave-skulled ancient and the gawky youth as fit candidates for such an honour. Others may be weighed down by a purer longing to join in this pilgrimage. Abler men than Trian and Cormac, for all Artt knows, better men perhaps; why didn't any of them appear in his dream?

But he must trust what was shown to him. *The last will be first,* he tells himself. *Blessed are the humble, for theirs is the kingdom of heaven.* It is too late for doubts now, and besides, three is the holiest number, even were there room for a fourth in the crammed boat.

A beam of sun spears through the clouds; several monks murmur and remark on that as a sign of divine favour.

The Abbot leans on his crozier. Waiting for further thanks? True, the man has surrendered some of his most valuable goods, as well as two monks. But it's God who has asked it, after all; God who's given a flawed leader a chance to back this holiest of ventures, and (as the Gospel puts it) *lay up treasure for himself in heaven that no moths or rust can eat.* So all Artt says is, 'Ready.'

The three take up their walking staffs—those of the monks plain blackthorns, simply curved at the top, Artt's topped with a T-shaped bronze cross.

'Well, go in peace.' The Abbot sighs the words.

(Is that worry in his voice, Artt wonders? *Or envy?)*

'Bring glory to our Mother Church.' Raising his crozier, the Abbot dedicates the boat, the journey, and the men to Christ. Behind him, dozens of voices rise in a psalm.

Artt steps down into the water and over the side of the hull, Cormac after him. Trian gives the boat a great shove off the bank before he gets in.

RIVER

HOURS LATER, CORMAC kneels facing backwards, gripping a narrow oar. Even with their reduced load, the shallow craft is so weighed down that its sides rise only a foot above the water.

Cormac's heard of boat sickness, but never knew it could rack a man so fast and so hard, like a malign spell cast by the motion of the river. The reek of wool grease and pine pitch isn't helping. Reaching dizzily for the nearest goatskin, Cormac takes a sip of water, then drives the wooden stopper back in with the heel of his hand. He rows on, his knees numb where they press on the slats. He swallows hard, breathes through his nose. But his throat emits small noises in spite of himself, and twice he has to thrust his head over the side to spew up his breakfast. Each time he begs pardon of his brethren.

On the other side of the bow, Trian's pivoting his oar with much more precision and power than Cormac. Of course, the young monk's well used to taking this boat up and down the Sionan, trading for the monastery. From the small bench in the stern, Artt—no, Cormac reminds himself, their *Prior* now—commands the steering oar, staring past his monks at what lies ahead. The slow but steady current is doing much of the work, sliding them south.

But how long will it take to get down the river to its mouth? Then how long at sea? How many days of this racking nausea?

The third time, when Cormac gags, all that comes out is a string of silver, as delicate as a spider's web.

'Should you lie down, maybe, Brother, and shut your eyes?' Trian suggests.

Through clamped teeth: 'I'll be all right.'

The Prior rises to his feet, and the boat wobbles. 'I've seen stronger men laid low for days, Brother. You're no good to us like this. Give me your oar.'

Cormac swallows sour humiliation.

Great frame bent low, the Prior steps around the sacks, making sure to stay on the laths so his feet won't hole the boat's hide.

Cormac ships his oar, and ducks out of the way.

'Sit in the middle, now,' the Prior orders.

So he hauls up his robe till it billows above his roped waist, and clambers past the stools, the creel, the cauldron full of crocks. He huddles on the piled dry goods, digging his fingers into the waxy sackcloth. He crosses his legs under him and leans leadenly against the mast.

To distract himself, he watches Trian's propelling strokes piercing the water in the shadow of the hull. Under the faint red beard, Cormac can still see the pimpled boy. Limbs too long for his body, spindly as willows; elbows and knees given to bending too far back.

Now that the Prior's taken up Cormac's oar and the boat's speeding along, no one is in the stern to steer her. Sick or not, Cormac should at least keep an eye out for hazards—mudbanks, logs, whirlpools, rocks, or rapids. If the boat were to capsize, they'd all drown. Also Cormac really should be scanning the banks for hostiles. He's lived behind the stockade of Cluain Mhic Nóis for so long, he's forgotten what it's like to roam through strange territory.

He squints hard at the water ahead, then at the land on both sides. But he's realising on this journey that his sight's not what it used to be. Mostly he sees gorse, to north and south, vast sheets of the prickly stuff blooming butter-yellow already. The occasional silhouette of a farm defended by a round ditch and fence or blackthorn hedge. A blur in the distance must be a man with an ox ploughing criss-cross, dragging a wooden spike to break up the winter-clogged soil; Cormac remembers doing that, how his forearms shook from the strain.

After a while, another fellow, riding, and leading one—no, two—packhorses. Cormac's never been on a horse. He imagines how lofty it might feel, and precarious. He wonders whether it's harder for a wellborn man such as the Prior to vow poverty; how rough a woollen robe must feel to smooth fingers. But their new master seems zealous for all hardships, as if dearth is sweet to him.

Jaw clenched, Cormac can't stop himself from retching again. Nothing comes.

'Try fixing your gaze on the horizon, Brother,' Trian offers under his breath.

The Prior's voice booms: 'Have you always had this weakness?'

'I...have never been in a boat,' Cormac admits.

Trian gapes at that. 'But you've lived so long. Been to battle, even, I heard.'

'I walked, that time,' Cormac tells him wryly, 'and got a javelin through me, so my kin had to bring me home on an oxcart.' Touching his waist, where his skin bears two puckers still. Beside him on the cart, in a tangle of guts, his third brother had died sometime along the way. That's twice Cormac's life should by rights have ended: the slingstone above his ear and the javelin in his side. Three times, if he counts the plague that took his wife and children.

The Prior tips his face back to reckon the dazzling point of white in the clouds. 'Noon.'

Time to recite the holy hour of Sext.

The Prior lifts his oar into the boat and lays it down. On the other side Trian does the same, and jerks his head from side to side to relieve the muscles of his neck with loud creaks.

Cormac realises the Prior doesn't intend to moor; drifting south on the current, this trembling vessel is their chapel now. Though he longs to get off it and be still, even for half an hour, he says nothing.

The Prior unbuckles the pouch on his belt and takes out a quadrangular bell by its loop, making its bronze-coated iron plates ring to ward off bad spirits. He rears to his feet in priest's pose, elbows by his sides and hands turned up. Trian follows, and then Cormac, staggering. The boat tilts, rights again. Cormac swallows hard, commanding himself not to spew during prayers.

The Prior switches from Gaelic to Latin

for the plainchant: *'Morning and noon and evening I pray and cry aloud—'*

Cormac joins in, and Trian after him, repeating the clear line of melody. *'—and God will hear my voice.'*

The Prior leads them in the three psalms. Having been a storyteller, Cormac didn't find it too hard to commit the whole Psalter to memory once he became a monk. Whereas Trian, even after his six years of training, still stumbles over words and loses track of the phrases. The young man's not stupid, Cormac knows, just shy, with a wandering air at times.

At the top of each psalm they genuflect by going down on the right knee, which makes the boat lurch and Cormac's stomach heave. When they've finished the service, they kneel again and murmur in Latin, *'God save me.'*

Trian digs out the holy chest and passes it over to the Prior. Of the two volumes inside, their master selects the Old Testament, drawing a small cross on its wooden cover and bending to kiss it. He reads aloud a passage from the Book of Isaiah. Since neither Cormac nor Trian knows more than a little Greek, afterwards he puts it into Gaelic for them.

God's word in their mouths, then their ears, then their hearts, that's the order; every holy hour of the day ends with quiet contemplation.

Cormac sits very still, pressing his chapped lips together and locking his throat. He prays to God to mend his stomach.

Afterwards, as they float on, Trian doles out food from the basket. Cormac makes his best effort, chewing on a piece of oatcake, and taking tiny bites of a slice of dried pork. He still has his teeth, even if they are worn short.

'Any better, Brother Cormac?'

'It'll pass, Father,' he says. 'I'm sorry for being a hindrance on this journey.'

The Prior shrugs grandly. 'Between the helplessness of the cradle and that of the deathbed, hasn't every man his times of frailty?'

Cormac nods gratefully, though the motion brings up another sour wash in his throat.

'The old may be weak, but the young are ignorant.' Trian quotes the proverb in such a stern tone that the older men both burst out laughing.

The river is more easily navigable than Trian expected. In places it's under two feet deep, but the boat's draft is even less, so with a push of the oar in the mud she slips on by. The heart-shaped leaves of aspens rattle, giving off a sweetness that makes him snuff the air with pleasure. Downy birch and willow are woven thick on both banks in the first haze of Eastertide green. Tall alders dangle reddish catkins against glossy ovals that have only just opened.

When evening draws in, the Prior directs them to moor under a spreading oak tree. Trian takes off his shoes to spare them a wetting. Robe bunched in his fist, he jumps off the hull and wades to the muddy bank, hauling the boat like a stubborn cow. Once he's tied her up—the rope hitched around a half-submerged willow—his elders climb out, though they still get wet to their shins. Cormac helps Trian pull her up a few yards more until she's well wedged in the rushes.

The Prior presses his right thumb and first two fingers together to stand for the Holy Trinity, and makes the sign of the cross over the place to banish any evil, calling out, 'In the name of Jesus!'

The men all stretch their arms and roll their shoulders to ease them. Trian and Cormac already have leathery palms from working with oars and spades, but the Prior's are swollen and blistered—not that he says a word of complaint.

Trian tops up the waterskins in the river

before he fills their wooden bowls with pork and cheese. Cormac, still green in the face, barely touches it. Trian eats fast, then waits for the food to reach his belly and give him that lovely feeling, not of fullness, exactly, but at least the lulling of his savage hunger.

Cormac brushes off the crumbs. 'Where's your home, Father, may I ask?'

'I have none.'

That throws the old monk. 'I only meant—'

'I was born in the West,' the Prior concedes.

'And your people?'

Learned judges going back generations, Trian's heard.

The Prior's mouth twists. 'They hoped I'd make an archbishop, for the clan's advancement. It's been a long time since that word *home* has held any earthly meaning for me, Brothers. I am an exile for God, and I love nothing here below.'

Trian has never met anyone like this. Where others speculate, the Prior knows; when others merely say, he does. Somehow he's cut himself free of the ropes that keep lesser men bound to the world.

After the Prior leads them in reciting Nocturns, they roll themselves up in their sheepskin cloaks. Trian finds he's not missing his old hut at all, with the three other young monks always chattering, the stink of feet.

'A spell cast over the senses,' the Prior murmurs.

Trian tries to puzzle that out. 'What is, Father?'

'Sleep.'

'A necessary evil though, no?' Cormac asks out of the dark.

'Unfortunately so. Really we should succumb only when we're dropping with exhaustion, and break our sleep to pray at least once every night, and get up early, still a little weary.'

'Amen,' Trian makes himself say. He's an awful gorger of sleep, but he still hopes to grow out of that. Right now he finds himself wary of dropping off, in case the three of them won't manage to wake for Vigil without the bells of the night watch.

But hours later, when the Prior's big voice rouses him, Trian realises that their new master always knows the time, even in his sleep. Or maybe—he wonders as they settle back on the ground after their psalms and brief prayers—a man this holy never closes his eyes, but lies all night interceding for the weaker souls on either side of him. Still brooding over that, Trian plummets back into the dark.

In the morning, they row for hours. When

they stop to eat, Trian notices Cormac's managing his apple and oatcake. 'You've a better colour today, Brother.'

Cormac produces a smile. 'I suppose I must be getting used to the motion.'

'It's a matter of humility,' the Prior tells him. 'Once your senses stop fighting and accept the constant bobbing, your suffering lessens.'

Trian frowns. He's been taught that suffering is good, since it lets you enter a little into the agonies of Jesus on the cross. But so is humility; a monk should be *humble as a slave*. If humility happens to lessen your suffering, is that allowed, so long as that wasn't your aim? Trian's head wasn't meant for wrestling with such abstractions.

The boat glides past a few river islands today, occasionally even a peopled one. 'This sea island we're seeking, Father,' Trian ventures to ask, 'it will be quite empty?'

'More than that: untouched.' The Prior jerks his head with scorn at the huts they've just passed. 'If an island's ever been settled, that means it's too fertile for us. No, our gleaming rock will be set apart from men and all their wiles. Bleak and harsh—a desert place in the ocean.'

All Trian knows is the coastal farmstead where a dozen of his people scraped a living by fishing and birding, and then the crowded monastery. He tries to picture this sea island; to smell the cleanness of it.

Gradually the Sionan opens out into a long lake the Prior calls Loch Deirgeirt. They pass a fragment of land with a small wooden rect-angular structure that Trian recognises as a church, and a cluster of round wattle huts sending up trickles of smoke. He half-expects the Prior to moor here and speak with what-ever saint's claimed the lake island for God. But no. And after all, they're in search of solitude; Trian supposes they will be stopping only when they need to trade.

So the laden boat floats on down the end-less water. On low green slopes, far off, black cows and brown sheep with curly horns look to Trian to be the size of flies.

That evening they rest on a hummock of dry bank fringed with marsh. A great thumb of stone has the name of this territory's chieftain notched in ogham script down one side. Or its onetime chieftain, rather, given how thick a coat of moss has grown on the stone. Trian wonders why men vie to amass possessions, when they can't even hold onto their own skin for longer than God allots.

He watches the green glistening head of a mallard parting the reeds, drab brown mate behind. A white-masked coot cuts between the ducks, leaving a rippled line in his wake. Why are all other creatures born knowing how to swim, whereas most human beings sink like stones? So few men trust the water enough to learn how to lie flat and stay afloat, but Trian—he knows this is one of his oddities—doesn't remember a time when he couldn't.

A pair of silent swans glide around the bend, their white shine catching the last of the setting sun, their beaks orange rimmed with black. One dips and comes up bearded with weed. The other arches and spreads gleaming frilled wings. Five grey cygnets chirp along in their wake. Trian remembers the rich, lingering taste of swan meat. He thinks of the swans in the legend who were king's children under a spell, imprisoned in feathers. He would not much mind being a bird, himself. This family pays the boat no attention, he notices. Do they mistake her for a hulking dead tree caught on the bank?

On the third day, Artt takes a turn at rowing and sets a faster pace; he can't bear how long it's taking to get to the western sea. Lake narrows into river again, the stretch known as the Luimneach—the last before the estuary.

He watches herdsmen, tiny at this distance, moving their flocks upland for spring pasture. He thinks of something to tell Trian. 'Pádraig, the holiest of our saints—he who was the very first to bring the Gospel from Albion to Hibernia—when he was young, he minded sheep and pigs.'

'Captured by pirates as a boy, and made a slave, so they say,' Cormac adds in his storytelling voice. 'Six years Pádraig endured herding on the hills, but the rain and the frost did him no bit of harm.'

'*Ora et labora*,' Artt rhymes. 'Work and pray. Young Pádraig recited a hundred psalms a day and the same number at night, and the love of God was a fire inside him. His prayers revealed to him at last that his shackles were made not of iron but of sin—something every true Christian must learn.' He can almost feel the metal chafing; he rubs his wrists. 'It was through solitary meditation in the wild that Pádraig won that wisdom. As Jesus told his apostles, *Come away to a quiet, remote place.* That's what we're looking for, Brothers: our own lonely hill.'

Both monks nod and say Amen.

But Artt wonders whether the brethren truly grasp the nature of their quest or are only paying lip service. That's the problem with a vow of obedience; it tends to make sheep of men. He'd almost rather monks with the fiery natures of wolves, who've harnessed their forces to follow him in all things.

Around a bend, the Sionan splits now and a fortified island looms in the middle of the water; an earthen circle topped with a palisade, lines of smoke rising. Fisherfolk, Artt guesses. Huts, but nothing that looks like a chapel. This could be one of those pagan holdouts where they still brew potions and cast charms. He mutters a prayer in Latin: *'Against the spells of druids and blacksmiths and women, I summon your aid.'*

Artt thrusts the steering oar straight down, then braces it against his torso and rotates it, slowly angling the boat into the wider west channel, as far from the island as possible. His monks don't need to be told. Trian seems more excited than afraid; he gouges the water with his oar to hurry the boat on.

Close to, the riverbank is webbed together by fibrous roots. Alder doesn't rot even in water, Artt finds himself remembering; it makes the hardest shields and the sharpest spears. Not that his party is carrying any shields or spears, only the small iron knives in their belts. They're men of God, after all. They come in peace, though that doesn't mean they'll find it. Artt rows faster. The boat rocks. What if the monks capsize their heavy craft and go down with her?

Cormac mutters a protection: *'Gabriel, be my breastplate. Michael—'*

'Be my belt,' Trian intones.

'Raphael, be my shield.'

Artt glimpses no faces through the island's blank palisade; no movement. Is the boat more than a spear's throw from the line of stakes? He pictures the three of them through enemy eyes. The triangular tonsure marks them out as monks, as does the wooden four-armed Greek cross on a thong around each neck. Are these marks likely to help or hurt their chances, if they're captured? Their vessel and all its goods seized, the holy chest cracked open and its treasures ripped out, the monks kept chained for labour here, or sold on?

Artt berates himself for his scuttling thoughts. He prays, like Jesus to his Heavenly Father when the soldiers were coming, *Not my will be done, but yours.*

A whizz, a splash.

Another.

Someone behind the fence whirling a sling,

shooting stones at them. More than one at-
tacker?

Cormac huddles down, clutching his skull.

Panic, a pebble in Artt's throat. He swallows
it down and steers even more sharply away
from the island, almost driving the boat into
the rushes on the bank. His monks stab the
water. 'Are you hit, Brother Cormac?'

'I'm not,' the old man gasps.

And now they're out of range of danger, gliding fast and beautifully. This broad channel
joins up with the narrow one again. The whole
skirmish has lasted no more than a couple of
minutes. The river widens, stretching its greedy
mouth, as the fortified island diminishes in the
distance.

Cormac keeps his head down, ashamed.

Trian's panting a little, exhilarated.

'See?' Artt demands. 'Fear nothing. We travel
under God's protection.'

Sun reddens in the west. Cormac's knees are
raw and his shoulders ache, but he's still dizzy
with relief that they weren't caught, or even
injured. His hand keeps going up to his misshapen scalp to marvel that it's intact. Also,

his stomach's quite sound now, for which he thanks the Lord too. To travel is to turn the pages of the great book of life.

The bank is interrupted by a silty creek, where water thrashes behind a weir of woven willow. Cormac's suddenly ravenous for something fresh. 'Fish, Father?'

Trian frets under his breath: 'Unless that would be thieving.'

The Prior shrugs. 'As no one's come to pull them out of the river yet, they still belong to their Maker, and the riches of creation are for all to share.'

He steers them to the right, and the others work their oars to bring the boat to a standstill. Pinned, she resists the current.

Cormac rummages around for the hand net and passes it to Trian. The young monk leans overboard to dip it into the busy water behind the weir, and brings up a salmon right away. Stuck to its flank, a long silvery lamprey has already gnawed a red hole. He stuns the pair against the gunnel. Cormac watches with interest as Trian inserts and jiggles his knife behind the salmon's eye, then dispatches the lamprey the same way. He stabs each fish in one gill to bleed it, cuts off the fins, slits it from jaw to vent, and pulls out the guts to drop in the water. Then he sets down the gutted fish and rinses his bloody hands over the side.

Cormac can see that the *ciotóg* is deft with all water matters, even if those dangling arms have a clumsy look to them; Trian handles the fish as fluently as he used to touch the holes of his pipe. Cormac's reminded of their last time playing music at the monastery—the night of the roast swan, though neither of them had any idea it would be their last time. He considers that he may never have an instrument again, and it hits like a blow to his gut. Only his ragged voice to lift in song as best he can. *Well,* Cormac reminds himself, *all treasures must be left behind in the end.*

The Prior gestures to him to push them off from the weir.

They row on till the sun's edged behind a hill a little to the left of them. 'Time to moor.' The Prior points out a flat place under trees.

When they get out and genuflect on dry land, Cormac's knees almost buckle. It's dim and faintly fragrant under the lower branches. His arms tremble as he starts collecting twigs for kindling—but the bell recalls him. First, Vespers.

'Three foes attack me: my eye, my tongue, my thoughts,' the Prior teaches this evening. 'But the Psalter'—he holds up the bigger of their books—'is armour against them all.'

Making camp, Cormac lifts arches of bramble out of the way, but a stinging nettle gets him; he sucks the heel of his hand. He finds enough stones to ring their fire and stacks the twigs inside this circle, with tinder of dry leaf mould at its heart.

Meanwhile Trian's rinsing the two fish. He sets them down on a flat stone, in the last of the twilight, and scales them with the blunt edge of his knife, scrape after patient scrape. Soon he has the salmon and lamprey spitted on two iron skewers to set across the rocks for roasting. He whistles as he works.

Cormac smiles, recognising a snatch of a dance. He takes the fire gear from his belt pouch and uses a fingernail to lift out the horn's fitted stopper, made of clay, pierced with holes to let the flame inside breathe. He shakes out the grey ash that blankets the glowing embers from last night, then scatters them lightly on the tinder; he cups it with his hands, and blows the flame to life. He feeds the new fire with a few lengths of charcoal from their sack; once it catches properly he adds twigs. The green wood smokes and fills the dusk with hissing.

The fish finally start to sizzle, and the six damp shoes Cormac's put by the fire release their steam. He drags over a rotting log for the Prior to sit on, then skinnier ones for himself and Trian. He stares into the blue flames, grateful for this respite. To be at rest, steady on the motionless ground. Alive, and free, too, when they might well have been chained up on the island of the fisherfolk, or floating facedown in the river.

The fish spit like live things as Trian turns the skewers. 'You put me in mind of the hero Fionn Mac Cumhaill,' Cormac tells him, 'when he was a boy, and in the service of the poet Finegas.'

The familiar names make Trian look up as he sets out their bowls.

Cormac glances to make sure their master doesn't object to heathen legends. But the Prior says nothing, so he goes on. 'Now Finegas—all his study and thought was to catch the magical salmon in the well of wisdom that's the source of this river Sionan. The well was ringed by hazel trees whose fruit dropped into the water and soaked up its powers, and the salmon that ate those hazelnuts absorbed all the wisdom. Learned Finegas dipped his hook in that water every day for seven years, until the hour came at last when he landed that magnificent king of fish!' Cormac lets the triumph have its moment. 'So Finegas set his young servant to roasting it, forbidding him to taste a bite. But a drop of fat leapt out of that pan, and onto Fionn's hand. It was burning the boy's skin, so he licked it off.'

'Sure who wouldn't?' Trian asks sympathetically.

But the Prior shakes his head. 'Rebellion, our downfall, ever since Adam.'

'In a trice,' Cormac hurries on, 'young Fionn was filled with all the wisdom there is.'

Trian's eyes flare. 'His master must have been furious.'

'He was, of course, having worked and waited all those years, but it couldn't be helped.' Cormac finds himself wondering whether the poet beat his boy. He pictures Fionn bruised, hungry, aglow with what he'd learned, what could never be taken from him now.

The Prior grunts. 'As if knowledge is a treasure that can belong to only one man, and must be stolen or fought over!—when the truth is, God pours out his wisdom like honey.'

Cormac feels a flicker of resentment that the Prior's scorning his story. But he says Amen along with Trian.

The salmon and the lamprey look flaky now, so Trian doles them out with stale oatcakes. (Cormac remembers with a pang that jar of pickled cabbage they left behind.) Trian sets down the Prior's bowl, with a deep bow, and then Cormac's, with a little dip.

The Prior makes a cross in the air and asks a blessing on the food and on their voyage and fellowship.

Head down, Cormac mulls over that word. The three of them hold their goods in common, like the first Christians, and share according to need...but the Prior commands. Is there a word for a fellowship of unequals?

Now that he's recovered from his boat sickness he eats with relish, stopping every now and then to pick a fish bone out of his teeth. It's not true that old men always lose their taste. Or rather, he thinks, *What they have left of it they prize all the more.*

The Prior, though—Cormac hasn't yet seen their master finish a portion. He sets aside his bowl now, with a good piece of fish still in it, and wipes his hands on the grass. 'There's a different legend told of the same mysterious well,' the Prior remarks. 'Some say the river is named after a maiden called Sionan, who longed to get all the well's wisdom for herself.'

Cormac's never heard this one.

'So one night she dared to approach the water, in fear and trembling, since it was forbidden to her sex.'

Trian asks, 'Why was it forbidden?'

The Prior answers with a hint of exasperation, 'The wisest Church Fathers, and the ancients before them, all agree that a woman is a botched man, created only for childbearing.'

Cormac wonders what his wife would have said to that. A contraction in his chest, like a muscle ripping. After all these years, he has trouble calling up her lovely face.

'Well, this perverse daughter of Eve, Sionan, lifted the lid of the well,' the Prior goes on. 'She sucked up the sacred waters, and gobbled all the hazelnuts too.'

Cormac imagines the thirsty, ravenous girl.

'Trying to coax the great salmon into her grip, she tickled its belly with her finger, but it began to lash about in fury, till its gigantic tail raised the waters so high they swallowed Sionan up and drowned her.' The Prior's arms shoot out. 'The flood spilled right across the country, as far as the western sea, and when it subsided at last, what was left was this vast river.'

Trian nods in rapt appreciation.

Something's rattling and squeaking in the trees overhead: a sedge warbler, maybe? Cormac recognises a magpie and a quarrelsome robin; the repeated phrases of a song thrush. Also the soft rise-and-fall whirring of a nightjar. The darkness thickens around their fire.

A whine in the distance, then another. Some farm's watchdogs, set free to roam now that the cattle are stalled?

A howl.

No, not dogs, he decides. Wolves. The countryside is rife with them. Pray God these ones aren't too hungry.

Trian's dipping the bowls in the river and rubbing them clean. Each man goes a little way into the woods to crouch and wipe himself with leaves. Then Cormac gets down stiffly on his knees to bank the fire, using a piece of log to scoop the embers into the middle, between the charred branches, and swaddle them in ash for the night.

TO SEA

ON THE FOURTH morning of their voyage, Trian wakes in grey twilight and lies still. Only when light prises open his lashes does he force himself to his feet. It still feels odd to sleep in his clothes; he brushes down the dishevelled layers. But he likes thinking of himself as a traveller, hardy, ready for anything. Making the sign of the cross, he whispers, *'From the rising of the sun to its going down, praised be your name.'*

The Prior's on his knees already, of course, locked in prayer. Around the snoring Cormac stretches a carpet of bluebells, sprinkled with dog violet and small suns of coltsfoot, the odd spike of red plague-flower.

Trian leans over the river to splash his face. The water tastes green, with a tang of vegetation. He smoothens his hair, reknotting the leather that ties it back. He gets a scrap of cloth out of his pouch to rub his teeth and gums.

A repeated whistle makes him look around for the kingfisher. There's the gaudy thing, motionless on a low branch, watching the water. It's good luck to spot a kingfisher, the first creature with nerve enough to leave the Ark, which was rewarded with the blue of the sky daubed on its back and tail and the orange of the setting sun on its breast.

Trian tightens the rope around his waist. *Gird me, O Lord, ready to serve.* He tugs on the three knots at the end to remind him of his vows: poor, chaste, obedient. Loyal to his master without reserve, like Christ who died hanging from nails through his hands and heels, without murmuring against his Father who ordained it.

The Prior's ringing the bell for Terce, so Trian hurries to fit his feet into his shoes and pulls their thongs. Cormac lurches off the ground, haggard. By the lapping water's verge, they kneel and sing three Latin psalms: *'See how good it is when brothers live together in harmony.'*

After the Prior reads a passage in Greek, he switches back to Gaelic for the prayers. Protections always go in threes in honour of the Trinity. The last one starts, *'Christ shield me today against poison.'*

'*Against burning*,' Cormac responds.

Trian finishes: '*Against drowning*.' Which always reminds him of his uncles.

He passes out two roasted eggs apiece, and a few soft apples. His share barely takes the edge off his appetite.

With his sleeves doubled over his hands to ward off stings, Cormac's ripping up a patch of nettles. Trian goes over to help, and asks, 'Are these for eating?'

A nod. 'One good dose and we'll keep our health all year.'

'God willing,' the Prior corrects him.

'God willing,' Cormac echoes. 'Mortar and pestle, Brother?'

Trian reminds him, 'We left them behind.'

So Cormac crams the serrated leaves into a bowl, and pulps them laboriously with a wooden spoon.

They each take the waterskin in turn, to wash the stuff down. The nettle mush tastes so sour, Trian knows it must be doing them a power of good.

He watches Cormac pack up the fire now. The older monk beckons him close to show him how it's done. 'Take touchwood—' He picks a big flake out of a rag from his pouch.

'What is it?' Trian has to ask.

'Fungus off a fallen tree, boiled in urine.'

Cormac lights it from last night's embers, tucks it deep into his fire horn, and adds crumbs of moss to keep it smouldering. He scoops in some soft ash before he stoppers it up, then puts the horn in his leather pouch.

'Doesn't it burn you?'

Cormac grins and pats his belly where the pouch sits. 'I keep a thin board behind the fire horn, to save my skin. I fear I'll never make a saint.'

The Prior speaks up from the boat, where he's fitting their baggage snug against the mast: 'The blessed ones aren't greedy for pain for its own sake, only for its teaching. Holy Brigit's pupil Darlugdach, for instance. When one night she was tempted to go to a man, she sprinkled embers in her own shoes.'

Trian's startled. 'So that she wouldn't put them on?'

'Oh, she did anyway.' The Prior's tone is grim.

'And went to him?' On sore, smoking feet? He tries to imagine a want that strong.

'No—once she felt the burn, she ripped her shoes off again, and went back to bed. She needed the pain to keep down her lust, see?'

Trian wonders who the man was, and how long he'd waited in vain for the holy woman.

Cormac's kicking dirt over the embers and stirring them with his staff. Trian dips a bowl into the river and dowses the ashes.

He holds the boat steady for Cormac to get in, then shoves her off the sucking mud and out into the current before leaping in.

The banks recede, as he and Cormac row, and the Sionan keeps widening. 'We're in the estuary now,' the Prior remarks. 'That was our last night on land.'

That thrills Trian. He wonders if their master has a map of the whole world in his head that unscrolls as he travels, showing the landscape from overhead as angels must see it.

Cormac kisses the cross on his thong, and mutters a protection.

'Just wait till you set eyes on the sea, Brother,' Trian tells him.

Plunging his long oar into the river, Trian notices all the signs of spring. Swallows wheel and cavort overhead in shrill numbers, the odd little brown flier dipping low enough to beak an insect off the water between one wingbeat and the next. Now the whole mass forms a spiralling, swirling cloud, speckling then darkening into a winged shape that smears like ink, rips and dissolves again. So many! What can drive them to flock in such urgent numbers, to form one great bird shape of their countless pointed bodies?

Long-legged herons stand frozen in the shallows as if hoping the monks floating by won't

see them. A godwit ignores the boat and stabs
its bright head over and over into the water.
Trian spots a few wading snipe. One of them
flies overhead in a display to its mate, swooping downwards and making a loud drumming
with its tail.

'Brother Trian, are you dreaming?'

How long has he been kneeling, letting the
oar drift in his hands and the boat go askew?
'Pardon, Father.' He whacks his chest.

'*Age quod agis*,' the Prior reminds him. 'Keep
your mind on what you're doing.'

Trian nods, hot-cheeked. He rows on.

The estuary is so broad, now, the monks seem
to Cormac to have shrunk to the size of three
ants on a floating leaf. But in the afternoon,
when they stop to sing None, their voices spill
across the water.

As they set off again, Trian yelps, 'A boat!'

At this distance Cormac can see only a
smudge.

'Traders, maybe,' the Prior speculates.

Cormac sniffs the air, sensing something
unfamiliar.

Trian leans over the edge of the boat and lifts

some water to his mouth. He grins as if it's fine wine. 'Brackish—half-salt. That means we're getting close.'

'A man who takes a sip of one sea tastes all of them,' the Prior says from the stern.

That mystifies Cormac.

'The various seas of the earth touch and form one ocean,' their master explains.

Really? Cormac inhales the strange saltiness. As he and Trian row on, he begins to feel the incoming creep of the sea, the turbulence as it tussles and mingles with the last sweet out-pouring of the river.

A while later they pass a different vessel, close enough that this time Cormac can make out figures on board, working their nets, in-different to the monks.

Slim gulls fly overhead with unnerving grace. Cormac and Trian are beginning to have to put their backs into the rowing. Salt stings in the oar-blisters on Cormac's hands. He sees blue veins stand out on Trian's sunburned forehead and arms.

Now the sea is a vast surge coming down the throat of the estuary. The wind against the current kicks up a real chop. 'Shouldn't be long, Brother,' Trian assures him. 'The tide's at its height, so in a little while it'll reverse and pull us with it, outerly.'

'God moves the very waters for us,' the Prior says.

Cormac frowns. Doesn't the tide turn twice a day, heedless of who floats on it?

He reminds himself that their master sees deeply into things and discerns the secret ways of heaven. Maybe both things are true; the tide always turns, but today God's making sure it'll lift his monks just when their arms begin to fail.

Sure enough, soon the oar work eases. The mainland slips away behind them.

Are they at sea now? The blue vista widens and widens, alarming Cormac. The boat is starting to revolve; a slow skimming one way, then back again, a leaf-dance under darkening clouds. He grips the gunnel with one hand. 'Is it always like this—the spinning?'

'She's a river boat, not made for seafaring, a round-bottomed dish,' the Prior says without concern. 'Hard to sink, but with no keel to help her hew a path through the waves.'

Cormac's distracted by a slopping sound under the slats. He keeps talking to soothe his nerves. 'Here's a saying I've heard but don't understand: *Never turn your back on the ocean.*'

'Even on a calm day, Brother, a roller can come in without warning and lick a man off the shore,' Trian tells him. 'Our mother had two brothers taken that way.'

Cormac winces.

'So *keep watch*,' the Prior quotes, *'for you know neither the day nor the hour.'*

Trian licks one finger and holds it up to the wind. 'Our island will lie to the southwest, you said, Father?'

The Prior nods.

Trian eyes the heavy yard above their heads. Diffident: 'We'd catch this bit of a northerly if we let out the sail.'

'Do it, then.'

It occurs to Cormac to wonder how much their Prior knows of navigation. For all the man's voyages, maybe he's always been a passenger. Whereas the young monk has seemed to grow in confidence from the first day he stepped into the boat.

Trian clambers onto the sacks of supplies, now, to tug at the yard's thongs. As the ties come loose the great square of leather drops with a loud snap. Trian's pulling a line from the bottom to an iron loop on the gunnel and tying it taut. On the other side, the Prior follows suit. The sail bellies, filling; four brown hides pieced together.

The boat straightens and speeds along, fast enough to grip Cormac with dread. To distract

himself, he squints at the line of the coast to
their left. There's a huge bay, like a giant's
wet foot giving the countryside a savage kick.
Then a sprinkling of tiny pieces of land, flat
and green, dust shaken off the mainland.

Trian asks the Prior, 'Is it true what they
say, that no pestilence can travel over nine
waves?'

A shrug. 'When is man ever safe from
contagion? God visits ills upon whomever he
chooses.'

Trian dips his head. 'I didn't mean—'

'This much is true,' the Prior tells him, 'that
when folk huddle together in numbers, for
fear of cattle raiders or slavers, death can still
find them out in their comfortable beds. Every
settlement I've visited has its plague-grave outside, where the people leave small stones as
they pass.'

That's to honour the dead in the old pagan
way, Cormac remembers, but keep down the
rot too. He can't turn his thoughts away from
his own beloved four, whom he laid out and
keened all in the one night, half a lifetime ago.
He remembers lighting candles and setting a
full bowl on his wife's flat chest, and one on
his little daughter's, and on each of his sons'.
Foolish, Cormac knows now, to try to provi-
sion the dead with food for wherever they

might be going—but it was some comfort. He didn't hold the traditional feast in their honour, not even for his kin, because who'd come to a plague-struck hut? In the morning he laid his wife on the ground outside with her arms wide, her three young gathered back into her, and then he piled on rocks until he couldn't see them anymore.

He doesn't say a word of this, for fear he'll weep.

But as if reading Cormac's mind, the Prior turns to him. 'Whatever lands or houses, parents or wives or children a man loses, he has Christ's word it'll be returned a hundredfold.'

The image bewilders Cormac: hundreds of unfamiliar sons and daughters and wives waving to him from unfamiliar fields. Frankly, he'd rather have back the ones he had.

Then he rebukes himself for taking the Gospel too literally. It's like a song; the meaning comes roundabout. Cormac's no scholar, only a tired old man, and he doesn't need to fathom the depths of scripture, only follow and obey.

'Is it true you came through the pestilence, Father?' Trian asks.

A calm nod from the Prior. 'My case was the choking kind. Great swellings all over me, leaking, and my fingers and toes so black I expected them all to drop off, not just one.'

Cormac stares at the tarry stub on the man's mighty right fist.

'I was sure my time had come, and I didn't fight it. Hadn't I pledged myself to God as a child, and stood ready for the call to heaven, all those years—almost longing for it?'

Joy, Cormac hears in their master's voice; an eerie joy at the prospect of dying.

The Prior stretches his marred hand now, as if it pains him. 'My Maker took only an inch of me, as an earnest of his love. And here is a miraculous thing—I've never been sick a day, since.'

Trian marvels at that.

'Of course he may come back and claim the rest of me whenever he likes.'

Trian crosses himself and mutters 'Amen,' and Cormac does the same.

'Remember, too, Brothers'—the Prior turns his gaze on them like a flaring torch—'in seeking out this island, we're fleeing not contagion of the flesh, but of the spirit. We're taking refuge from the nine evils: pride, vanity, anger, envy, avarice, lust, gluttony, apathy, and sadness.'

'We are,' Cormac agrees.

Trian almost shouts: 'Let's get nine waves away from them!'

Trian feels as lively as a dog who jumps and whines for a scrap of meat. The salt scent is making a child of him again. He remembers how he used to pick his way along the fore-shore to find the food the sea scattered for free. Shinning up tufted, slippery cliffs for eggs, and for the glee of it.

He undoes the line nearest him to angle the sail a little, keeping the boat scudding due southwest. Hundreds of little kittiwake gulls are settling on the water, letting out quacks and yelps, plucking up small fry with no effort. Birds always seem to stick to their own kind, even if they sometimes squabble over a scrap or a place to land; strength in numbers, Trian supposes. The kittiwakes' movements chime together like bells; one flutter will prompt an-other and another till the whole flock's shifted from water to sky. He can't spot a leader among the kittiwakes; at any one moment, he wonders, how do they decide which of them to follow?

Up ahead, an island with a long, rippled silhouette, almost like a man lying on his back. As the boat nears it, Trian makes out a few thatched huts plumed with smoke. People cutting and stacking turf, none in monks' habits that he can see. A couple of knobbly-legged cows.

A whole cluster of islands reveals itself behind the first. What looks like an old cliff fort. On the next island, a chapel cobbled together from boulders, swaybacked under the weight of time. Built of rock for lack of trees, Trian realises. *Who prayed in this now-slumped chapel, and when? And how did they come to abandon it—bad luck, sickness, pirates? A faltering in faith?*

The Prior leans on his steering oar, setting course to thread through the cluster.

Trian points out an outlying island on the western edge. The waves are gradually gnawing an arch through it, and it's crested with circling seabirds. 'What about that one, Father?' His voice comes out half-choked with excitement.

'What about it?'

'Might that be the one in your dream? It's bare and bleak.'

The Prior's tone is almost contemptuous. 'Not half a mile away from its neighbour? No, no. The farther from men, the closer to God.'

Trian subsides.

They're passing close by the black slope of the nearest island, where turf-cutters are working.

A woman straightens up. A man does the same, and raises a hand. Friendly? None of them seems to be raising an alarm, or running for a weapon. Trian waves back.

In a little harbour below the turf-cutters, three boats lie at anchor. Cormac voices what's on Trian's mind: 'Father, should we maybe pull in for a few provisions?'

'I see no need. We still have drinking water.'

'We're nearly out of cheese, though, and we're low on pork.'

A magisterial shrug from the Prior. 'We have enough.'

For the first time it strikes Trian that even if they stop, they've nothing surplus to offer in trade for provisions. Although those folk, if Christians, might offer hospitality in exchange for nothing more than the holy man's blessing. But the Prior's right that there's no real need to break the journey yet.

On they sail, and the cluster of islands shrinks behind them till it's gone. High on the coast to their left, Trian spots the occasional farmstead, ringed by a stockade. But no more islands. The ocean is an empty, sparkling dish.

The boat spins again. The steering oar is slack in the Prior's hands.

'Father?' Trian prompts him. 'Still south-west?'

'Who knows?' The Prior says it so low that Trian's not sure he heard right.

He tries again. 'Which way?'

'We are off the map now.' The Prior lifts the dripping oar out of the water and rests it. He opens the pouch on his belt and unrolls a piece of linen. 'See, this is Hibernia.'

Trian twists his neck to make sense of the image.

'We've come right down the Sionan and out its great mouth, and some way farther down the west coast.' The Prior fingers the line. 'Now, west or south—from here on, it's all a blank.'

Trian looks at Cormac, who meets his gaze with unease.

'Oh, our island is out there,' the Prior assures them as he rolls the map up again. 'But we cannot find it by ourselves. God is our pilot now, and we'll go wherever his breath blows us.'

That sounds incongruous to Trian, not to plot course; to let the currents seize the boat like any detritus. But he sits back on his heels quietly, and watches the sail plump with wind. *God's breath*, he tells himself.

So they are blown on, still more southerly than any other direction. A raft of hundreds of great black cormorants stains the water ahead. Thousands, more like, foraging busily. The

boat drifts right through the indifferent birds.
Guttural grunts: *Ark ark ark!* One cormorant
pops out of the water beside Trian with a
big fish, and sucks it whole into his throat
pouch. By some collusion a gang will suddenly
take off, running along and kicking the water
till they gather enough momentum to heave
into the sky. Another group swoops down to
take its turn forming a dark raft on the sea.
One cormorant—a good four feet long, Trian
would say—stands on a protruding rock,
snake-necked, holding out its angular, powerful wings.

'Like some demon carved on a pillar,' the
Prior mutters.

'Just drying its feathers, could be,' Trian
suggests.

'What's that bird?' Cormac asks.

'A cormorant,' Trian tells him.

'Ah. Famous for greed, aren't they?'

Trian shrugs. 'My folk said they brought
good luck.'

The Prior huffs his breath. 'Those sinister
creatures?'

'Luck for the catch, anyway, Father. They
know where the fish are.'

The boat lolls, rotates. Trian says prayers in
his head to pass the time.

When he first came to the monastery, he

found it almost unbearable. He was always roaming off or shinning up trees, which earned him beatings. Gradually he learned the knack of sitting still, but it's against his nature.

His knuckles and wrists feel tight now, so he has to crack them. But when he catches himself whistling a tune, he stops at once, because his people always said whistling in a boat could wake rough wind.

The invisible force of air curves the sail one way, then another. The boat spins. God's breath will blow them where they're meant to go, Trian promises himself. Wherever that may be.

The three psalms of None float out over the waves. Seabirds of various kinds that Artt doesn't recognise interrupt the singing with raucous coughs and honks. He's never liked feathered creatures, especially in numbers. They seem like harbingers to him, bad omens. Not that he would invent meanings for their flights or cries, practising divination like some druid. But there is something uncanny about creatures that won't confine themselves to land, water, or sky, moving at liberty through all three.

Artt calculates it will take his monks a week to complete the full cycle of one hundred and fifty psalms. The Desert Fathers used to go through the whole Psalter over the course of each day, but he must be patient; this is a softer generation.

By the time he has finished saying the Scripture passages—from memory this time, so as not to risk a wave spraying any of the two precious books—the afternoon sky is dark blue overhead and a northerly's sprung up and filled the sail.

Cormac is bracing himself against the gunnel, clearly rigid with nerves. A wash slops over the side now, wetting their feet. Trian takes up his bowl and starts bailing out, and Cormac copies him. The young monk murmurs a reassurance: 'She's balanced nicely, Brother. We shouldn't be swamped.'

But as each wave smacks the side, the boat skids. Stirred by greater swells and chopped by the new wind, the sea forms a lumpy gruel. Artt feels no panic, only uncertainty, which he finds rather harder to bear. He demands silently, *What now, Lord?*

'Father, could we...maybe I'll turn us face-on into each wave, at least,' Trian suggests, 'so her prow can ride the crests?'

'As you like.' Artt's voice is almost blown

away. He swaps places with Trian to let him take the steering oar.

The young monk twists it to straighten up the boat a little, but she's still bucking at the whim of the wind. Cormac is breathing as loudly as a horse, nostrils flared. Artt supposes he should give the old man something to do. Feeling a drop of rain on his jaw, he tells Cormac to unpack their waterproofed leather hats, and the cloaks. The three put them on oiled side outwards, fleece inwards. Artt fastens his cloak with an iron brooch, a simple pin piercing up through a ring, and the monks use thorns, which work just as well.

Soon the smoke-grey clouds let down their burden. Quick-thinking, Trian sets out the bowls.

'See, God's gift to us of fresh water.' Artt has to shout to be heard.

A shaft of low light spears through. The scudding clouds take on a reddish tinge to the west. The boat drifts on more smoothly. Once the shower's over, Cormac shakes diamonds off the cloaks, and rolls them up.

Artt gazes west, then south. The view's appallingly open now, empty of even a fragment of land. What if there are no more islands?

What if Artt's dream, which seemed like a true vision—

These are doubts, the foul whisperings of demons; he should know better than to lend his ear to them. He punches his fist against his chest so loudly, his monks startle like sparrows.

Artt despises himself for his momentary lapse in faith. A priest owes a greater tariff than a mere monk for the same weakness; more is asked of him. Should Artt do penance by standing in cross-vigil now, arms out? But the boat's moving too fast; he might topple, which would be undignified. Instead he kneels down on the slats, shuts his eyes, and mutters the 119th Psalm, the one used to atone for sins, as it is 176 verses long. In a harsh whisper: *'I am a stranger on earth; do not hide your commands from me.'*

When he has finished the last verse, Artt sits back on the bench in the stern, avoiding the others' glances. An absurd vanity—he'd rather they didn't know when he sins. But he must be an example for his flock, both in avoiding error and in atoning when he fails. How lonely it is to be the leader; to stand as his own soul-friend, his own confessor, his own guide.

Thirsty now. Artt picks up a bowl, with its puddle of rain, and allows himself a sip. To their right, the sun is sinking in scarlet fire. He takes the bell out of his pouch and rings it for Vespers.

They all work to keep their balance, standing, in the slowly pivoting boat. Cormac sways and lurches, and grabs at the yard. As a concession, Artt lets them kneel instead.

Afterwards, before the evening meal, he lifts his robe and undoes the drawstring of his woollen braies to make water over the side. He notices Trian avert his face sharply. Some youths just can't shake off that squirming shyness about the base needs of the body.

Sitting, they pass around their half-bare joint of pork, chipping small pieces into their bowls with the very last of the cheese.

A dusky face rises behind Cormac in the twilight: big-eyed, womanly. Artt jerks backwards.

Trian lets out a whoop.

Cormac spins around, but there's nothing there. 'What? What?'

'Only a seal, Brother,' Artt says gruffly.

The creature reappears a minute later, nosing the hull with interest, then sinks away.

Artt is reminded of a story. He jerks his thumb north. 'One of those old chapels on the estuary back there was founded by holy Senán.'

'Blessed be that saint's name,' Cormac murmurs.

'Now Senán was so strict,' Artt goes on, 'he

laid down as a rule that no female should ever set foot on his island to tempt his monks.'

'An act of kindness in him, to spare them,' Trian comments.

Artt thinks, with a flash of revulsion, of those sinners back at Cluain Mhic Nóis. 'Senán came from a devout family, and his own sister was a nun.'

'Conainne, I believe her name was,' Cormac puts in.

Artt would rather not be interrupted, but he knows the old monk's used to being the storyteller. 'Well. On her deathbed the nun asked to be buried near her dear brother. Her sisters in Christ rowed Conainne's body to Senán's island and made humble petition. Now what was he to do?'

Trian squirms. 'Surely, Father, especially once she'd departed this life...'

Cormac fills in, with a little chuckle: 'A corpse could hardly be an occasion of lust.'

'That's neither here nor there,' Artt snaps. 'If Senán had broken his own rule, it would have been rank hypocrisy. Once the track is marked out, there can be no wandering.'

Trian sounds confused. 'So Senán turned away the body of his own mother's daughter?'

'Not that either,' Artt says with satisfaction. 'He told the nuns to wait till low tide and bury

her in the wet sand of the foreshore, because
that wasn't part of the island. The saint was as
clever as he was clean-hearted, see?'

His monks are nodding in the thickening
dark.

'Father,' Trian asks, 'maybe we'd furl the
sail now?'

Artt should have thought of that; otherwise
they might run onto rocks in the night and
be wrecked. He gets to his feet and finds his
balance before loosing the cord. The leather
is sticky with salt spray. Trian does the same
on the other side. Between them they roll up
the square of skin and bind it tight against
the yard.

Now the boat's movement slows, becomes
aimless again; it's a toy for each wave. 'Drop
anchor,' Artt tells Trian.

The young man grimaces.

'What is it?'

'This far out, Father...I doubt the anchor
would come near to reaching the seabed.'

Artt peers at the grooved stone in its tangle
of thorny branches. Its looped rope can't be
more than a dozen fathoms long; why didn't
he think to ask the boatwrights to add more?
'Well, let's try.'

Trian gnaws his lip.

'Speak,' Artt snaps.

'It's only that...the weight of the rock might tip us over.'

Artt can see that now. There's a lesson in that: the very thing they have lugged along as a safeguard could be what capsizes them. As the Gospel warns, *Whoever seeks to save his life will lose it.*

So. In open ocean, drifting blind now, and with no way to stop moving through the dark. It is Artt who's brought them to this extremity, and it's too late for doubt. 'Never mind. We won't founder,' he assures them. 'We travel in the palm of God's hand.'

He retrieves one of their beeswax candles from the holy chest. 'Your fire, Brother Cormac?'

Cormac gets the gear out of his pouch and unstoppers the horn.

Artt leans across the boat and pushes the taper down into the embers until the wick flames up.

The boat dips and sways, pivots, circles. Silence stretches. The candle in Artt's hand gutters, leaking hot wax. He registers the pain in his fingers; waits as it fades. He had better recite Nocturns soon, before either of the monks drops off or the flame goes out.

BECALMED

CORMAC GETS BARELY a wink of sleep. The relentless creaks and whirlings of the boat, the screechings of birds, the bell summoning the monks for Vigil by the light of a candle stub, Cormac so groggy that he slurs his psalms like a drunk...

At dawn he wakes and reckons in his head. The fifth day of travelling, but it feels endless. At the moment they don't seem to be moving at all. White in his eyes, white all around: fog.

The ocean is all the more disturbing now that Cormac can't see it. The appalling breadth of it, one maw eternally drinking and spewing. He shivers, rubbing his arms and legs through the wool. Greenish-white spatters on his robes, on all their robes, he sees; the birds have fouled the monks in the night as if to say, *The sea is ours*. Still, though, being shat on is said to be good luck.

The Prior prays: '*I arise today through the strength of heaven.*'

'*Through the light of the sun,*' Cormac answers.

'*Through the swiftness of wind,*' Trian finishes.

The bell for Terce. Cormac staggers to his knees, clears his throat, and joins in the psalms. (Seven rather than three, at each of the hours, since today is the Sabbath.)

Afterwards they munch on very dry oatcakes. Cormac thinks it's just as well the fog has come, because there's not a breath of wind to fill their sail, and they're not allowed to row. No lifting, no cooking, no work of any kind; what would count as idleness another day is virtue on the Sabbath.

A bird flaps by, yelping almost in his ear. 'I'm put in mind of the voyages of holy Breandán and his seventeen companions.'

'I hope they had a bigger boat than this,' Trian says under his breath.

Cormac grins, nodding. 'They found one island made of clear, shining crystal, and another covered with grapevines that were heavy with fruit.'

'Ah,' the Prior says with an odd tenderness, 'I don't suppose either of you has tasted a grape? I ate them right off a wall, in Gaul. They burst in the mouth like balls of juice.'

It's the first time the Prior's shown the slightest enthusiasm about food.

Cormac goes on with his tale. 'Another island had a well whose soothing water put the monks to sleep. But the next, now—the next actually rained fire. Spurted it upwards, shot flames into the sky.'

Trian's mouth hangs open.

'The holy man and his followers sailed on and on till they came to a rock with no human mark on it at all,' Cormac continues. 'Birds were perched all over it, singing praise to the Creator day and night. Breandán called that place the Paradise of Birds.' It's quite clear in his mind, the tufted embellishment of every crag. And the polyphonic chorus: not ordinary, shrill birds, but a heavenly choir. Maybe they were the souls of the blessed dead in disguise. Or sinners' souls, more like, Cormac thinks now—encased in feathers as a penance, to work off their crimes by singing hymns for hundreds of years.

'The island in your dream, Father.' Trian's peering into the fog. 'May I ask, what did it look like?'

The Prior sounds nettled. 'It was not drawn like a picture, or illuminated in colours. It was more the idea of an island.'

'Somewhere out there in the ocean.' Cormac

means that as confirmation, but it comes out almost sceptical.

'It's out there, all right,' the Prior insists. 'Since God has given me—given us three—this holy mission of serving him in absolute seclusion, he will have prepared a fit place for us.'

'Amen,' Trian murmurs.

Cormac's thinking, it will have to possess a spring or a well, to supply them with water. So, a scrap of land far from the mainland, and well south of all the other islands. Capable of cultivation... but where no one is living, nor ever tried living. For the first time, Cormac registers how unlikely that sounds.

'It will be defended by waves against the world's encroachings,' the Prior goes on. 'All we have to do is wait for a wind, Brothers, and let it take us there.'

This is sounding to Cormac less and less like an actual island. As if the three of them have stepped out of everyday life into a magical boat, and their journey is a fable.

Trian asks warily, 'If we go on and on, Father, over the ocean... won't we come to the rim?'

The Prior laughs a little. 'Aristotle teaches that the earth is as round as an apple.'

'Round?'

Cormac has heard the same thing, though he's always had trouble picturing it.

The Prior explains, 'Hibernia is called by some *Terra Finalia,* the far or final country, but that only signifies the last before the great western ocean. If we crossed this whole water,' gesturing into the thick white, 'we would come to unknown lands, and beyond them the Indies, and Africa, and the European continent again, and on its edge, Albion and our Hibernia—as if we'd thrown a rope around the globe, you see?'

Trian's clearly straining to follow.

It's not the risk of sailing over a rim that's worrying Cormac, but a much more mundane prospect: death by thirst. Their food will not last a week, and their fresh water—unless more rain falls—only a matter of days. His throat contracts at the thought. He has an impulse to reach down for one of the goatskins, but stops himself.

'And how will we recognise our island?' Trian wonders.

'By a sign of some kind.'

Cormac realises something: the Prior doesn't know.

Trian hesitates as if about to say more, but doesn't.

It comes to Cormac that maybe it's their fault the boat hasn't reached the island yet, his and Trian's. *We of little faith.*

He speaks rapidly, to hide his treasonous thoughts. 'Didn't holy Ciarán's bell begin to ring, all on its own, the moment he reached the site where he'd build his monastery?'

The Prior rewards him with a nod.

Cormac lowers his eyes.

Say the island in the Prior's dream is real, but even when the monks get a wind, they don't pass close enough to spot their destination, because two of the three are having trouble believing it's there? Say they slide right past it in the fog tomorrow, and blunder on into open ocean, and starve and parch and die in their own ignorance? Fit punishment, Cormac supposes: they will be lost, for lack of conviction. *Christ, my true friend,* he prays, *strengthen my faith. Cherubim lift me, angels support me, archangels bear me up.*

Artt sits quite still, trying to forget the fact that his robe is bedaubed in droppings. The fog is as thick as ever; the sun's only lit, not lifted it. The boat stands as if the water's thickened and congealed around it. Becalmed, not a breath of wind; everything is motionless, except for the flocks overhead keeping up their complaint.

He rebukes himself for his itch to be sailing on, even on the Sabbath. Isn't it enough that he has time to sit with eyes shut and contemplate the holy island that God has set aside for them? *Pray without ceasing,* Paul told the Thessalonians. That's the only true urgency.

A peculiar rumbling makes him open his eyes. Birds floating all around the boat; black and white plumage and snubbed beaks of riotous orange, red, grey, and blue. Such a deep growl for such little creatures.

Trian's watching them with interest. 'The puffins have put on their gaudy faces already, to find mates.'

Yes, now Trian's said it, Artt can spot pairs of them rubbing bills, like any man and maid: the endless, predictable rhythm of it. 'Time for Mass.' He pushes himself to his feet and the boat shakes.

Cormac blinks and stirs from his doze. Trian scrambles to open the holy chest.

Artt unrolls the narrow white linen stole—the mark of priesthood—and hangs it around his neck, crossing the ends over his breast and fixing them in place with his belt so they hang down to his ankles. He lays the linen cloth over the flat lid of the chest, as a tiny, makeshift altar table. He unwraps the cloths that hold the chalice and dish—not gold, but the best the Abbot could spare them, a small bronze cup and a thin stone plate inlaid with amethyst.

'Holy water,' Trian remembers, and leans over to retrieve the little flask from the bow.

Artt takes it from him, pulls out the stopper, sprinkles the draped chest, and makes a cross in the air over it: 'The sign of the living Christ.' He picks up one of the beeswax candles.

But when Cormac opens his fire gear, he tuts. 'Gone out, Father.' He gives his chest a token smack. 'Beg pardon, I should have kept a closer eye on it.'

Such disrespect to the Mass. Artt breathes out his annoyance.

The old monk fusses about, unwrapping a rag and choosing three big flakes of touch-wood. He sets them into the horn, then uses his grooved flint to strike against the back of his knife over and over. He makes sparks, but none of them land on the dried fungus.

Artt catches himself grinding his teeth.

At last, a spark flares up. Cormac blows on it gently and feeds it some moss.

Finally Artt can light the taper. Palms pressed together, heads down, the monks pray silently, preparing for the sacrament.

Artt fills the little gilt jug with fresh water, and pours some over his hands, murmuring,

'*Lord, wash away my crimes. Cleanse me of my sins.*'

No need of a book; he knows all the parts of the Mass by heart. For want of a deacon, he nods to Cormac to sing the antiphons in his hoarse voice. 'Now let us offer each other peace,' Artt says, 'and when your lips approach those of your brother for the Pax Tecum, do not let your heart shrink from him.' The boat lurches under their feet as they embrace each other in turn.

Taking up the wine jar (bound in coils of rope), Artt pulls out the wax plug and pours a trickle into the chalice. As ever, he adds some water from the jug and the blood-red pales to pink. It is not yet clear to him how he's to get any more from Gaul, but he pushes that qualm aside. Now he opens the silver box which holds the Host—three small rounds of wheat bread, the *Chi Rho* symbol baked into their tops to mark them as Christ's. After the Greek blessing he goes on in Gaelic.

Trian is already ringing the bell to mark the beginning of the Consecration. In Latin Artt says the words of power: 'On the night before Jesus died, he took bread and gave thanks, broke it and gave it to his followers, saying, *Do this to remember me. This is my body.* He took the cup and gave thanks, and said,

This is my blood.' Artt elevates the Host in both hands, as high as he can reach. Squeezing his eyes shut, he stares past the treachery of appearances, to the very substance of the bread and wine transformed into the flesh and blood of Jesus. As always, the miracle makes him shake.

Next Artt raises the chalice so the monks can adore the Presence in that form too. He breaks the Host into three roughly equal triangles and puts one into each mouth, the last in his own. He passes the chalice around. When he swallows, his throat is sour with ecstasy. 'We three are made one.'

As Trian washes the holy vessels afterwards and swaddles them in the chest, the glare of sun intensifies behind the fabric of cloud. The white thins, lightens, finally tears. At last a spring breeze starts up. The boat slides broadside to it and lolls and rolls. Relieved to be moving, even if only uncontrollably, Artt watches the fog meandering off and leaving a sky only ribboned with cloud.

Is that shock on Trian's face? He turns to look where the young monk's staring. On the horizon to the southwest of them, two islands side by side, thrusting up from the sea. One larger, both weirdly pointed. 'What a pair of skelligs,' Trian marvels.

Cormac skews around and shifts his head from side to side like a bird. 'Skelligs?'

'Spikes of rock in the sea—sheer, sharp islands. I suppose our eyes were on the setting sun yesterday,' Trian adds uncertainly, 'so we didn't look any farther south.'

'It's not that.' Artt's voice comes out like a lion's roar. 'Christ is revealing them to us only now. Our island—it must be one of these two.' He makes a cross on his forehead, his mouth, his chest. *If God is for us, who can be against us?'* he sings out. *'Ask and you will receive. Seek and you will find. Knock and it will open.'*

'Amen,' the monks chorus, catching his fervour.

He watches the islands in a loud silence; his gaze eats up the distance. The boat rotates and drifts, more or less in the right direction but with a languor that racks his nerves.

Trian must feel the same way because he begs, 'Can we go faster, Father?'

'The Sabbath,' Cormac reminds him gruffly.

Artt stares at the two great jagged outcroppings. The small pyramid floats beneath the level of the clouds; the broader, higher one rears up, wrapped in vapour. It seems ungrateful not to harness this bit of heaven-sent wind. 'Well, I don't suppose it would count as work to drop the sail, at least.'

The others rush to follow his lead, unfurling the great square and stringing it to the sides of the hull. A light puff fills it at once and speeds them south, just where they want to go.

Closer, the great shards of grey are dabbed with green, as if a pair of mountains slid off the land into the sea and sailed away. Like some desert mirage; a miracle worked on a floating altar. Little by little the skelligs grow. Their crazed cones seem to Artt to be merging, the lesser slipping in front of the greater, two becoming one. He wonders aloud, 'Could that be snow on their tops?' Well past Easter, so surely not. Unless these unique rocks have their own rarefied weather.

'Bird droppings, more like,' Trian says.

'Ah, yes.' With misgiving, Artt jerks around to reckon how far these extraordinary islands lie from the mainland. Seven miles, eight, no more; will they have been claimed by impure folk long since? 'I see no signs of settlement yet.'

'Nor I, Father.' The young man's voice is shrill with excitement.

'Maybe they're uninhabitable.'

Artt glares at Cormac.

'I only mean... they seem all up and down. But my eyes aren't what they were,' the old monk admits.

It strikes Artt that the combination of the light current and breeze is going to take the boat right past the skelligs, too far south. He grabs the steering oar and pushes it deep into the water, just to nudge them west. He wouldn't call this work, only sitting, holding on, feeling the pulse of the sea, his gaze on the islands' splintery silhouettes. His throat is locked as the boat inches nearer the smaller one, and the greater one looming behind it. They are like nothing he's ever encountered in all his travels, two broken fists of rock held up in prayer. He sings out, *'Be before me, O Lord.'*

'As a bright flame,' the others chant back.

'Be above me, O Lord.'

'As a fixed star.'

'Be below me, O Lord.'

Cormac and Trian finish: *'As a clear path.'*

As they approach what Artt is thinking of as the Lesser Skellig, it reveals itself as entirely possessed by an army of birds. He can't hear anything like a hymn of praise in the screams of these vermin. Nor can he see any spot to moor around this whole stained crag. Could it be too steep to land on?

The boat is past already, gliding slowly, straight towards the bigger island, which is still a mile or two off. Its rough cone is veiled in cloud, but the breeze is already beginning to wipe it clean.

Now the Great Skellig is revealed in all its strange glory. Twice the height of its neighbour, sharply fingering the sky. Eroded by wind and water; littered with rockfall, smeared with emerald vegetation. Its crags are capped with the droppings of the wheeling flocks who keep up their harsh cacophony.

'This is the place,' Artt proclaims. 'The higher up, the closer to heaven. On this island's peaks, our prayers will be halfway to God's ears already.'

'Amen, Father.'

'Amen.'

The Great Skellig is an abandoned fortress, awful in majesty. No, Artt tells himself, not abandoned, just lonely, waiting for its commander. The most gigantic of cathedrals, ready for its priest.

Belatedly he realises that the boat is getting close enough to run aground. 'Furl the sail!'

Trian and Cormac hurry to bind the leather against the yard.

'Now drop anchor.'

Trian heaves the thorny stone over the side. Its rope slithers, and slithers, and finally stops.

They kneel there, in the bobbing boat, pinned

in the shadow of the island. Artt demands, 'Any signs of occupation?'

'Not from this side at least,' says Trian.

No possibility of landing today; it would be too late to make a start, even if it weren't the Sabbath.

As the sun goes lower, his neck aches from staring up at the Great Skellig, which takes on new colours in the dying light. Seabirds wing by, shedding the odd acrid spatter. Trian hands him a bowl with some salt pork and an oatcake. Artt makes himself eat; the body is a beast of burden that must be fed and watered.

'Our second evening without a fire,' Cormac remarks.

Artt narrows his eyes; is the old monk complaining?

'A fine, mild night it is too,' Trian hurries to say.

'Holy Éanna and his men lived in caves, on their island, and never lit a flame,' Artt points out.

Cormac nods apologetically. 'And one of our strongest saints, blessed Comgall—he too preferred to deny himself that comfort. Though one time, in the deeps of winter, his companions broke down and begged him to make them a fire.'

Trian asks, 'Did the holy man take pity on their weakness?'

'He did, in the end. He picked up a few dry sticks,' Cormac says, half-laughing, 'and kindled them with his breath.'

Artt pictures that: a puff of warm air sparking to red life. The weaklings—ashamed, but grateful—holding out their hands to the flames, their renewed faith glowing inside them. Well, he supposes there are times mercy may do what strictness can't.

Evening is drawing in; he shivers and reaches down for his cloak. Around the boat a flock is gathering to preen and bathe, thousands strong, glossy black on white, pure white underneath. 'Brother Trian, do you know what these creatures are?'

'Shearwaters, Father. My people used to call them night birds, or devil birds, for the awful racket when they visit their burrows after dark.'

A pair of them come in stiff-winged now, scraping the water and leaving a fine wake; like gliding crosses, to Artt's eyes. Everything is a sign if you look at it hard enough.

The water laps; the tethered boat bobs. After a while the first lights stand out in the sky.

Trian asks, 'Are they holes, the stars?'

'Bodies of cold fire,' Artt corrects him, 'fixed

in a sphere around the earth. God spins it westwards every day. That's what makes the air and the clouds move.' He cranes up, a little dizzy, imagining that giant hand flicking the globe.

The dark shape of the Great Skellig looms above them, blotting out half the sky. Staring up at it, Cormac asks, 'Has either of you spotted any marks of a spring on this island?'

Trian doesn't answer, meaning no.

Nor has Artt, not yet. But he doesn't like the question's implication—the sneering hint that there may be no fresh water here. He'd like to crack their two heads together for doubting him, the haw-red one and the grey-wisped one. He bites his lip, tasting salt. 'Trust me, the island must have water, since we need it to live. This place was set aside for us when the earth was made.'

LANDFALL

CURLED UP AGAINST the skin of the boat, Trian breathes in pine pitch and wool fat, but behind it all, the savoury sting of the sea. The long night's paling at last. The air above and around him is awhir with birds. He makes tiny crosses on his forehead, mouth, and chest and says his dawn prayers silently, so as not to disturb his elders: *From the lures of the world, protect me. From bad men and demons, protect me. From plagues and accidents, protect me.*

The mainland lies like a black smear to the east; light rises over its low hills, tinting the sky pink. *From the rising of the sun to its setting, praised be your name.*

The sea is quite glassy, as if God's poured oil on it. As the red berry of the sun floats up into the sky, Trian can see everything: the silken fabric of the ocean, stretched out smooth with barely a ripple; flocks of voracious cormorants and moaning puffins working the waters.

Looming over the boat, the Great Skellig's sharp magnificence. To Trian it almost looks as if its rock was formed in flat layers, then the whole thing tipped sideways. *Every valley shall be lifted up,* Isaiah promises in the Scripture. This is a tiny, perfect land, stood on end; a bridge to the sky. *O bringer of good news, go up on the high mountain.*

The Prior's bright granite eyes are fixed on the peak. 'A perfect day for making landfall.'

Trian's heart leaps at the word.

With his bell, the Prior summons them onto their knees for Terce.

Afterwards they share a few eggs, roasted flesh gone rubbery. Then the Prior takes his place at the stern, with the steering oar. Trian eyes the northernmost headland. 'Which way around the island, Father?'

'Sunwise, of course.'

He feels foolish for having asked, since that's the luckier direction. He heaves at his oar, to angle the boat to the left of the protruding spit.

The Great Skellig looks to Trian to be not much longer than its sister, but twice as wide across and twice as high. Greener, too; grey scree patched with vegetation. On its eastern

side the rock slopes rather more gently down
to the water, but he sees no landing place to
moor the boat. They pass a cove like a little
bite. Then a deeper one.

'Might this do for an anchorage?' Cormac
asks.

The Prior shakes his head.

'The walls are too sheer, Brother,' Trian
points out.

While they circle the ragged pyramid, it
seems to unfold and come apart. Two great
breasts of rock, divided by a cleft, as if the
Great Skellig has been cracked almost in half.
The south side's quite different; cliffs tower
above the little boat. But on the other side of
the headland, a gigantic cove opens up.

The Prior leans forward. 'Now this is more
promising.'

Trian doesn't like the look of the open sea to
the west. 'Maybe too exposed, though, Father?
No shelter at all if a breaker were to roll in
while we were landing.'

He can't help thinking of his kind uncle and
his mean one, plucked off the shore in the
same moment.

They row on, sweating in the still air. A
splash to the left, a flurry of water. 'Dolphins!'
Trian hasn't seen one since he was a child.

The old monk's eyes bulge at the sight of

the sleek creatures leaping along in the boat's wake.

A pair—*or is it mother and infant,* Trian wonders? They speed up to come alongside and pass the boat, then double back, clearly curious.

The Prior stares past them. He steers farther out to give a wide berth to a reef of islets and sea stacks that trails off to the west of the Great Skellig.

Trian watches the water, wary of any rock that could hole their hull. Stroke by stroke, they work their way along to the northern face. This side is just as steep—incongruously, impossibly jagged. No hint of human presence; no level ground except the tiny ledges crowded by kittiwakes and guillemots, hundreds of feet in the air. Trian spots another great cove without any flat ground to get out on. Stone walls lean over, becoming precipitous overhangs.

A while later, he makes himself speak up. 'Father...isn't this where we started?'

The Prior nods, frowning. 'Keep on, Brother. We'll moor in the first cove we saw, just to the east of this point.'

'The little one?'

A nod.

At least it's sheltered there; with no swell at all, they should manage to scramble onto the rocks. As the boat moves in, Trian asks for the sounding line, and Cormac passes it to him. Trian heaves the lead, tossing the pointed plummet well in front of the prow. It sinks a surprisingly long way before it finds bottom. He pulls it up, counting by the leather ties that each mark off the height of a man. 'Still more than five fathoms, right here, but I'd expect off-lying rocks.'

The Prior gestures impatiently for them to close in on the island.

Next time Trian heaves the lead it sinks only two fathoms. He scrutinises the shoreline for any level perch at all. In the shadows, what looks like a sea cave. Beside it, a descending diagonal of rock, almost flat at the base, washed by the surf. 'There, Father?'

'That's it.' The Prior leans forward, using his steering oar to push the boat.

Trian eyes the slippery platform and the boulders around it, slick with rotting kelp. Twenty feet of water between them and the Great Skellig, he guesses.

Just then, a bump, an awful lurch.

The Prior lets out a groan.

'What is it?' Cormac asks.

'Aground,' Trian whispers.

Just the bow, maybe. The boat's skin is four layers deep, a full inch of cowhide. But the baggage she carries must be weighing her down, and if the spike of rock presses hard enough to pierce her...

Trian toes off his shoes and leaps over the side.

Cold water closes over his head. The shocking brine in his eyes makes him splutter and laugh.

When he comes up blowing like a whale, the Prior's barking: 'Brother Trian!'

Trian churns the sea with his legs and grabs the gunnel with both hands. Gasps, 'Just trying to shift us off the rock.' He flails at the stony knuckle the boat's wedged on, till his soles hit slimy stone; he plants them, heaves and pushes.

'Get back in,' the Prior's ordering.

'I nearly have it,' he protests. But what if his efforts to dislodge the boat only push her harder onto the sharp point?

The outcropping under his feet seems to move, or rather the boat's pulling sideways, slipping free at last. Trian heaves himself up on the gunnel, panting.

Cormac pulls him into the boat. 'Well done, lad.'

First thing, Trian checks under the laths. All the water there seems to be running off his own soaked robe; no sign of any rips in the hide.

But the Prior's voice is steely. 'You should

have asked before you leapt into the water. I thought you were drowning.'

Trian's thrown. His master didn't know he could swim. 'I...I beg pardon, Father.'

'Impulsiveness *and* insubordination.'

Cormac looks wide-eyed from one man to the other.

Trian's eyes brim. *No excuses,* he reminds himself.

'This is our testing ground.' The Prior speaks through his teeth. 'In the face of new difficulties and dangers, I ask you again, can you hold to your vow of obedience?'

'I can. I will.'

'Our mission depends on brotherhood. Divided, we'll fall.'

'Father,' Trian weeps. He slams his fist against his chest, a dozen times.

After a long silence, the Prior moves his oar and the boat inches forward. Cormac pokes the water ahead to make sure there's room to pass. The hull touches the platform at the base of the rock—scored with fissures, encrusted with limpets—and bumps away.

Shoes off, staff in hand, the Prior steps forward, edging around their goods. Trian doesn't dare move until he's told. Cormac offers a hand but the Prior ignores him, gripping the edge of the prow instead. (Is he still angry?)

He springs forward like a much younger man. The boat recoils as his feet find purchase on the wet slab.

Trian has the mooring rope ready to throw. Catching the coil, the Prior hitches it around a shard of rock and pulls, drawing in the boat as close as he can. He makes a tight knot. Then he reaches out to Cormac.

The old monk grasps his hand and uses his staff to get up onto the platform.

Trian hangs a waterskin around his neck by its horsehair strap before he joins them. He ventures to say, 'We might be the first men ever to set foot here.'

The Prior's voice booms, exultant: 'Like Adam in the Garden.'

Three Adams, one of them drenched, two of them caked in dried bird droppings. Trian shivers a little. He tips his head back and scans the cliffs, which are thick with clamouring birds.

The Prior quotes, '*When they had brought their ships to land, they forsook all, and followed him.*'

'Well now.' Cormac squints upwards, looking daunted.

The Prior's almost chanting: '*Neither height nor depth nor any creature can keep us from God.*'

Trian crosses himself. 'Amen.'

Their master gives him the nod. 'Brother, lead the way.'

And like a rabbit gratefully released from a snare, Trian is off up a ledge that offers just enough purchase for his feet. He's left his staff in the boat, along with his shoes; he prefers to rely on the grip of fingers and toes. His wet robes cling to his limbs, but he springs from rock to rock. Finding one handhold and foothold after another, he spider-dashes up the slope, setting course towards the bump he thinks of as the North Peak, the slightly lower of the Great Skellig's two.

Greasy, weed-scummed rocks give way to cliffs covered in nests. A reek of bird droppings, fish scraps, sea. The dusting of white reveals itself, up close, as fragments of eggshell. Left over from last summer, Trian supposes.

He glances over his shoulder. Cormac's hunched, grasping each rock as if in hand-to-hand combat. Trian calls, 'Close one eye, maybe, Brother?'

'What's that?'

'Shut your seaward eye and look only at the rock beside you.'

Cormac nods.

Below them, the Prior climbs with neither trouble nor grace.

Wherever Trian can, he picks his way along the carpet of cliff plants. Only low, hardy things seem to thrive on these salt-sprayed patches. Tufted fescue grass; low-growing mayweed, splotched with white daisy-like blooms already. Dense tussocks of thrift, sending up the odd stem of pink. Mounting higher, he spots more and more spurrey with its little pointed leaves, as well as tiny yellow buds of vetch, and white sea campion that some call *dead men's bells* because it seeds in unreachable niches. Where there's no vegetation, Trian follows firm slants of bedrock, rather than the scree that's so treacherous underfoot. Once or twice his step dislodges something and he shouts, "Ware rocks!' so his elders below can shield their faces.

Puffins poke gaudy beaks out of burrows. One launches itself into the air in front of Trian, then returns to the hillside with a crash of feathers. The squeaks and screeches of kittiwakes rise above the other cries; in their grass nests mudded to inaccessible perches, they face inwards and display their forked tails like knives. High ledges bristle with guillemots—duck-sized and upright in their black and white plumage. Some massive birds of a similar kind, too, that Trian's never seen before, bigger than geese.

The Great Skellig's feathered inhabitants are all so tame, they may shriek in surprise but they don't so much as flutter out of Trian's way. No, not tame, he realises: wildly innocent. They don't know enough of men to fear them.

His robe's beginning to dry already, and he's warming up. On the next turn, he passes a bizarre rock formation like a woman looking out to sea—her jaw jutting in grief, her hair blown behind her, her hand gesturing at the Lesser Skellig. Could the wind and the rain really have carved this? It's only a trick of perspective, Trian tells himself.

His mother wasn't crying when she and his father left him at the monastery, or not that she let him see.

Trian goes on, till he comes out onto a narrow plateau. Such a relief to stand on a patch of flattish ground and let his arms hang. He crosses to a rowan no taller than himself, growing out of a crevice in the rock. Three wizened red berries from last autumn cling on, but new toothed leaves are showing already, and the first blooms coming.

The Prior catches up, breathing heavily and swaying a little oddly as he stands surveying the island.

Shyly Trian asks, 'Does the earth feel like it's moving under you, Father?'

A guarded nod.

'You may be a touch landsick, then.'

The Prior stares at the word.

'When a man comes home from sea, and it takes him a day or two to get his land legs again.'

A shake of the head. 'So many varieties of frailty of the flesh.'

Here comes Cormac. He drops to the ground beside them and lets out a wheezing laugh. 'Good to take one breath at least without fear of dropping off a cliff.'

'You're a strong enough climber,' Trian says.

'Ah, but I haven't the balance anymore. It leaks away with age.'

Behind the little rowan, bare bedrock stretches up diagonally—no more than forty feet, Trian would guess—to the island's North Peak. The Prior's already heading up the slope. Trian and Cormac follow him to where the land drops away as if a giant's sliced it with a battle-axe.

Cormac lurches back from the brink. 'Too close for me.'

Trian keeps an eye on the Prior, ready to grab hold if need be.

Below them, birds arc and dive. Farther down the delicately etched water spreads out as far as Trian can see. No more islands. The three men have reached the edge of everything.

'There must be a spring here somewhere.' The Prior turns and strides down the hill.

Cormac struggles to his feet again. They head inland, towards the cleft in the middle of the Great Skellig, down a slant steep enough that once or twice even Trian has to sit down and slither, grabbing at the rock. This landscape is pathless, quite untrodden—because it has no four-footed beasts, he supposes. A great blank page, and these travellers are the first pens to touch it.

A grassy depression is opening up—a U-shaped saddle between the island's two high points. In the very middle, the Prior stops and spins in a circle. To north and south, empty sky, empty sea. 'Still no water,' he complains. 'Besides, this part is too exposed to build on. The winds would whip right across it.'

Cormac gives no opinion, only bends to examine a tiny flower.

Trian goes ahead, working his way up the conical tusk of the South Peak. He swings himself between narrow ledges. He supposes it is dangerous, but aren't they here on God's orders?

At some point he realises he's left the others behind, or they've dropped back. But he has to find water. Not out of vainglory, just to prove himself of use, despite his failings. To make the Prior glad, after all, that he brought Trian along.

So much seems wrecked about this island: stone shattered or worn, with deep vertical cracks, stained with droppings and lichens, rank with decaying seaweed. But in another way it feels quite new. As if Trian is being permitted to see a piece of creation at the very moment the world was made, more than six thousand years ago.

The valley's far below him now, an emerald patch with two tiny sitting figures. He moves on, without effort, without doubt, weightless, as if in a dream. The risk buoys him up. He follows a ledge that twists around a blind corner where he finds himself above a pure drop of hundreds of feet. The only way forward is a cleft in a great wall; he squeezes through. It's narrow enough to claw at his damp robe, and he thinks of Jesus's parable about it being easier for a camel to get through the eye of a needle than for a rich man to reach heaven.

Trian stands at the very top of the island now, where a horizontal spit of rock leads forward. He steps along it, then drops to a crouch. The spit's several times his length, thrusting into the sky. He crawls along, out into the blue. The rock slopes down a little; now it's no wider than his hand. He's inching on his belly,

his hip bones hanging free. Where the spit runs
out, Trian lies still, not even holding on; his
hands rest on the air. His face floats in open
space. Like flying. The hugeness, the glory.

A screech behind him.

Trian spasms and nearly rolls off. Gripping
the needle of rock under him, he cranes up
over his right shoulder—

And an enormous bird screams down, blotting out the sun. *Jok-jok-jok!*

The eagle's deep-fingered wings are as big as
a pair of doors. It grips a crag and settles its
bleached brown feathers with its hooked beak.
Gripping a large, twitching fish in one yellow
foot, it makes no move to swallow it. Its crop is
bulging, the size of a fist, Trian notices; maybe
it's gorged itself already. These seas must be
one great board spread for this king.

Nearby, a different cry: *Krau-krau-krau-uik-ik!*

The eagle goes on the alert again, throwing
back its pale head and answering more shrilly:
Kri-kyi-kyi-kli-kliek-yak!

His mate. Of course, this male must be warning Trian away from their eyrie. With a single
flap the eagle wings away, out of sight.

When Trian stumbles back down to the cen-
tral valley he's dubbed the Saddle, he expects
a rebuke for having been gone so long. But the
Prior only asks, 'Anything to our purpose?'

Rock. Air. Eagles. 'No water, Father, sorry.'

The Prior looks up at the bright clouds. 'Noon.' He opens the pouch on his belt and takes out the iron bell.

The other two press their palms together and follow him in chanting the three psalms.

Trian's belly growls. They brought no food up from the boat, since they were so keen to explore. He contents himself with a drink of water.

'Father.' Cormac sounds troubled. 'Can this really be the place? Without a spring...'

Trian stiffens at the hint of dissension.

For answer, the Prior flings his huge arms wide. 'Does God not visit those who love him in the wildest wastes?'

'He does,' Cormac acknowledges.

'This is an island unlike any other on earth. Do you doubt that?'

Both monks shake their heads.

'Then it must be meant for us, Brothers. It must have water, if only we have eyes to see it.'

Trian doesn't know what to say to that.

Leaving the grassy Saddle, the Prior retraces his steps up to the little Plateau below the North Peak. The monks follow. Out of the corner of his eye, Trian watches the Prior stare past the spiked pyramid of the Lesser Skellig to the gauzy country they've left behind, with its hills that look like low tents. A small fishing boat is rounding a headland; there must be a settlement around there.

Is their master waiting to be guided by a vision, Trian wonders? An angel who'll come down and make sweet liquid shoot up out of this bony ground? *Water, water, water.* His thick tongue presses against the ridged roof of his mouth.

The stunted rowan is the only tree they've seen here, and trees live longer than anything. Trian goes over and reaches down beside her roots, fingering gently, prodding. Is he imagining it, or does it feel a little damper? He scans the huge inclined surface of rock and pictures it during a rainfall, trickling, streaming. If there were a way of collecting that water...

In one slab, Trian finds a slanting fissure. In the next, a crack that runs to join the first. A shallower groove that looks like it's been worn by water. Where the lines drop out of sight, he pokes his left hand into the darkness, cramming it between the rocks. He wriggles, scrapes, struggles to decide what he's touching...When he pulls his hand out, one knuckle's bleeding, but the end of his middle finger's wet and clear. He examines both liquids, the scarlet and the

see-through. Puts his tongue to his fingertip.
'Father!'

The other two come hurrying.

The Prior's eyes flare. 'A well!'

'Not water springing out of the ground,'
Trian hastens to say, 'just a basin that seems
to hold rain.'

They each dip a hand deep into the crack and
taste it. 'Fresh water at such an elevation—a
miracle,' the Prior pronounces, sketching a
great cross in the air.

'We could dig it out to make a proper cistern,'
Cormac says.

The Prior thumps down onto his knees.
*You who makes a way in the wilderness and
streams in the desert,'* he recites, *'praised be
your name. You who told Moses to strike the
rock so water gushed out for all the Israelites
to drink—'*

Trian joins in, with Cormac: *'Praised be your
name.'*

*'You who splits the mountain and gives us
drink—'*

'Praised be your name.'

'And blessed be the rowan,' Trian adds, 'for
leading us to the water.'

'Isn't she known as the quicken tree, for
how fast she grows?' Cormac is almost
gabbling. 'And as for her fruit'—he strips

the three gnarled red balls from their yellow stems—'they're famous for cleaning the
blood.' He hands them out, one to each man.
Trian chews his; it's tart enough to make his
mouth pucker.

'Right here is where we'll camp, and then
build,' the Prior decides. 'This flat part has
the well, and the peak to our backs to keep
off the wind. Of what, maybe fifty acres of
land, only this one's level enough for us to
live on without rolling into the sea in our
sleep. I could wish we were facing away from
the world we've escaped, not towards it,' he
adds with a scowl at the mainland, 'but that
should remind us to stay on guard against its
temptations.'

'We'll get the warmth of the southern sun
here, too,' Cormac points out. 'We could ter-
race our garden to make it flatter and more
sheltered.'

The Prior raises both hands. 'Lord, I beg a
blessing from heaven on this Great Skellig, and
on us who'll live out our days here.'

'Amen.'

'A home for whatever time we may be
granted, where our bones will lie.'

That gives Trian a shiver. Of course he knew,
when he said yes to this great man outside
the dormitory less than a fortnight ago, that

there'd be no going back. But somehow it unnerves him to think of dying here, on this gargantuan sea-hill.

Descending the slippery cliff after they've sung their psalms for Sext is harder. Trian's stomach rumbles and he finds his legs wavering under him.

When they're nearly at what Trian thinks of as Landing Cove, Cormac stops short in fright. 'The boat's not there!'

The Prior lets out a bark of mirth.

'The tide's gone down, that's all, Brother,' Trian murmurs, 'and the boat with it.'

Cormac's quick to laugh at his own mistake.

Reaching the shell-pocked platform, they find the boat sitting a fathom lower, her rope pulled taut. 'Will I jump down and pass things up?' Trian asks.

But the Prior's already sitting down on the slithery edge. He lands on a lath with a loud creak, and the boat wallows. He heaves each item over his head to Cormac, who passes it to Trian: the holy chest first, then the stools, the great iron pot, the creel full of tools. 'Set everything down farther up the rock. Keep this flat place clear.'

'Mightn't the tide wash them off, even up there?' Cormac frets.

Trian points out the seaweed mark below.

'Unless there's a storm, Brother, the water won't come up any further than this line here.'

As they unpack, he finds he's almost sickened by their quantity of stuff. So unlike the birds and the beasts, who accumulate nothing, have nothing but what they seek out when they need it.

Their one spare robe Cormac hands to the Prior, who puts it on in place of his spattered one. Trian drops his eyes while the Prior's changing. He knows himself to be modest to a foolish degree. In all his years at Cluain Mhic Nóis he never took off his clothes in front of anyone, and washed only under them. On the rare occasions when the monks bathed in the river, Trian hung back until he could do it alone.

Now Cormac pulls his own tunic over his head and kneels down in his braies, trying to reach the water. Trian can't help noticing a blue-grey marking—an animal?—tattooed on his wrinkled back. 'Let me, Brother!' Eyes still averted, Trian takes both men's filthy robes, moves lower and crouches to rub them together in the sea. He gets the bird muck off and wrings as much water as he can out of them before handing Cormac's back up for the old monk to put on wet, since they have no other. The one the Prior was wearing, Trian stretches over a boulder to dry.

Joining in the chain of hands again, he passes up the sacks of charcoal, oats, wheat flour...

Cormac catches him staring at the food basket. Trian looks away, sheepish.

'Father,' Cormac asks, 'might we take a bit of nourishment to strengthen ourselves?'

'Very well, but don't waste the daylight.'

After an apple, Trian finds his hands are steadier. Cormac eats even the seeds and stem of his. The Prior only takes a drink from a waterskin. Trian's curious—is their master fasting as penance for some minor offence, or just caught up in the work?

From the rocks above, a derisive quack from one of those great waddling birds, the size of a child. Trian asks, 'Has either of you ever seen the like of that creature?'

The Prior shakes his head impatiently.

'Such comical white circles around its eyes,' Cormac points out.

Some sort of auk, Trian supposes, a hugely overgrown cousin to the guillemots and puffins. It rattles its stumpy little wings, then flops to its belly and slithers away. How odd—a bird born landlocked, like a goose with one wing clipped by a farmer's wife to stop it from flying away.

The Prior heaves himself out of the boat, onto the platform, and considers the rocky slope.

Trian is worried about how Cormac's going to manage the journey back up, heavily laden this time. 'Father, maybe I could go up first and rope the steepest spots, for us to hold as we climb?'

The Prior gives permission with a wave.

So Trian rummages around to find their iron pegs, the mallet, and a long, thin skein of nettle cord.

By the time he comes back down the cliff, Cormac is ready, with a sack slung evenly, front and back, over each shoulder. He grips his staff for balance. The Prior has lifted the wicker creel onto his own back, sliding his arms through the straps. What's more, he's got a stack of earthenware crocks under one arm. Trian wants to say something—to suggest their master is carrying too much—but it's not his place.

So he crams the iron cauldron with as many tools as it will hold, and leads the way.

It's slow, precarious work, even with the rigging he's pegged into the rocks. They pant and sweat; they kneel on rocky knobs and cling to wiry plants. Looking down, Trian spots a faint pale line in Cormac's wake. 'Brother, you're shedding flour!'

'Ah, no...'

A puffin runs over to peck at the trail. Cormac staggers, struggles to find the hole in the half of the sack that hangs down his back and lift that corner before—

The bottom rips loudly, unseams, and sheds a choking cloud. Released, the heavy front half of the bag falls through Cormac's flailing hands and scatters itself across the rocks.

This stock of ground wheat is all they have for making Communion bread.

Cormac's frozen, chalk-faced. 'Father,' he coughs. 'I beg pardon.'

'Nothing to be done,' the Prior says disgustedly. He turns back to the cliff with such furious momentum that the stack of crocks he's holding sways and the top half-dozen crocks fall, rebounding and smashing in pieces below.

Puffins flap away in outrage. Neither of the monks says a word.

The three push on, the Prior gripping the rest of the crocks with white-tipped fingers, Cormac clutching his remaining sack as if it's a baby.

When they've finally mounted up to the Plateau, they're all in a lather. Cormac folds up the ripped bag dolefully and begs pardon again and again.

They make a great pile of their stuff. Anything

light, they weigh down with stones. But they can leave it all sitting here without fear of theft, Trian realises, because there are no enemies. The monks have the place to themselves, and the birds pay them no attention. The whole island's a royal treasure house, locked tight by the sea.

The Prior scowls in the direction of the cliff. 'If only there was some better way to get the rest of our necessities up here.'

Cormac's eyes brighten in their nests of wrinkled skin. 'What if we hoisted them?'

An hour later Trian is kneeling with him at the top of the cliffs, beside a protruding rock. Cormac's leaning all his weight into the pulley they've pegged into a cleft. Sweat stands out on his forehead as he winds the handle.

'I can take a turn, Brother,' Trian repeats.

Cormac ignores that. Trian waits for the lumbering bundle the Prior's attached down at the shore—stools, cloaks, nets, the spare sail; he leans over to haul it in and untie the rope.

By the time the monks have winched up three bundles, the sun's low in the enormous sky. Trian guesses the job must be almost done by now; he can't think of anything still missing. 'Stay up here, Brother, while I go down to the Prior.'

Cormac objects: 'It must be nearly time for Vespers.'

'This is a hard climb even in full daylight,' Trian tells him. 'Say your prayers and get a fire going for us, maybe?'

Cormac nods and lets himself down on the ground.

Trian finds the returning tide has lifted the empty boat closer. The Prior breaks his pose of contemplation and looks up. 'Help me lift her out, Brother.'

This puzzles Trian. Won't they be needing to set off on a trading trip soon enough—to a farmstead on the mainland, or that island where they saw the turf-cutters? But he holds his tongue. He supposes it might be safer to store her on dry land for now, in case a spring storm breaks her on the rocks before they go to sea again.

First the two of them lift out the oars and the anchor stone. They draw the heavy mast out of its socket and lay it along the landing platform.

'The sail,' the Prior orders. 'It could come in handy.'

So Trian unwinds it from the yard, undoes its laces, and rolls it up.

Then they heave the hull out of the water, the effort nearly knocking him off his feet. 'Upside down,' the Prior grunts, 'to keep the rain out.' They tip it over, inverted like a gigantic shell against the rock wall.

The Prior pants with stern satisfaction, 'Nothing's won without pains.'

The sun's already slipped below the cliffs overhead, making a black jagged line. Trian shoves the anchor stone and the oars under the hull. He wedges the folded sail under his arm and goes up the cliff in the dimming light, on all fours this time.

He remembers to take a few eggs from a ledge as he passes, and tucks them into the pouch on his belt. Where the path turns left, there's that outcropping he thinks of as the Wailing Woman. Trian's starting to feel almost at home on this weird mountain. He mouths the old prayer to Mary the Virgin: *We fly to take refuge under your wing, Mother of God. Don't ignore our pleas in times of trouble, blessed one, but rescue us from danger.* Then he catches a whiff of smoke from above—what must be the first fire ever lit on this island.

THE CROSS

THE GREAT SKELLIG reminds Artt of Jacob's dream, in the Book of Genesis—a ladder planted on earth and reaching up to heaven, angels going up and down it all the time. This must be the most pointed place on earth; horns, spears, spikes, and blades of rock as far as he can see.

He walks at dawn. The sheer relief of being alone, after the week in the boat packed in so closely with the young monk (who seems to have no sense of how loudly he cracks his joints) and the old one (with his endless stories).

My island: Artt tries out the phrase in his head. Here he and his followers can live sequestered from the corruptions of society, and have some breathing space from each other too. But the heavy yoke of authority sits on Artt's shoulders. *The first shall be last;* a truly

Christian master must serve his men. It's Artt who bears all the responsibility for lighting a beacon of prayer in the ocean, now. A way-mark pointing up, one that will stand till the Last Day.

Rays of light sword out from the east, illuminating patches of glowing lichen on the grey rock. Birds spread their wings to catch the dawn's warmth. Artt would wish the Great Skellig not already occupied by so many feathered pests... but they're a useful reminder that there's no perfection to be found this side of heaven.

Artt takes out the iron bell and jangles it hard and fast now. He calls on Michael the Archangel, to whom all high places belong ever since he cast Lucifer's rebels into hell. 'By the power of Michael, I expel and banish any evil from this place!'

Silence, except for the odd yip from the birds.

This island's mine, Artt reassures himself. Meaning, his to hold in trust for his own Master. '*You bring them to your mountain, Lord, your own dwelling, the sanctuary made with your own hands.*' He rings the bell as he walks, drawing a musical line of blessing along every scaly rise and dip. '*His rule will be from sea to sea, and from the river to the ends of the earth.*'

At the south end of the island, where Artt finds he can go no farther, he kneels and kisses the ground. Its thin skin of green; its hard skeleton of stone. He shuts his eyes and quiets himself. Becomes as firm as rock. Begs to be as clear as crystal, so God's light can shine right through him. *Christus, Christus, Christus,* over and over more times than Artt can count, calling on his beloved.

When he emerges from his daze of prayer, he turns back, heading towards the green Saddle. One of those gigantic auks waddles straight across his path and stops, giving him a stupid, round-eyed stare.

Artt's reminded of a purifying rite from his childhood in honour of holy Martin—the blood-sprinkling. For lack of a cockerel, won't this creature do? Shaking off squeamishness, he walks up and takes the great auk by the neck, which is as thick and warm as a baby's arm. He says aloud, 'I dedicate this bird to sainted Martin and to our Lord Christ.' He gives one hard yank, hoping that will do it.

But the huge creature still struggles in his hands. Artt has to kneel on it. Pulling the knife from his belt, he lops off its head, and the thing is done. Having no bowl with him to catch the blood, he lets some spill into his left palm and asks Christ's blessing. He dabs a wet X on his own forehead with his right hand.

Carrying the heavy auk under his arm, Artt makes his way back to the camp on the Plateau, sprinkling the dark liquid to cleanse the land, the sea, the air.

Waking, Cormac's bewildered. Last night he was glad to stretch out on the ground after so long cramped in that wretched boat. But in his dreams he found himself crazed with vertigo, pursued up and down pinnacles by honking birds. His back's aching, this morning. He has salt in his mouth, the air's so strongly flavoured with it.

No sign of the Prior. There's Trian, back turned, hunkered down; a trickling sound. Cormac himself has to crouch to make water, these days—easier to get out the last dribbles that way—but he's never known a young man to do it that bashful, girlish way, and it makes him grin. 'Good morning, Brother.'

Trian straightens and pulls down his robe before turning to bow. 'Can you believe it, Brother? We're like the lords of the great ocean!'

For Cormac, the immensity of the sky seems to shrink them to the size of insects. 'I'm just relieved to be on dry land that's not wobbling about,' he tells Trian, searching for a pair of socks. He works them onto his feet, then ties on his shoes; the wool and leather should keep off the chill and soothe his aching toes.

A gull flies past so close, Cormac feels the waft on his face. He stumbles aside; laughs under his breath. He remembers sayings about birds being in-between creatures; maybe the souls of the dead, hovering above the land of the living for days or years before they'd drift west to what folk called *the other land*, or *the land of youth*, or *the land under the wave*? Since his conversion to Christ, Cormac knows all living things are simply part of God's creation, but birds still give him the odd shiver.

Breakfast. He pokes last night's embers and feeds the little flames with charcoal from the sack. He sets the three-legged griddle over the fire to heat up. In a bowl he grinds oats with a roundish stone till they're smooth enough to mix with a lump of butter, salt, and water, and form into a ball.

Cormac's head is crowded with practical concerns. The party is down to less than one full waterskin, so they really must start gouging out that crack in the rocks above to catch the next good rain. By the time the weather turns, they should also have put up some rough shelter, because getting soaked through is a recipe for illness. But their garden, shouldn't that come first? Every day they haven't put the seeds into the ground is a lost day of growing.

Cormac shoves the oatcakes around on the hissing iron with his finger. 'Such a fool I was to spill that wheat flour.'

'Ah, come,' Trian says, 'something must have torn the sack in the boat. And which of us makes no mistakes?'

'True, we're all cracked vessels. God must make the best use of us he can.' Cormac uses a wooden spoon to press together a crumbling oatcake. 'Now blessed Molua was so celebrated for his hospitality, God granted him a remarkable power.'

Trian always pricks up his ears at a story. 'What was it?'

'The saint could sow common grain—oats and barley—and have fine wheat spring up in its place.'

Trian laughs at that.

Cormac leaves the oatcakes to cook. He folds away the three cloaks. He takes the three long ticks and looks for something to fill them. There's fescue grass; he rips out handfuls. Cushions of thrift, too, its first pink tufts feathering, its grey-green blades sharp enough to cut any hands less leathery than his. He thinks he recognises a sprawling mass as spurrey; its hairy foliage leaves his fingers sticky. Sea campion, too—the small waxy oval leaves look rather softer for lying on.

As he forms the mattresses, Cormac fills a pouch with any greens that seem edible. Spinach-like goosefoot, even spoonwort with its heart-shaped leaves that make the eyes water with their mustardy pungency. Until he can grow a few potherbs, he must gather any healthful forage he finds.

'Brother Trian, do you know this succulent one?'

'Sea beet. That's good eating.' Trian drops to his knees and starts helping to sort food from bedding.

'You didn't take a chill yesterday, from going in the water?'

A shake of the head.

'Your uncles who drowned, God bless them. Had they not learned to float like you?'

Trian shakes his head. 'My people thought, if the waves were going to take you, better to die fast than slow. And they had a saying: *The sea must have its share.*'

'Its share of... people?'

'Right. If you saw someone struggling in the

sea, you'd make a grab for him, how could you not? But you knew if you managed to haul him out, you'd owe the sea a life—yours.'

Cormac murmurs, 'What our Prior would call a heathen superstition.'

Trian's abashed. 'Of course it's God who decides, not the sea. My people were baptised, but they still held to some of the old ways.'

Who understands that better than Cormac? Even though he's been Christ's man for a decade and a half, those ways still flow in him like an underground stream.

It occurs to him that if Trian's family lived far off on the east coast, they can't have been serfs of the Abbot's clan. 'Your parents, I wonder why they made an offering of you at thirteen—was it in thanksgiving for an answered prayer?' Like Brother Ronán, a quarrelsome character; his parents gave him to Cluain Mhic Nóis at eight, Cormac remembers, and kept the other twin.

Trian shakes his head. 'Our priest spoke about the monastery on the great Sionan, and how it was famous for the teaching of the young.'

'Had you a longing for education?'

A shrug. 'My mother told me I was made for a monk.'

It doesn't sound to Cormac as if the boy

balked at the prospect, though. Trian seems to have a natural talent for working, obeying, and doing without. 'And how did it—how did we seem to you, when you first came?'

Trian grasps for words. 'So many men, cheek by jowl.'

Cormac chuckles. 'The stink.'

'And the noise.'

He remembers finding that a shock, himself, when he woke up after the surgery with his astonishingly mended head. But he stayed anyway, out of gratitude, and embraced a second life. Cormac never imagined, all these years later, that he'd find himself beginning a third one, on a great rock in the ocean.

The three ticks are stuffed with foliage now. Misshapen, bulging oddly, but they'll do for sleeping on. Cormac unrolls the leather that holds the bronze needles, which are among their most irreplaceable tools. He chooses a small one, handling it with great care so as not to drop it. He cuts off a length of strong wool thread and sets to tacking up the ends of the bags to hold in their scented green.

Trian's head is up, his eyes on the skinny rowan that led them to water yesterday. Buds just on the verge of blooming. A small brown bird perches on one of her branches, then wings away.

Cormac thinks of the tree in the Scripture, a mighty cedar where birds of all kinds nest and find shelter—not like this puny bush. Still, rowan's known for warding off evil spirits. 'The hardiest of all trees.'

'Is she?'

'Some call rowan *the lady of the mountain*,' Cormac tells him, 'for her skill at rooting herself in the rockiest places.'

'I wonder how big this one will get, when full grown.'

'Oh, she's old already.'

Trian looks confused. 'But she's still only child-sized. *The quicken tree*, you called her, because of how fast—'

'They thrive in good soil, but this one's stinted and stunted. No, you can tell her great age by the bark.' Cormac puts his finger to the scaly, cracked black. 'It starts out smooth, with a tinge of yellow to the grey.'

Trian strokes the furrowed rowan.

'Trees were so precious in the eyes of holy Colm Cille, when he heard that to build his church facing east in the customary way would require cutting down a stand of ancient oak, he laid out the foundations facing north instead.'

Trian smiles and crosses himself. 'What an act of mercy, to spare those trees.'

Cormac spots the Prior coming towards them, bloodied on head and hands. Has he had a fall?

They jump to their feet and make their bows.

But the Prior's unhurt, and exhilarated. He drops a great dead bird on the turf and steps up close to mark Cormac's forehead, then Trian's, with its warm blood. 'The blessing of Christ on you.'

'Amen, Father.'

'Amen.'

The Prior takes the jar of soap and the goat-skin of water, to wash his hands.

Cormac hopes their master doesn't use up too much of their drinking water, but doesn't dare say so.

Then the Prior rings the bell for Terce.

After the service, they share the browned oatcakes, and the Prior tells Cormac to put the great auk on to roast. 'Fat and flightless—could we have more plentiful or easy prey?'

The notion seems to make Trian uneasy. 'We shouldn't take more than we need, though, surely Father?'

The Prior looks at him, one eyebrow tilted. 'What else are they for?'

'I only mean ... they were here long before us.'

He corrects Trian: 'Ready for our arrival.

This whole island's like one great banquet table that God's spread for us.'

Trian's tongue-tied now.

'Didn't he give man *dominion over the fish of the sea and the birds of the air*?' the Prior quotes.

There's no arguing with that. Cormac offers a story, to ease the mood. 'I'm put in mind of a tale told of holy Columbán that's known as the Manna of Birds.'

The Prior nods.

'One winter, our blessed countryman's followers hadn't eaten for three long days, but he told them to fear nothing because God would surely feed them. And sure enough,' Cormac goes on, 'on the fourth day, the monks woke up to find an abundance of birds covering the ground, as white as snow.'

'Were they singing,' Trian asks, 'like the ones on the paradisical island you said holy Breandán discovered?'

Cormac shakes his head. 'Frozen, as if under a spell. Or rather, held by God's command, so they wouldn't startle and flee. Meekly those birds offered themselves up for the famished monks to wring their necks.'

'Of course, God offers us all the like abundance,' the Prior points out.

Cormac looks at the limp great auk. 'You mean...'

'The one nourishment that truly sustains? That feast that all may approach, without one man's share reducing what's left for his brethren?'

'Oh! Holy Scripture,' Trian guesses, before Cormac can say it.

When the Prior goes off to pray, Cormac wakes up the fire, putting on more charcoal. Since there's no timber or even peat here, before this sack runs out they'll have to sail in search of more. Well, leave that worry for another day.

He concentrates on plucking this bird. A great auk can't be so different from a goose or a hen, surely? He starts by yanking out the primary feathers—the tail ones he pulls directly, but for the wings he goes against the grain. He wishes he had shears to snip off the last joint of each wing, but the big knife will do. Anchoring the auk's legs in the grip of his right fist, with his left thumb and knuckles he grabs the breast feathers and rips them upwards, towards the missing head. He moves on to the smaller feathers farther down the belly and the undercoat of fine down. This grown bird's tough, and even though the body's still warm, the plucking proves such hard going that Cormac begins to think he should have skinned it instead, especially as a sea bird will have a rankly fishy skin. Ah well, he'll finish what he's begun. Legs, then wings, the hardest spots to pluck. The auk's naked skin is yellowish and looks coarse-woven; he has to dig into the armpits to tear out the little feathers. Finally, the back, where the feathers come out almost as easily as from the breast.

Trian's collecting them before they can drift away on the spring breeze. 'Separate out the down for trading, would you?' Cormac asks. Trian nods and opens a smaller bag for that.

Cormac feels around inside the auk's limp neck and digs out the crop with its mess of undigested stuff: shells, bones, scales, and beaks. Two fingers in one end of the bird, he wrenches out a tangle of entrails; two fingers in the other, the rest. The little heart he snips off. It's a tidbit that some prefer raw, but that seems savage to Cormac. He spikes it on an iron skewer and sets it almost in the flames, so it begins to sear and juice at once. After a minute he holds it out to Trian.

The young man waves it away.

'Aren't you hungry?'

A half-smile. 'Sure I'm always hungry, Brother.'

'Go on, you're still growing. A bit of heart meat will do you good.'

Trian thanks him and takes it off the spit with his teeth, blowing to cool it; he swallows it in one gulp.

Cormac reaches for the knife again to hack off the auk's feet. He adds a very sparing slosh from the goatskin to rinse the bird through. He'd use salt water for that if he had it, and for washing hands and implements. 'Brother, could you ever haul us up some water from the sea?'

Trian grabs two of the buckets, and sets their straps over his shoulders. He heads off without a word.

Cormac pulls the leather stopper out of their big jar of salt and takes a gritty handful to rub over the carcass. He spears the great auk on two crossed iron skewers. Under the skin, the meat's a dark red. Cormac knows little of the arts of the kitchen, but he doubts the Prior would approve of fine cookery anyway. He sets the spitted bird across the stones to roast. He goes over to a patch of fescue and rubs his bloody, down-flecked palms on it.

The Prior comes back to the fire. 'I've never seen so many birds,' he complains. 'Huddled in their thousands, or tens of thousands.'

'I suppose they must like the company,' Cormac says.

He puffs out his breath. 'Each jostling for

his foul few inches of ground, more like. Like
those stinking cities, on the Continent. I suppose you've little grasp of what a city's like, or
even a town?'

'Only from books,' Cormac admits, feeling
ignorant. He's pored over drawings of towers,
amphitheatres, buildings tall and uncountable,
all packed with people living like grubs in a log.

The Prior shudders. 'Charnel pits, I call
them. Sin spreads there as fast as infection.
The noise and filth I witnessed in Autricum,
Cenabum... or poor ruinous Rome, where
refugees drop down starving in the streets.'

Just then Trian staggers back into camp with
both buckets half-full of seawater.

Cormac points along the Plateau. 'Father, I
was thinking I might tackle a proper cistern to
catch the rain for us, even before I start on the
garden, or some kind of shelter—'

The Prior puts up his hand, silencing him.
'Does it not strike you that these are low
concerns?'

Cormac's face heats.

Their master's tone is serene. 'Having landed
on this holy island, should our first thoughts
be for the body's wants?'

The rising aroma of the meat seems to mock
him. He finds himself wishing Trian weren't
there to hear him put to shame.

'Instead,' the Prior says, 'our very first task will be to claim this Skellig for Christ with a great cross.'

Cormac's carved high crosses before, of wood with metal ornaments, but that's impossible here. 'Incised on a boulder, you mean?'

The Prior shakes his head, his smile gleaming. 'Freestanding. A tall cross-slab chiselled out of the bedrock, so it can be seen from all directions.'

Seen by whom, Cormac wonders?

'Like a standard carried into battle, a banner to mark this as sacred ground.'

All he can say is, 'Right, Father.'

Soon the great auk's blackened, so Cormac takes it off the fire and sets it on a flat rock. He carves pieces off it, still bloody at the centre. He turns the third bucket over as a seat for their leader. He and Trian sit on the grass and wait for the Prior to bless the meat. Each man makes a cross over his own bowl and thanks God before he eats.

'Liverish?' the Prior wonders aloud.

'Beefy, more like,' Trian suggests. 'Or gamey, maybe.'

'A bit fishy, but not as much as I was expecting.' Whatever about the taste, it's rich, fresh meat; Cormac tries not to bolt his too eagerly.

When he's cleared his bowl he feels more solid; more able for whatever will be asked of him today.

'Come,' the Prior says.

Cormac and Trian follow him down the Plateau to where an outcropping more than the size of a man thrusts up, almost like a thick pillar.

The Prior touches an indentation on one side, at the top.

'See this piece of our cross, Brothers—already cut out, as if God's begun the work for us?'

Cormac nods, less certain. 'We should test the stone for soundness, first, I'd say.' He goes back to fetch the short-handled oak mallet, which is less likely to damage the rock than their iron hammer. He taps the pillar all over.

Trian asks, 'What are you listening for?'

'That ringing, like a bell. If there are fissures inside, they'll suck in the sound, deaden it.'

The Prior persists: 'But this pillar sounds right?'

Cormac nods. 'To be quite sure, though, we'll need water.'

Trian's already hurrying off to get one of the buckets.

Cormac trickles seawater all over the great rock, a drip at a time. He can detect no cracks. He runs his leathery hands over the grain, from top to bottom. 'The wet shows the bed lines, see?' He points out the pattern to Trian. 'Every rock's strongest along its bed. Where we cut across it, that's where we'll have to take most care.' Turning to the Prior: 'Is it a Greek or Latin cross you want, Father?'

'Latin, with a long leg, to suit such a tall slab.' The Prior picks up a shard from the ground and begins to scratch out his design on the rock: the pyramidal base, the giant cross rising from it. 'Sturdy enough to stand until the end of time.'

Cormac's relieved to see that a thick ring will connect the short arms and bear their weight; they'll need to protrude only a few inches past that.

'The circle symbolises the heavens, the celestial sphere,' the Prior declaims. 'The heavens turn, but the cross stands still.' He steps back and considers the pale lines. 'You can start blocking it out now, Brother Cormac.'

A few mornings later, in faint drizzle, Trian's fowling.

This island is one great festivity of birds—more of them every day, swooping in and scrambling across the rocks, which are increasingly whitened by a snowfall of creamy droppings. Each bird seeking out its kind, he supposes, longing to pair and breed little copies of themselves.

A funny thing he's noticed—once shearwaters land, they have to drag themselves across the rocks, because they can fly but not walk, which is the other way around from great auks. Maybe each creature's granted only the powers it needs to live? The Creator doles out talents at his pleasure, Trian supposes, and brooks no argument.

He remembers how his kinsmen used to go out roped together in pairs for some measure of safety. They pursued the birds all over the cliffs with their nets, or three men would dangle a fourth from an overhang so he could pick a whole basketful of eggs out of the nests. The most talented cragsmen scorned the ropes; they claimed to scrabble up and down cliffs better that way, knowing one misstep would be their last.

On the Great Skellig the hunt is so easy, it troubles Trian. He's already caught a kittiwake by holding the hand net under a ledge and knocking the bird in with his staff. And the bright-faced puffins, in their burrows, like juicy turnips waiting in the ground. He chooses a dark hole now and inserts his left hand, all the way to his armpit. Nothing but the smooth blockage of an egg. In the next, a peck at his finger; Trian pulls back, to check he's not bleeding, then goes in again fast, winding his wrist around a corner, and at the very back lays hold of a puffin on its egg. He pulls out the bird, calms it by stroking, and says a quick thanks to God before he twists its vivid head. With his knife he cuts a slit right through the puffin's limp neck and pushes its head under his belt and through its own neck gash, pulling it into a knot.

Should he leave that egg in case the other parent comes back to sit on it? It seems unlikely; he's only ever seen a pair manage to raise young. (Not like the she-cats at the monastery, who rear their litters alone.) Trian decides he'd better take the egg, so it won't be wasted. Pure white, and oddly big for such a neat little bird. He holds it up to the morning sun; no sign of anything growing yet, only a little spot darkening the oval. He places it at the bottom of the cloth bag tied to his belt. An egg and two birds—that seems more than enough to feed three monks for a day.

Another puffin walks past Trian, toting a feather the size of itself into its burrow. He's struck by how industrious they are. Another picks up a little dried root of some plant and scratches its underbelly with it. This impresses him, that a bird can make something into a tool. Trian's learning to distinguish a neutral greeting from an alarm call, from a boast to attract a mate. Now a cormorant flies by low with its neck stuck out, a long ribbon of sea-weed in its beak. All these different birds, on the same mission of nest-building, and with such energy and inventiveness.

Time slides away from Trian, here on the cliffs. The crosswinds flare his rain-damp robe and he finds himself wondering what it would feel like to be equally at home on land, in water, and in air. To be powered by the breeze, wheeling and soaring, free from the weight that keeps other creatures shackled to the earth. Could a man make a cloak of feathers that might bear him up, gliding over the sea?

When Trian gets back to the camp up on the Plateau, he takes the birds off his belt and sets them by the fire with the egg. He follows a clinking to where Cormac's toiling on the stone cross. Its right arm is already emerging from its shielding ring, as if the shape's always been hidden inside, ever since God first formed the rock.

'Your carving goes well, Brother.'

'So far.' Cormac wipes his rain-slick forehead

on his grey-fuzzed arm. 'Well, as the saying has it, work as if all depends on you, but pray as if all depends on God.'

'Amen.'

'Maybe it's time you learned to cut stone. Come here.'

Taken aback, Trian goes to stand at Cormac's side.

'Always carve towards the centre of the rock. The edges are thinner and can sometimes break off without warning.'

Trian flinches at the idea.

'First we rough out the shape with the mallet and the pitcher'—Cormac shows a flat-ended tool in his left hand. 'I hold this pitcher halfway down its length, and tuck my thumb into my fingers so I won't hammer it with the mallet. Though you being the way you are, I suppose you might wield the mallet with your left, for more force?'

'If that's allowed,' Trian says uncomfortably. 'My two hands are about the same in strength—it's just that the right isn't as nimble.'

Cormac sets the tip of the pitcher tool to the spot on the cross's arm where he's been working. 'Keep the tool coming in low, nearer to flat than upright.' He hits it with his cylindrical mallet, and the stone chips. He moves

on half an inch and does it again. 'If your
tip gets stuck, it means you're digging in too
steeply. And don't strike the stone head-on, or
you'll leave a shiny bruise, and nothing can
rub that out.'

Trian's trying to commit these warnings to
memory.

'Nor too shallow either, or your blade will
skip right off. If you find yourself sliding about
on the surface, go deeper.' Cormac cuts on,
every move clean. 'Now, keep your tip pressed
to the stone all the time, no jiggling about.'

'Right.'

'Here's the rule: *pitch, punch, claw, chisel*,'
Cormac tells him in a singsong voice. 'After
you've roughed it out with the pitch, you'll
need the punch—the pointed one—for clear-
ing away all the leftover stone, but don't get
carried away and take too much.'

Trian fears he's muddling up the various
tools already.

'The claw is this toothed one,' Cormac says,
'it'll level the surface nicely. The last is the
chisel, with a narrow flat end, for the fine
details.'

He's finding it hard to imagine he could ever
do such subtle stonework.

'What's the rule?'

'*Pitch, punch, claw, chisel*,' he repeats back.

'Let me try? I pick things up better in the doing.'

Cormac hands over the tools. 'Get above it, and carve down—that way you'll have more force.'

'Like in battle, bringing a spear or sword or axe down on an enemy?'

A shrug. 'Fighting goes by in such a blur, it's hard to recall.' He pats Trian's right hand on the mallet handle: 'That's a fierce grip. Looser, looser. You'll be keeping this up hour after hour, so if anything's a strain it'll wear you out in no time.'

Clutching the punch, Trian chips the stone away.

'Oh, and guard your eyes from motes and specks, they could blind you,' Cormac warns. 'Veil your eyes with your lashes.'

Trian nods, half-shutting his lids, and hammers again.

Cormac stares at the tiny puddle on which their hopes rest. Now that Trian's taking a turn on the cross, at last the Prior has given Cormac permission to dig out a cistern.

He's already pried up three boulders with the

crowbar to find the precious rainwater, which
fills a depression only the size of his palm.
A bullaun, that's what such a hollow's called.
When Cormac was young, you'd drop a pebble
into the puddle in a bullaun stone and turn it
rightwards first thing in the morning to work
a cure, or leftwards for a curse. Now he makes
a cross in the air with his thumb and first two
fingers, blessing the water in the name of the
Father, Son, and Holy Spirit.

He starts with the wide punch and a rounded
rock the size of his fist, since he's left Trian
the lump hammer for carving. Cormac gouges
delicately, widening the rut; when the water's
thick with stone chips he pauses to rake them
out with his fingers. If in a careless moment he
cracks this strong base, the liquid will trickle
away into the hill, and they'll have to resort to
setting out bowls to catch the rain.

But the hollow grows, little by little, and Cormac's mind leaps ahead. He'll make the basin
as deep as his forearm, with small scoops out
of its base to catch any sediment that settles.
Then he'll start cutting shallow channels down
the rock wall above, to feed the cistern. The
whole bare scarp, he could cover with grooves
like a spiderweb. No, more like silver snail
tracks, many trickles joining in a thick flow.

And if the cistern works so well that it fills

up in heavy rainfall and brims over? Cormac will make a notch in the side, and hollow out another basin underneath to catch the overflow. What's more, he can raise and reinforce their sides with thin slabs of slate. His arms are throbbing now, but he works all the faster. He repeats the Scripture in his head for encouragement: *So lift your tired hands, and straighten your shaking knees.*

When the bell for Sext summons Cormac back to the fire, Trian already has a great auk sizzling. He shows what he uses to noose them: a loop of string stiffened with beeswax and tied to the end of his staff. 'Though it hardly seems fair,' he says under his breath, 'when they can't fly away.'

Cormac nods ruefully. 'Every kind of creature needs to eat, I suppose, and we're no different.' He hurries to grind some meal, to make oatcakes on the griddle.

The Prior comes up, ringing the bell for silence. The monks stop what they're doing and stand to recite the holy hour.

As Cormac joins in the psalms, his mouth is watering like a cavern behind a waterfall. He'd forgotten how fierce a hunger a man can get from hefting stones. At Cluain Mhic Nóis, he had a hand in many tasks, but there were always younger men to do the heavy lifting.

Cormac hasn't felt so tired, or so needed, in long years.

After their prayers, he takes the charred oatcakes off the griddle. He watches Trian poke the auk's blackened breast. The juice runs clear at last, so Trian wraps a cloth around his hand to yank the bird out of the fire.

At last, the day's come. Artt's stone cross stands as tall as him, and beautiful.

His followers are blistered and sore. They've stood for hours on upside-down buckets to shape the top arm where it pushes up from the ring like the branch of a petrified tree. They've bevelled the edges with the claw tool. They've scrubbed the droppings off every time a bird dares to dirty it.

The rock faces are still nibbled, but Artt's decided that is as it should be. 'There's nothing smooth about this Great Skellig,' he muses aloud, 'so it should be a rugged cross, to command a rugged place. No, there's only one spot that needs a touch more work.' He sets a chisel to a darker lump that blurs the lovely line, where the ring meets the protruding right arm.

Cormac grimaces. 'There seemed a weakness in the stone there, Father, so I was afraid to go any deeper.'

'Oh, it only needs a stroke or two.' Artt taps once with the mallet—

He doesn't hear a crack, or see it grow, but the whole arm of the cross drops away.

Artt recoils. The white-dusty wound; the lump on the grass, like any fallen rock. He thuds to his knees and the tools drop from his hands. 'God forgive me!'

Trian crosses himself and mutters a prayer to avert evil.

Cormac speaks hoarsely. 'Not your fault, Father. Pure accident.'

'There are no accidents.' Inadvertence, inattention. Worse: the reckless arrogance of a priest who insists on going one better than his simple monk brethren; the devilish pride of a man fonder of his own judgement than God's.

Artt's mind races. If he could cement the piece back on...but how can he make mortar with no slaked lime, with no sand even? No, his awful blunder can't be fixed.

He reaches out and hefts the fallen arm; fingers the jagged point where it fractured. He could bring that down on his own fist right this minute; he longs for the blow. But which hand is the sinful one—the left, which set the blade to the weak point despite the old monk's warning, or the right, which must have landed the mallet too hard? Artt should smash both his hands, and his eyes for misjudging, and his ears for not listening, and his brain for its willfulness—

No. He reins in his rage. Founding this monastery is going to take all three of them, and all their limbs, and all their powers. Even with all their weaknesses.

'Father?' Trian whispers.

Artt finds he can't speak yet. He gets up and stumbles away.

What penance should he set himself to make satisfaction? He could roll in nettles, except that he's seen none here. Lie in cross-vigil? No, stand—that's harder. Or kneel—that's even better punishment. Artt crashes down, in the middle of the Plateau, and holds his arms straight out from his sides, the position of Jesus on the cross. He starts his prayers of contrition. He waits for discomfort to ripen into pain.

The man who masters himself rules a mighty kingdom. Pain is one way to do it. Those who love Christ, he grants permission to suffer for his sake. Pain's a privilege, a gift, a grace. The more Artt's knees hurt, the more he'll be atoning for his sin—albeit never quite enough, because every wrongdoing leaves a faint mark. Isn't every child born bearing the smudge of Eve's sin of eating the fruit the serpent offered, and Adam's sin of letting her persuade him—that deep-dyed human tendency to stray from the loving Father?

Sever me not from your sweetness, Artt begs.

He straightens his aching back and stretches out his arms. Remembers Moses, who was already eighty years old when God called him. During the battle against the Amalekites, didn't Moses hold up his hands to encourage the Israelites? When his strength began to fail and his hands sank down, the fight started going against God's people. So Moses asked his elder brother Aaron to hold up one of his arms, and their companion Hur to support the other. With his comrades' help, his hands stayed high till sunset, when the Israelites triumphed. Artt clings to the image of those three men, bearing each other up. So few, but indomitable.

A puffin walks right up to him now, motley-coloured, like some jester jeering. Artt squeezes his eyes shut. Holy Cóemgen, who lived in a glen in a hollow tree, knelt in cross-vigil for so long, one time, that a crow made a nest in his hand. The saint didn't move a muscle all the time the bird was laying her eggs and brooding on them; didn't let his arms down while the chicks were breaking out and cheeping to be fed; never moved from his penitential posture all those long weeks until the fledglings flew away.

Artt will be as strong as Cóemgen. He chants, emptying himself out so he can be filled with God: *Sanctus, sanctus, sanctus, sanctus, sanctus.* Truly hurting now. He opens a door to the pain. Penance is balm to the soul; it releases sorrow, softens the hardest heart. God teaches by tears, and he wounds only to heal.

The next time Artt feels his hands failing a little, he imagines himself held up by a long nail hammered through each palm. He recites fiercely: *I am crucified with Christ.* He tries to be the man on the cross—not Jesus, but one of the lowly thieves by his sides, the penitent one.

Artt will stay in cross-vigil all afternoon, all evening if he can, until the sky's quite black. God is all he strives for, all he thinks about, his very breath. He'd like to level the botched high cross, first thing tomorrow, but he won't. Let it stand as a warning to himself and his monks, a sign of their imperfection, the crippling weight of it. That's the lesson stone teaches: even after it falls, it endures.

SEEDTIME

THE HEIGHTS ARE mysterious with cloud, today, and Trian can't see a thing. Fog makes an island of every man. Trian can find his brethren only by calling out, as he picks his way around the Plateau, and he has to restrain his usual lope so he won't fall. He pops his neck muscles in loud frustration; he prays; he waits.

Then a breeze clears away the wreaths of white, and the Great Skellig dazzles like an emerald.

The Prior asks Trian to catch them some fish.

So it must be the weekly fast, the day Christ was put to death. (Trian's lost count. Time runs differently here; sometimes when he hears the iron bell, he's bewildered, because it seems only minutes since the three gathered for the last service.)

What he doesn't mention to the Prior is that he's far from sure how to fish here. He remembers his father and uncles rowing in to their coastal farmstead with nets full of shining catch, but the monks' boat is upended on dry rock below, in Landing Cove. He knows better than to suggest putting her to sea again to catch fish in quantity; the Prior would call that greed. Instead, Trian will have to cast a line from the rocks. But where to begin?

He knows he'll need juicy bait, anyway. So he climbs down the cliff, carrying the fishing gear. The tide's going out; it looks like a massacre. It's only gaudy red kelp fringing the rocks. Small pools hold opaque spills of white, lumps of startling green that wave in the water like hair, and little air sacs of bladder wrack. Smears of foam are drying out already, and the seaweed's begun to decay in clumps and twists, tiny flies leaping and biting.

He leaves his shoes near the upturned boat, above the tide line, and scrambles over giant boulders across the strip of cove that gets wetted and dried twice a day. This is a good time to harvest shore food, he realises; any shellfish still clinging to the rocks should be healthy, now the weak or dead have been washed away.

Looking for limpets, Trian finds dozens of the oval cones with their blue rays and pearly sheen. Approaching quietly, he slides his knife tip under one to prise it off its rock. Such strength for a little thing! It gives in at last, revealing its snail-horns and puckered gripper, as round as a baby's mouth. It comes back to Trian that you can knock a limpet off its perch if you hit it sideways, so he tries that on the next few. It works only when he surprises the creature; if the first blow doesn't do the trick, the limpet takes fright and clings twice as hard. He supposes it's a sign of life if it resists being seized. Like a mussel, which claps its two shells together when it feels a hand.

His bag's starting to fill. Would the Prior consider it a sin to eat between meals? Distracted by hunger, Trian decides to allow himself one limpet. He makes a cross over it and pulls off the head and guts before he bites the meat off the shell. Deliciously salty and chewy, though he has to spit out the grit.

When he opens the next it smells wrong, and he's about to throw it aside before he remembers that fish find the tang of decay irresistible. He unrolls the fishing gear and takes out a short line—no more than three times as long as he is tall—with tiny iron hooks knotted on at intervals. He scrapes and yanks the rank limpet out of its shell and pushes it onto the first hook. He baits the next, and the next.

He finds himself wondering what makes it

permissible to eat fish on a fast-day. Is it because fish are less like men than pigs or cows are, so less likely to rouse the baser appetites? Trian's never understood why, in the Garden, at first Adam and Eve ate only fruits and nuts, but after the Flood God told his people, *Everything that lives and moves will be meat for you.* Well, the important thing's not to grasp the rule but to obey it.

He's hoping for bream, today, maybe, or pollock. Wrasse? Whiting or scad, even? Unless the fish on this coast are quite other than the ones of his childhood. When he's loaded all his hooks with bait, he scans the water. There's a good rock out there, though its furry green patches look slippery. Trian wades out and clambers on, finding a spot where his toes can get purchase. The sea's calm enough that a rogue breaker is unlikely to roll in. He ties a pebble onto the bottom of the barbed line to weight it; he whirls and casts it out, well away from him. He loops the end around his left hand and waits.

Trian perches there for what feels like hours, watching the tide shrink away from the foreshore. The sea stacks seem to be rising, and his own little pedestal too, like a hill budding out of the sea, but that must be an illusion. He shifts his weight from left to right and back again, over and over, like dancing. He whistles a tune under his breath. He misses his bone pipe, the one he carved with the guidance of Brother Blathmac. That's something Trian did love at the monastery: making music at dinnertime. Here on the Great Skellig, when the birds sing out their different calls, Trian would like to be able to answer them with human tunes.

No flicker on the line yet, no feel of anything alive at the other end, only the gentle fluctuations of the sea. The fish aren't there, or they're sleeping, or not hungry enough to bite. The water's too low; it must be slack tide now, the hour before the turn, when nothing's moving. Is it too bright for fish at this time of day, the water too riddled with light, despite the gauze of clouds? The air's sprinkled with gliding birds; puffins land on the water with a splash or an undignified roll. Divers occasionally duck under and come up with fat fish, effortlessly, as if taunting Trian.

A light shower of rain begins. His stomach creaks; he's tempted to pull another limpet off a hook and eat it, but what if that's the one bit of bait that might catch their noon meal? And he doesn't know which is the graver offence: to miss Sext because he doesn't hear the bell down here, or to get back on time but empty-handed.

Cormac hurries to help the Prior cover the baggage. They push the stuff most vulnerable to wet (the chest of books and writing supplies, the sacks of oats and charcoal) into the middle of the pile, then drape it with the two sails and fasten down the edges with rocks.

As the rain thickens, he's excited at the thought of his cistern being put to the test. It's drizzled on other days, but this is the first heavy shower since he's had the cistern dug out. He hopes the elaborate grooves he's carved will direct the little runnels down the rocks and into the pair of basins. Foolishly, he finds he can't bear to go and check.

Without a word, the Prior withdraws to the edge of the Plateau, head down over clasped hands. Cormac marvels at the man's ability to immerse his mind in silent meditation for hours on end; he himself finds manual work more prayerful.

Cormac is tempted to find somewhere to shelter, but if their leader won't hide away from the rain, nor will Cormac. It's high time he broke ground on their garden, he decides.

The turf is slick. No matter where he tries it by prodding, it's no more than a fingernail

deep, a thin green cape thrown over bedrock. At least there are plenty of stones lying
around. Hood up to keep the water out of his
eyes, he starts by gathering a great pile on the
south-facing part of the Plateau. He lays them
out in lines: the small, the middling sized, the
large. He'll stack them three courses high, to
make an oval enclosure around his plot; not
a proper drystone wall, only a rough rim to
shield the seedlings from being scoured away
by the wind, and to catch and hold the sun
when it shines.

First Cormac pulls out the ground cover.
Quantities of spurrey, great hummocks of
thrift so dense at the base he has to fetch the
hatchet to hack through. He can't remember
which severe saint it was who wouldn't let
his followers use any tools to clear the fields.
What Cormac wouldn't give now for the sharp
billhook they left at Cluain Mhic Nóis! *Never
contented,* he teases himself. No matter what
the monks brought with them, even in a boat
twice the size, he supposes there'd always
be some so-called necessity he'd find himself
hankering for.

A low mat of stonecrop. Under its multitude
of fleshy leaves, its wiry stems grip the wet
ground so hard that when Cormac tugs it out,
he bares a patch of bedrock. He shakes and

rubs each clump to make it cede its crumbs of soil. He takes the tiny leather pouches out of the herb box. He hasn't opened them till now; hasn't wanted to risk it. He hunches over to keep his shoulders between the seeds and the rain.

If only he had an iron trowel, or even a bone one. And a dibber—Cormac thought he could make do with a sharpened stick, and never imagined he'd be somewhere there are none. He supposes he could break a twig off the solitary rowan, but he hates to do any harm to the only tree on the island, and such a thin old one. He wipes water off his nose, and tells himself to stop griping.

Cormac begins with the onion sets—orange scaly bulbs from last season, dried and saved—which should be much quicker to grow than seeds. He uses his index finger to dib each hole a handspan apart; it should be a full inch down, but the dirt's barely half that. He drops the onion sets in, one by one, and paws up the soil to cover their brightness, though only barely. The gardener monks at Cluain Mhic Nóis would shake their heads to see him grubbing around in such inhospitable dirt, like a small child at play.

The rain's stopped, he registers.

Next he puts down sorrel seeds, and the

smooth brown pods of fat hen. That's all he can chance, this early in the spring. He fears he may be throwing the precious specks away. Never in his life has he sown in such a poor skin of earth.

Whatever about potherbs, this scanty soil will never be able to grow grains. The monks will have to barter for those, offering the mainlanders—what, down? Bird meat? This little monastery will also need more charcoal, candles, wine, salt, soap, butter...How will they ever be able to afford it all?

That's the Prior's concern, Cormac reminds himself. He kneels outside his oval garden and starts setting the enclosure's first course of stones. This patch, stripped bare, harrowed and rock-ringed—it's hard to believe it'll bring forth anything to feed three men.

Next time Cormac looks up, to stretch his neck, Trian's ginger head has appeared against the grey sky. Then the rest of him, as he comes up onto the Plateau; what a long-legged, spindly bird.

Cormac straightens up, brushes down his wet robe, and goes over. Trian has a heavy bag dangling from his belt. Feet wrinkled from the sea, he wipes wet strands of red out of his eyes. 'I see you covered the dry goods, Brother.'

Cormac nods.

'If we hung the sails from that overhang over there, could we maybe make a bit more of a shelter?'

He looks where Trian's pointing. 'There's a notion.'

Trian drapes the wet leather squares from the rock, while Cormac finds four heavy boulders to pin down the top edges. Now they move the baggage behind the hide curtains. 'Room to spare,' Cormac says with satisfaction.

Trian comes over to examine Cormac's plot. 'I thought it would be a bit bigger.'

'Better to do less this first season, but do it well, than take on too much and fail,' Cormac tells him. 'Do you know the story of holy Brigit's cloak?'

Those pale blue eyes light up. 'I forget how it goes.'

'Well, the holy woman had a vision telling her to found a convent, so she called on Christ to convince the King of Leinster to give her land for it. When that bad lord refused, Christ put it into Brigit's mind to ask for just a tiny patch, then, only as much as her cloak would cover. That made the King laugh and say yes. So clever Brigit put the corners of her cloak into the hands of four of her nuns.' Cormac spreads his arms. 'One ran to the east and one to the west, one to the south and one to the north . . . and her cloak stretched and stretched, till it covered a fine estate of land, and that's where the holy women built their convent.'

Trian laughs. 'Could our little garden grow in all directions like that?'

'God willing. Now, what have you caught for us today, Brother?'

He empties out his bag by the steaming, hissing remains of their fire. 'I had a wrasse twice the size of this one, but it dived and ripped the hook right off the line.'

Amid the scattered limpets and mussels, Cormac recognises the wrasse's long fin, its scales shimmering between green and orange. And a ray beside it: bat-winged, diamond-shaped, with its gasping mouth on the upturned underside. As for the third—'What's this huge flat-faced fellow?'

'A sea devil, we used to call it, or a frogfish. There's good eating in that thick tail,' Trian assures him.

Brown, warty; the jaws are agape. 'Is that seaweed stuck to its head?'

'No, bits of the fish itself.' He lifts one of the fringed filaments to show him.

Suddenly the Prior's behind them. 'Throw back the shellfish. We're told in the Book of Leviticus that every water creature without scales and fins is unclean.'

Cormac frowns. He's come across that passage in the Old Testament, but never thought it a rule; river mussels were often served at Cluan Mhic Nóis.

The Prior flicks his finger disgustedly. 'The ray too, and the devil.'

Trian's jaw drops. 'They're fish, though.'

'But the flesh of these kinds is well known for stirring up lust.'

'I never heard that,' Cormac remarks, so Trian will feel less foolish.

A hard gaze, turned on Cormac. 'Are you contradicting me?'

'Not at all, Father! I only meant—there's so much you know that I don't, for all my years.'

The Prior nods, mollified. 'Well, inquiry is the beginning of knowledge.'

'Pardon my ignorance.' Trian snatches up the sea devil and the ray by their tails, and starts scooping the shellfish back into his bag. 'I'll get rid of the dirty creatures.'

Cormac puts his hand out. 'I wonder could I cut up the fish for planting?'

'Planting?' the Prior asks.

'I've heard of sowing seeds with the heads, to nourish poor soil.'

A shrug, which Cormac takes as permission. As Trian starts scaling the lone wrasse for their meal, Cormac picks up the spurned ray and sea devil. He hacks them into bits on a rock. He tries to find each spot where he buried a seed; he fingers the earth open, and pushes in a chunk.

When Trian slits the wrasse's belly, a whole fish slithers out, smooth and unchewed. Cormac jokes: 'Jonah, returned!'

Trian grins. 'A sprat. We'll roast that too.' He rubs the backs of his hands as if they irritate him. 'Extraordinary little things, scales.'

'Are they?'

The young man comes over and puts a palm right up to Cormac's face. The tiny discs speckling his skin are transparent but dabbed with silver. 'Soft and thin, but they form a coat so strong a knife can barely cut it.'

'Brother, what else do you think you could find me to dress my beds—to cover the seeds against the first stiff wind, then rot down fast?' Like a shivering patient who can't get warm, Cormac thinks; you pile on the blankets and spoon broth into his mouth.

'How about...bird droppings? That's the most plentiful stuff here.'

He makes a face. 'Too harsh. The smell of it makes you blink, so it'd scorch the seedlings.'

'Seaweed, then?'

'Too salty, surely.'

'It'd just need a wash. If I spread some out,' Trian suggests, 'and we wait till it's been rained on a few times...Maybe green from the tide pools, and brown thongweed? Maidenhair, that'd shrivel down fast for you.'

'That sounds good.'

'My folk made soil out of nothing but seaweed and sand and time.'

Yes, a midden, that's what Cormac really needs, with its promise of richer earth for next year, at least.

He's chilled from standing still in these rain-soaked clothes; best to get moving again.

Just outside the low garden enclosure he chooses a midden site. He wishes he had some brown gold—cow dung—to get it started. Instead he undoes his braies, lifts his robe, and squats down. *Lord, thank you for all the food you grant us. May our dirt carry some of its goodness back into this earth.*

To his brown pile Cormac adds the ground cover he ripped out earlier, spade-chopped. In the creel he carries over all the stinking scraps from their meals so far: birds' wings raw or cooked, bones, heads, feet, stray feathers, and eggshell. The sea may nibble away at the land, he thinks, but she feeds it too.

Now, what can Cormac add? He fetches a spadeful of wet wood ash from beside the fire.

The mix could do with some grit as well. He goes to collect some fine stone dust, scraped up from around the base of the high cross. (*The poor cross,* he calls it privately, ever since it lost its arm.) He mixes it all together so the light stuff won't blow away. This should rot down together into good earth, given enough time.

Time, that's the thing. The old are meant to be more patient than the young, but sometimes those who've lived as long as Cormac sense the sand in the hourglass running out.

Trian has the wrasse cooking aromatically on skewers. Cormac goes over to the fire and points out his midden in the distance. 'Throw the fish guts on there, right? And the skins, after we've eaten. And whenever we make water or move our bowels, it should be on the midden, if we're close enough to get to it. Our hair-clippings, even.'

That amuses Trian. 'The parings of our nails, too?'

Cormac nods. 'Everything that was once alive has a bit of goodness left to give back.'

'The rain's filled your cistern nicely,' Trian mentions.

He'd forgotten his cistern. So it worked; they won't go thirsty.

'I set a pot for washing beside it, with a dish of soap.'

They can even clean their hands whenever they want. Cormac straightens up as if he's done some deed that will go down in the annals.

Next morning, the spring light blinds Trian as he stands chewing a rubbery tangle of dillisk from the seaweed he's hauled up the cliff for Cormac. He's considering the sails hanging from the rock over their most valuable goods; is there a way he can weigh them down with stones at the bottom so they won't flap?

'Brother Trian.' The Prior's at his side.

Trian swallows the seaweed, choking a little.

The Prior brushes the sail aside and digs their holy chest out of the pile. It looks unmarked. 'Today we begin the sacred task of copying.'

Trian blinks. 'Already? I mean—before we've built our monastery?' Surely they'll need a dedicated hut to work on the precious manuscripts?

The Prior's gesture takes in the whole sweep of crags and sky. 'This is our monastery, composed not of stone buildings but of our little family, our faith, and our works. And what could be more urgent than copying the Bible?'

Trian makes himself nod.

'Every day now the light lasts a little longer, which is a clear sign we should be using it for its highest purpose. Time to up and wage war on the devil with pen and ink, Brother.' The Prior lifts a thick leather pouch out of the chest. He takes out the Psalter and kisses its wooden covers before he opens it. 'This book here is a great sword of the spirit. Do you know its lineage?'

Unsure what that word means, Trian shakes his head.

The Prior touches one fingertip to the black markings on the first page, the elaborate initial capital letter of the psalm. 'Since God guided my hand, I think it no boast to say that my lettering was well done here. I was the humble midwife only—every codex is the child of the mother manuscript from which it's copied, as calf to cow.' He goes on, reminiscent: 'The one from which I took this was itself written out long before my time, in a Coptic refuge at an oasis in the desert mountains of the Red Sea.'

Trian's thrown by the image of desert mountains. Made of sand? 'You said—*oasis*?'

'A life-giving spot in the wilderness, where God reveals an unexpected well.'

'Like this Great Skellig, then?'

'Only much hotter and drier,' the Prior tells

him. 'The Egyptian psalter I speak of was the calf of a codex made long before, in Constantinople, known then as Byzantium. The Byzantine book was smuggled into the desert by Melchite monks fleeing the persecutions of the Persians.' He smooths the Psalter tenderly. 'The text of all these copies is holy Jerome's own revision of the Latin version of the Septuagint, which he corrected against the original Hebrew.'

Their master speaks as if of absent, beloved kin. For himself, Trian wishes he was still down on the shore, fishing.

The Prior fingers the page, making a rasping sound on the vellum. 'And now this calf, grown to a cow, will bear her own calf, on this lofty island, and so the light of Christendom spreads in glory.'

Trian says shortly, 'God be with the work.'

The Prior's eyes glitter. 'I'll take charge of the Old Testament, as you know no Greek, Brother, but you'll copy this Psalter.'

Trian is shocked; he thought he'd only be assisting. He clears his throat with a ragged gulp. 'You're the famed scribe, Father. I can prepare parchments, and ink, and pens, but—'

'The two of us will write side by side, but each on a different book.'

He shakes his head hard.

'Come, false modesty is no virtue. I know they trained you well at Cluain Mhic Nóis.'

'But I've no particular talent.'

'Then you must improve.' Steel in the Prior's voice.

'Father, for all the care I take...you know my hindrance.' Trian holds up his left hand, which is trembling. 'My own fingers obscure the letters they've just written, and cast a shadow over the one they're forming next.'

The Prior nods. 'Just as our sins overshadow our lives.'

Parables are no use to Trian right now. 'Also the side of my hand sometimes blots or smears the ink. I have to push the nib ahead of me rather than pulling it, which can make it trip or fray.'

'Many a scribe has struggled with your burden, or others. What matters is purity of heart.'

Trian gnaws his lip.

The Prior says, 'Go find us something to use as a desk.'

Trian manages to nod before he stumbles away.

Roaming the Plateau, he remembers his first teacher, the withered, unsmiling Brother Óengus. The scribe handed Trian a stone the size of a loaf with the Roman alphabet chiselled

on it, and ordered him to carry it everywhere.
Trian found this humiliating, like the millstone
in the Gospel that's hung around the neck of
the sinner to drown him. But gradually he
became fond of that incised boulder. Having
nothing else of his own at the monastery, he
guarded it like a lamb from the wolves. Trian
used to finger those letters at idle moments,
and their shapes cut deeply into his mind. His
teacher set him to practise forming them on
wax tablets and slates. He made a straggly
mess with his right hand for long months
before Brother Óengus accepted defeat and let
him use his left.

His teacher died of a cough that winter.
In spring, when a little boy came to the
monastery—Ronán by name—Trian was told
to pass on the alphabet stone to him. He cried
for it in secret, or maybe for Brother Óengus.

Right now he tries to keep his mind on
one worry at a time, the desk rather than the
book. He and the Prior will need a spot near
enough to their camp that they won't waste
most of the day coming and going. (And what
if they're carrying the books up or down one
of the steep slopes, and drop one like the Prior
dropped half their crocks on the day they
landed? What if its irreplaceable pages were to
be scattered or lost?)

Trian searches everywhere for a rock surface smooth enough that it won't pock the vellum. Ideally it should slant towards the scribe, too, so the nib can meet the page at a right angle. After a quarter of an hour, he finds one out-cropping that's almost flat enough to write on, but far too low; he tries to fit his legs under it first by kneeling on his heels, then by sitting cross-legged in the Eastern style, but either way the stone scores and grinds his thighs through his robe. He could dig out a hollow underneath, maybe... except that under the grassy tufts of fescue, his fingers meet hard rock.

Trian spots Cormac adding another course of stones to the oval around his garden, and goes over. 'What've you planted lately, Brother?'

'Now the days are warming a little, I've put in two long rows of turnip seeds'—Cormac points them out—'and nettle and spinach will be next.'

'I miss parsnips.'

'Ah, yes,' Cormac says with a laugh. 'What else?'

'Curds,' Trian murmurs. 'Blood sausage.'

'Beef. Fresh butter!'

The butter they have left is getting rancid. 'The Sunday gruel,' Trian says, 'all milky, with nuts and berries and honey.'

Cormac chuckles. 'I liked getting a clean pair of socks every week. And my lyre, of course.'

'Yes!' A pang in Trian's chest. 'My swan-bone pipe.'

'Ah, we're still allowed to play the five-stringed harp, though.'

He's at a loss.

'You never heard of that harp? What you hear, see, smell, taste, and feel.' Cormac touches his ears, eyes, nose, and lips, then wriggles his leathery fingertips. 'Though I must admit, a couple of my strings are frayed,' he adds rue-fully. 'I barely noticed at the monastery, but my far sight's failing.'

Trian comforts him: 'You seem to see what's in front of you well enough.'

Cormac nods. 'My weak eyes keep my atten-tion trained on the matter in hand, I suppose. *Age quod agis,* as they say—concentrate on the task!'

Which reminds Trian that he's supposed to be finding a desk.

He wanders farther up, towards the North Peak where there's a horizontal slab he remem-bers. But no, it turns out to slope away instead of towards him. He examines another, which proves too small to fit the exemplars, the copies, and all the supplies the two scribes will need. Yet another is huge but very uneven.

Finally Trian's eye lights on a slate surface that's smooth...except it's too high, sticking directly out of an outcropping at the level of his ribs and sloping ever so slightly towards him. The scriptorium hut at Cluain Mhic Nóis was furnished with a long-backed chair with rungs for the feet; here Trian and the Prior would need very high stools, and all they have are upturned buckets. Or they could always stand, he supposes.

Trian goes in search of his master and finds him deep in prayer, the Old Testament in his lap. He waits until the Prior looks up, then asks his question.

'Why would there be a rule against standing up?' the Prior demands.

'I just thought...it isn't the usual way.'

'We've left behind all the usual ways. No doubt our legs will ache,' the Prior adds with a smile, 'but we'll offer that up to our Lord.'

Now that they have a makeshift stone desk, Artt decides they will begin the sacred copying tomorrow.

He can't hold a candle to a legendary scribe such as Colm Cille, credited with some three hundred codices, but Artt has copied more than a score. He thinks of his manuscripts as his children, the only trace of him that will be left on earth once his bones have rotted. He has deposited at least one at every monastery where he's stayed, including Cluain Mhic Nóis. But the two they've brought with them are among Artt's best, the script elegant, without a blot. The Old Testament in Greek he made in Wales, from an exemplar he'd carried from Gaul, which in turn had come all the way from Egypt. When Artt turns the pages he imagines he's touching paper reeds, three times the height of a man, which once swayed in the Nile.

The fittings of these two books are metal, but unjewelled; only the words inside are treasure. To the ignorant, Artt supposes, all this ink would be so much soot scratched into kidskin. If the sling-whirling inhabitants of that river island on the Luimneach had seized him and his monks, they might have tossed these volumes on the fire; months and years of Artt's life, fuel for an hour. There's a lesson in that: man's flesh is grass, and often his works too. Artt shouldn't be too proud of these copies, or too confident that they'll outlive him.

But his exhilaration bursts out when he's speaking to the brethren in the evening. 'Think of it! God's words breathed into King David's ear, entrusted from scribe to scribe for centuries, unaltered, unadulterated, passed all the way down in unbroken descent to Brother Trian here.'

The bump in the young man's throat writhes as he swallows.

'Angels will guide your hand,' Artt promises him. 'Now, we're all looking a little ragged, so let's shave.'

He's the first to kneel, so Cormac—having sharpened his knife on a whetstone—can make his master's cheeks, chin, and upper lip smooth. Then Cormac blows away the tufts, and finger-combs and reties Artt's ponytail before he tidies his tonsure with the blade. Artt knows his hairline's receding somewhat, though not much for a man in middle age, so his forward-pointing triangle is more of a trapezoid.

Next Trian works on the old monk, who says a cropped beard will do him. 'And since I've only a few wisps left up top, Brother, just shave off everything in front of my crown.' So Trian rasps away. The arc of Cormac's skull is curved like an axe-head. Artt notices that Trian skims lightly over the shiny hollow where there's no bone beneath the scar. Cormac's long strands, pulled back tight, make a skinny rat's tail.

Artt passes the time trimming his fingernails. Finally Cormac and Trian swap places and Cormac shaves the young man's beard, which is reddish, but nearer to brown than the plentiful, bright hair tied back in a ponytail. Cormac scrapes the tonsure into Trian's sun-weathered scalp, making the line clean over the hill from ear to ear, the point of the triangle coming forward almost to his hairline.

Finally Artt nods approval. 'We look like proper monks again.'

Cormac's on his knees, gathering up their detritus to add to his precious midden. 'While you and Brother Trian are at work on the books, Father, could I start on a hut for us? Just a simple stone cell?'

Artt needs to be firm with this old monk. He reminds himself that Cormac must have grown accustomed to following his own path, all those decades before he took vows. 'No, Brother. God has ringed us with his sea—set the waves like shields around us, keeping attackers at bay whether animal or human. The air grows milder every night, too, so we won't freeze, lying on the ground. It's not our bodies but our souls that need protecting. No, what you must make us first is an altar on which to celebrate the Mass.'

Will there be any resistance?

Cormac says nothing, only bows.

Artt rings the bell for Nocturns. In the dancing circle of firelight, he leads them in the first psalm: *'Morning and noon and evening I pray and cry aloud, and God will hear my voice.'*

After they eat, they sit on their buckets by the last of the fire as the darkness grows and the shearwaters cackle and howl. They sound more like wolf pups than any flying thing Artt's known. 'The devil birds seem even louder this evening.'

'I suppose they're calling out to their mates on the eggs, as they fly in,' Trian murmurs. 'Otherwise they'd be hard put to it to find their own burrows.'

Artt wonders whether he could stop up his ears with some beeswax from the little jar. Then he reminds himself that the sound is a small trial to bear—one he should welcome. 'Well, they're here to try our patience, so we thank them for their service.' A different thought strikes him. 'Unless they're hell-sent? Antonius the Egyptian—the first holy man to go into the wild—even in the cave where he lived, he was tempted by demons in the form of animals.'

Trian asks, confusedly, 'Isn't this Skellig a refuge from temptation?'

Artt clicks his tongue. 'We're out of the

clutches of the world of men, Brother, but we've dragged along our heavy carcasses'—he gestures down at himself—'with all their low cravings.' Such as, in Artt's case, a longing for peace and quiet; for five minutes' relief from the feathered pandemonium. 'Aren't our souls as frail as ever they were?'

Cormac nods glumly at that.

'Besides,' Artt goes on, 'we've journeyed here not to escape from Satan like cowards, but to fight him off like soldiers, with prayer as our weapon.' He likes that; he warms to his theme. 'We're sentries standing guard on the outer frontier of God's empire—the last outpost of Christendom. We must expect attack. We're halfway to heaven here, and if our enemy snatches at our heels we must kick him off.'

'So...the shearwaters are the devil's messengers?'

Artt lets out a small sigh. This young man seems shackled to the literal. 'They're birds, Brother Trian. But Satan might be inspiring them to new heights of horrible noise, to see if they can chase us away.'

'Not us,' Cormac says.

'That's right,' Artt says. 'We stand fast.'

The fire crackles. Cormac remarks, 'I heard the tormentors of Antonius came in the shape of wolves, bears, lions, leopards, bulls, snakes, and scorpions. Imagine that hullabaloo of howling and hissing!'

Trian sucks in his breath.

'They hurt the saint terribly, too, with their claws and horns and fangs. But Antonius only laughed through the pain and told them, *Come on now! If you'd any power over me, a single one of you beasts would be able to tear me to shreds. The proof of your weakness is that you have to gang up in such a hell-horde. Then'*—Cormac pauses for effect, and pokes the charcoal to make the flames flare—'there was a bright light and the animals disappeared like smoke.'

'The devil called them home?' Trian asks.

Artt corrects him: 'God banished them.'

Cormac nods and goes on with the story: 'So Antonius cried out to the Lord, *Where were you when the demons were ripping and gnawing on me?'*

A child's cry, it strikes Artt; wounded petulance. What reason has any mortal man to expect to be spared pain?

Trian asks, 'How dared he? I mean—wasn't that a dreadful thing to say?'

Cormac shrugs. 'That's the story as I heard it. And God told Antonius, *I was here all along, but I wanted to watch you fight.'*

Artt finds himself wondering if perhaps tales

will be told about him. Is it arrogance to think it? The legend of how the priest and scholar Artt set off, with just two humble companions, in a small boat. The extraordinary pair of islands he found in the western ocean; how he claimed the higher one for God, and founded a great retreat in the clouds. The glory of the books reproduced there, and then generations of the copies' offspring. The ceaseless hum of prayer always rising from that little hive.

When in time to come Artt is buried in a rocky hole on the North Peak—Brother Cormac before him, presumably—will other pilgrims be miraculously drawn to sail this way, he wonders? To join Brother Trian, and live on together on these heights like unquenchable candles, forever blessing the name of their founder, holy Artt?

TO WORK

A DAY OF SUNSHINE and shadow, alternating as the clouds scud overhead. Cormac's gathering stones for the altar. It's to be a plain drystone square, knee-high. He's made walls before; a flattened cube can't be any harder, surely?

He collects mostly sandstones and slates, gritty to the touch. Sandstone is good stuff for building—soft enough to work, but stands up bravely to weathering. When Cormac peers at the shimmering greys, he finds hints of tan, yellow, green, brown, even red and purple. Many of these boulders have wavy layers, as if they were liquid before they hardened to stone.

He seeks out the flattest rocks, for stability. He pries up heavy ones with the crowbar, but leaves any that are too big for him to lift alone. He sets them all out in rows according to size. Drystone can stand for generations, if you take the trouble to pick the right rocks and give thought to how they'll sit together.

A mason at Cluain Mhic Nóis taught him that every stone has six faces—front, back, left, right, top, and bottom—though it often takes a few blows to reveal them. Cormac starts to shape his first rocks with the lump hammer, knocking off corners and humps flake by flake, always hitting away from the centre. Occasionally a stone cracks in two; if the break makes a smooth face on each half, Cormac keeps them both, but sometimes there's nothing left but debris.

Patience, he reminds himself. If he rushes the work, and cobbles together boulders that don't fit, the altar's own weight will make it sag or topple. But if he can remember where just the right shape is waiting in the gritty rows, he can pluck it up and set it in place like a key in a lock.

Cormac's calmed by the clink of rock on rock, the dust between his swollen knuckles. He mutters protections as he works. '*From temptations of vices, God's hand to steer me. From snares of the devil, God's shield to guard me. From all far and near who wish me ill, God's hosts to save me.*'

The dense, creamy flowers of the nearby rowan are sending out a musk that reminds him of the monastery church at night, crammed with sleepy-breathed men just out of their sheets.

Trian's making pens. For lack of geese on the Skellig, the great auks will have to do.

The flight feathers he needs for his own writing will have to come from the right wing, because those have a slight curve to the left, to fit his better hand; he'll use the left wing feathers for the Prior's pens. He finds a few in the sack that seem fit for the purpose: long, glassy quills below the soft plumes, as bendable as his own fingernails.

When God created men and women and set them apart from the beasts and the fowls, could it be that he made all of them from much the same stuff? It occurs to Trian that the difference isn't in the raw material, so much as in the making.

He'll prepare four pens for a start. With his whetted knife, he strips all the soft barbs off the shaft of the first right-side feather, and slices off the thin end. Then he does the same to a second. Then two left-siders for the Prior. They're all too soft, of course. Better if they could be left to dry out for months or years...At Cluain Mhic Nóis, the scribes sometimes set Trian to tempering and hardening quills with heated sand. But here there's only silt, down at the shore. And if he holds them over a fire, he's likely to singe them to a crisp.

He goes to find Cormac, whose square altar's looking firm and true, a handspan off the ground already. The old monk seems preoccupied, fiddling with a bob that hangs from a crossbar.

'What's that for?'

'If my surface is level, this string should hang plumb against the vertical mark on the bar.'

Trian remembers his own problem. 'For hardening quills, Brother, would boiling water work, do you think?'

A shrug. 'Why not put them right into the hot ashes?'

Trian thanks him and hurries off.

Once the quills are half-buried in the bed of grey ash, he gets the vellum out of the holy chest. The parchmenter entrusted three whole rolls to them, fully prepared, so Trian's spared the long and nasty work of purging them of flesh and hair in a vat of human excrement, pegging them out and scraping them.

He undoes the first roll now, counting a dozen bifolia. Good skins, soft and velvety, from white calves unmarked with shadowy brindles.

So as not to waste any of this, Trian decides to cut each page to about a quarter of a hide—bigger than the exemplar from which he'll be copying. For a start, he'll prepare just one gathering for himself and one for the Prior. He cuts three full sheets in two, chooses the five best half-sheets of the six, and lays them on top of each other, folding them over, with the calf's spine as the book's spine, making ten leaves.

Trian catches himself already fretting over how long it'll take him to fill up these twenty pages. How much of his life will be enclosed in hard oak by the time he's finished this book? (He makes a mental note that the monks will have to trade for the boards to make covers for each codex.) He soothes himself with Scripture: *Take no thought for tomorrow, for each day has trouble enough.*

He fetches the ball of thread and takes out of the roll the biggest bronze needle, the one with a triangular point for gouging leather more easily. He threads the eye, presses the whole gathering against his rock desk, and starts sewing the five skins together. Soon his fingers are marked with painful red lines.

The parchment has too much of a glassy

shine left on the hair side, so he gives it a rub all over with a pumice stone, then adds ground chalk from a bag. This is the skin of two and a half calves he holds in his hands; by the time the new book's finished, it'll contain a whole unseen herd. Trian imagines them nudging and bumping each other, lowing in the dark. He touches the first page. Its owner had no chance to grow into a great bull and sire others, and never fed a crowd with his vast haunches. All so a clumsy *ciotóg* can scrawl on his back. The fear of botching this makes Trian feel sick.

When he's formed the second gathering—a little more sure of his movements this time—he goes back to the fire to retrieve the stripped, opaque feathers from the ash and scrub off their greasy coating. What if there's some inherent weakness in the wings of a flightless bird? But when he clips off the very end of one quill, it doesn't shatter. He scrapes and cuts it gently, and uses the tip of his blade to clear old honeycomb out of the shaft. Now to shape the nib, ever so carefully. He cuts, splits, presses, cuts again, slanting ever so slightly to the left to suit his grip, shaping the two tines. A finishing touch: a tiny slit to channel the ink.

As he's cutting the last of the pens, the Prior's shadow falls across him. 'Have you everything ready?'

'I believe so, Father.'

His master takes the Psalter out of its leather pouch. 'If there's the least smell of rain, put it back in the bag before a drop can fall on it.'

'I'll guard it with my life.' Though this volume could be said to be worth a lot more than the life of one young monk. Trian gestures over at their improvised desk. 'Should I . . . '

'You go on the left.'

So Trian's writing hand will be out of the Prior's way.

As soon as Trian sets the Psalter on the slate outcropping, a new problem occurs to him: how to hold it open to the first page without one of those scribe's strings with a pyramidal weight at each end? He looks around until he finds two walnut-sized pebbles, then binds them to the ends of a length of twine from the ball he keeps in his pouch. If he had a real desk he'd hang one weight over its back. Instead he tries looping the twine over the wooden cover of the Psalter, but it threatens to drag the book right off the slab. Trian sweats under his master's cool gaze. He wrenches the stones off the string and goes to look for smaller ones. On the third try, a bee-sized pebble at each end of the string proves just heavy enough to hold the page open.

'Three things to bear in mind,' the Prior says

musically. 'The first two will make your copy even more beautiful than the exemplar.'

Trian swallows. That sounds almost heretical.

'First, as an illumination, you must start each psalm with a large and complex capital' —

Trian knows how to do that much.

—'and outline it with red dots.'

He's never been allowed to use colour. 'The capital letter only?'

'With tiny dabs all round the black. Also, embellish with diminuendo — form each letter after the capital a little smaller than the one before, until by the fourth or fifth they've shrunk to the size of the ordinary script.'

What if they shrink too much, till they're no longer legible? Trian's armpits are running with sweat.

'And finally, at the top of each psalm, in Gaelic, you'll interpret the Latin Scripture below.'

Trian shakes. 'Ah Father, I couldn't think of making up words to—'

'Don't be ridiculous. I'll compose the head-ings.'

He lets out a long breath. The Prior will tell him exactly what to put, much as God blew his thoughts into the minds of David and the other Psalmists.

'You may rule the guidelines, now.' The Prior walks away.

Trian feels calmer now that he's not being watched. Alone but for the wheeling, crying birds.

With the ruler and his knife tip, he measures and pricks the margins around the square that will contain his text, with bounding lines to stop the words from spilling. Twenty-seven lines, he decides, just under half an inch each. He rules them in hardpoint, scoring firmly with the back of his knife. (In training, he cut a page right through; Brother Óengus called it an error every scribe makes once, but that didn't ease Trian's guilt when the page had to be thrown away.)

Now he uncorks the wide-necked stone jar to make up the ink. He takes the stopper out of the sheep's horn that holds the oily soot and scoops some into the jar, mixing in water a few drops at a time. For a thickener to bind the ink to the parchment, he supposes white of egg will do. At the end of a snaking burrow Trian finds a little egg, pale, under the caking mud; shearwater, he'd guess. Having held it up to the sun to make sure there's no chick—why kill without a reason?—he cracks it delicately over a bowl. He asks a blessing on the dark yolk and tips it into his mouth so as not to waste it; stronger and wilder than a hen's egg. Then he beats the white hard with a spoon till it's foaming, and adds a little of the liquid underneath to the ink.

He does the same with vermilion, in a smaller jar.

Now at last Trian has all their supplies to hand. His desk is thick, irregular, stony; he feels the cold pressure from heart to gut. But the top is almost miraculously flat. *Like a table spread in the wilderness,* he tells himself—*made ready for the Word.*

He doesn't want to interrupt the Prior's prayers, so he stands and waits, trying to remember the perfect position for holding the pen. Quite high up its shaft, gripped between the tips of his left thumb and first two fingers, with the other two curled out of the way. He cocks his wrist a little to the left; he mustn't let his hand form a hook or he won't be able to see what he's writing. He sets the nib head-on, at a right angle to the parchment.

With no warning, the Prior is beside him, dictating: '*In this first of the Holy Psalms, God promises that the good man will endure and be blessed, but the evildoer will be blown away like chaff.*'

Trian whispers the entire line under his breath, and then again, so he won't have to ask his master to repeat a single word.

It feels strange to spell out the plain Gaelic

words of the Prior's preamble, when Trian's only ever written in the language of Rome. He's using the one script he knows, with a flat nib and wedge-shaped serifs. Rounded and distinct, with short ascenders and descenders, his letters don't touch even though they form one continuous track of black. (Like himself and Cormac and the Prior, it occurs to him—living close, but separate.)

The Prior inspects his work, squinting a little, and nods. 'Now the Psalm itself.' And turns away, to begin his own copying of the first page of the Old Testament—those curling Greek letters which are gibberish to Trian.

Large capital, Trian reminds himself (a great double-bellied black *B* for the start of *Beatus vir*, happy the man), red dots, diminuendo. He must faithfully replicate what he sees, splitting his attention between exemplar and copy, so as not to get lost in the gap. He dips his nib again. The ideal is a controlled flat flow, a gliding stream with no waves, no rocks, no gaps. Downward strokes are smoother, following the natural pull of the ink; upward ones are precarious. Lift the pen, reposition, as precise-footed as a wading bird. The key is never to let his own unworthy skin touch the surface. His left hand must hover in the air; only the arm moves, so lightly that a watcher mightn't notice. Trian should barely even put nib to page, transmitting the ink like the lightest of caresses.

The Prior's writing away intently, to his right. *It's not a race*, Trian tells himself. *Nor a contest*. The Prior's a famed scholar and scribe, as holy as he's wise. Trian's nobody. He repeats a different psalm in his head: *O Lord, hasten to my help*. He dips his nib again.

Sunday, and Artt's standing at the completed stone cube, which is draped in linen—a proper table to bear the Mass dishes at last, a fit altar for the sacrament of Communion. In a ringing voice, he blesses the tiny flasks of water and olive oil (carried all the way from Rome): 'May all fevers, maladies, and evil spirits be banished from him who drinks or is anointed with these liquids, in the name of Christ Jesus.'

The Great Skellig falls away below the Plateau like green silk, and Artt's suddenly filled with triumph. To think that he and his monks have travelled all this way, to the hidden haven saved for them since Creation. They've begun their work, and God looks on it and calls it good.

When it's time for the Consecration of bread and wine, Artt opens the silver host box and sees at once that the last wheat loaf is spoiled. Pale blue mould flares around the *Chi Rho* symbol.

He goes rigid, but only for a moment. Then he sets the loaf on the jewelled stone plate and carries on with the ritual. Trian rings the bell, and Artt intones, '*On the night before Jesus died, he took bread and gave thanks, and shared it with his followers, saying, Do this to remember me. This is my body.*' He elevates the Host over his head and his monks bow to it. This is not a loaf rife with mould, but the Bread of Life, the actual flesh of Christ. Breaking it in three, he puts the bluest piece in his own mouth and washes it down with the strong wine, which is not wine at all but the blood of their Lord. He hands out the rest, his eyes daring his brethren to say a word about the mould.

Each monk swallows his third.

Afterwards, at their midday meal, Cormac asks Trian, 'How goes the copying?'

Trian lets out a gloomy breath. 'Practise doesn't seem to improve my script.'

It seems to Artt that the young monk's letters are getting more awkward, if anything. But he fears that reproof will only make Trian's grip more cramped. 'Prayer can do wonders.'

'I hope so, Father.'

Cormac's face brightens. 'I remember a story about a novice scribe.'

Artt pulls a string of something rubbery from between his teeth. This stream of tales rather gets on his nerves these days, but he reminds himself that any company would be grating by now. That's the nature of congregation, he supposes—like the grit in a millstone that gradually smoothens down the soul.

'This young monk's writing was slow and ugly,' Cormac begins, 'like chicken marks in the soil.'

A chuckle from Trian.

'But he prayed to God to bless his eyes and hands and give him time enough to form the words gracefully. He set to work on the Four Gospels the next morning. Well, the hours passed, but the sun never set, so that scribe never put down his quill—and when the book was done, he thought it had been a single day, when in fact forty had passed!'

Artt dislikes these legends in which God takes away all his followers' troubles. Mere wishful thinking, like pagan stories of magic by another name. How do such fantasies fit men to live in this world, or find their way to a better one?

Trian doesn't seem fooled. He gnaws on a thigh bone without a word.

'Father,' Cormac says with no warning, 'of the supplies we need, I'd say charcoal's the most pressing. Maybe a couple of sheep to graze on the clifftops too? Soap, wine,' he lists. 'And wheat flour, of course, to replace the sack I so stupidly spilled down the cliff.'

So that's what this is about, the mouldy Host.

Trian puts in, 'I believe we'd reach the mainland in five or six hours, with the right wind.'

Have his monks planned this artless conversation, Artt wonders now—plotted behind his back? 'I thought you both understood. Our travels are done.'

Cormac meets eyes with Trian. 'Only a brief journey, I was thinking, to trade with fellow Christians.'

'What have *we* to do with other people?' Neither of them dares answer Artt. 'We've looked our last on the filthy world.'

Trian speaks up, childlike. 'But how are we to manage for supplies?'

Artt almost growls it: 'God will provide.'

'God will provide...charcoal and wheat?' Cormac asks.

Artt rears up, on his feet. If he can't instill conviction into this pair of Doubting Thomases, at least he'll put them to shame. 'Brother, do enlighten us, why was it wheat bread that

Jesus shared at the Last Supper? Because it's a holier grain than any other?'

Cormac hesitates.

Artt knows the convert can't debate theology. 'No, it was merely the common bread of the Holy Land. So if we've no more wheat flour left, we'll use what we have.' He pushes on. 'Next Sunday, make us oatcakes.'

Cormac's grey eyebrows go up. 'For Communion? Ordinary oatcakes?'

This may not be what Artt was taught, but it's what God's telling him now. 'Whatever we offer at the Consecration, with clean hearts, will be turned into Christ's flesh.' As he makes this guarantee, he feels his wrath fall away and he's their guide again, their soul-friend.

Trian's blue eyes are wide; Cormac's are lowered to the ground.

'Come now, pray with me.' Artt gets out his bell and rings it melodically. '*Christ be my shield.*'

'*My sword,*' Trian answers.

From Cormac: '*My stronghold.*'

'*Christ be my wealth.*'

'*My meal.*'

'*My delight.*'

Artt sings out, '*O arms of Christ, be around my shoulders.*'

HATCHING SEASON

TRIAN WAITS, PERCHED hundreds of feet up
over the southwest corner of the Great Skellig, the line between his fingers. He's caught
wrasse before, under this overhanging cliff,
and lost hooks to them too; they're hard fighters. Sometimes a bream, the odd mackerel or
gurnard. But it's too calm today. He's found
that sea fish show themselves only in lively
weather, something that ruffles or darkens the
water, or a strong tide at least; he supposes
it makes sense for them not to approach the
island unless they have a reason.

He looks down, all the way down. There
are days when the ocean's a playful, bubbling
cauldron. Trian's seen wonders. A school of
porpoises cavorting, unless they were great
dolphins—he couldn't guess their size. A bask-
ing shark, lolling and rolling to the south of
the Skelligs; when it surfaced, with black fin

and long snout, water poured out of its gills. Trian calls the indent below him Seal Cove, because seals often haul out there, to keep company and squabble on the rocks. Their big eyes are so childlike, they remind him of tales of mermaids.

Trian is beginning to be able to interpret this sea. At low tide, the swirl of a sunken reef troubles the water. Farther out, currents meet, scribbling a message that he tries to read before it melts away. Even on a day this quiet, an ocean breaker can flash white as it rolls in to take a chew of the island. He stares at the horizon now and tries to grasp what the Prior's taught him, that the earth is a ball with the stars and heavens spinning around it.

Stray beams shard through gaps in the vast sky. The clouds shift, the light tints the Great Skellig brown, then grey, then green, as if God's nib is inking in an illustration. Land and sea like opposite pages, intricate and be-jewelled with colour, in a book laid open for all to read.

Scrutinising the rock faces below, Trian counts eggs, just out of curiosity. He's found that a kittiwake will lay two or three, in a tiny nest. Whereas a cormorant has a huge nest with as many as four, pale blue; those are the only eggs the monks agree are inedibly foul.

Anytime Trian's delved into the burrow of a puffin or shearwater, he's found only a single egg. Once he encountered a shearwater, in the daytime, and it spat a stinking oil at him. Great auks and guillemots, they too lay one pointed conical egg, left carelessly on a ledge—the guillemot's egg a dark-blotched green ovoid, the great auk's marbled white and a good five inches long. As for the new eagles on the South Peak, they've hatched already, though only one chick seems to have lived.

'Brother.' Here's the Prior, panting a little.

Trian leaps to his feet.

Is their master a little leaner than when he first came to Cluain Mhic Nóis? But the outline of his shoulders seems even stronger, grey eyes more sparkling in his weathered face. The whole island spreads out behind him like holy Brigit's magical cloak.

'Were you in a trance?' The Prior stands, catching his breath.

'No, Father.'

'Remember the dangers of idleness, Brother. Any moment not filled with work or prayer is a chink left open to the cold winds of hell.'

If Trian says he was contemplating the glories of creation, but that comes down to mere daydreaming, is he doubling his error?

'What have you caught for our meal?'

He hauls up the twine hand over hand to check: the hooks have nothing on them but winkles and whelks, his tiny scraps of bait. 'Sorry, Father. I'll try casting from another spot.'

The Prior frowns. 'Well, don't stay much longer—I need you to work on the Psalter. And while you're waiting for a bite, let your head be bent, Brother. No one can pray with his eyes open.'

Trian nods. The Prior's hard on him, but only to mend him, he reminds himself.

Cormac makes sure to keep his garden moist under its mulch, now that the weather's getting warmer. When the seaweed shrivels down, he asks Trian to bring up more and spread it on rocks for the rain to rinse. The midden, too, he tends so it won't dry out and be scattered by the wind; after washing the bowls and spoons in a bucket he always throws the water onto the rotting pile, which he slices and turns with the spade every day. He's glad to see it is alive with little springtails, those jumping flies that swarm on anything damp or rotten. Earth-worms, now, they'd be a big help, but he's found none on the Great Skellig; he supposes they've no means of crossing the water from the mainland. If only he'd thought to bring a few, alive in a jar; if he'd had the slightest idea what it would be like on this island.

Cormac's far sight is going fast now. In the distance he can make out coloured shapes, that's about all. He's reminded of the blind man in the Gospel. Jesus spat on his eyes and touched them, asking whether he could see anything now, and the man replied that he saw people but they looked like walking trees. So Jesus touched him a second time, and then he could see perfectly. It's the other way around for Cormac. The gift of vision is being taken from him in stages, maybe so he'll grasp what he's had and be grateful he's had it so long, since many folks' eyes turn milky long before they're old.

And sure what does it matter, really, when Cormac's sight at close quarters remains as sound as ever, for a chisel or a leaf or a needle? Everything he needs to see and do is contained on this small piece of high ground.

Today he makes a stew of fish heads and tails, just for a change from the endless roast birds. He throws in handfuls of bitter greens, and lengths of seaweed: translucent frilled green, fronds of carrageen, red leathery dillisk. He can't say what good the monks will get from each food, but he knows they need variety, or they'll sicken.

'Brother Cormac.' The Prior, standing at the altar. Has he been beckoning for a while?

Cormac adjusts the pot on its tripod over the fire, and hurries to him.

'This altar was well built, Brother.'

'Thank you, Father.' Their master's less stern, today. Might this be a good moment for Cormac to admit what's weighing on him? 'I must tell you something. These days, anything far off... it's a blur to me.'

The Prior nods, unsurprised. 'Well, no one picks an old companion for his sharp eyes.'

Cormac bows deeply.

'We all have flaws, Brother. Some that may be hidden from us, even.'

Since the Prior's in a benign mood, Cormac chances it: 'Maybe now I could start on a hut for the safekeeping of our goods from rain and wind, and for us to sleep in, when winter comes?'

A shake of the head, inexorable.

Cormac should have known.

'We can lie on the ground for many months yet. God must be housed before man,' the Prior tells him. 'What we need next is a chapel around our altar.'

To Cormac's mind, the whole Great Skellig is a church; can't the three of them pray undisturbed on every inch of it? And what more glorious windows than the ever-changing sky?

But as the reed told the oak tree: *Better bend than break.* He says, 'Right, Father.'

'A plain rectangle, I think, with sides sharply pitched.'

Cormac pictures this chapel as a sharp-bottomed boat turned upside down—a sign of their pilgrimage being complete, he supposes. 'Triangular gables at the ends?'

The Prior nods, sketching it on the air. 'And the door here at the west end, of course, and a triangular window opposite, to let in light over the altar.'

Because Christ will come again from the east. Cormac nods. He's resigning himself to the task of building this church. It would be a simple enough plan if they only had timber, but Cormac must work out how to do it with loose stones. 'How big would you want it, Father?'

'It's not my desire you must satisfy, but God's.'

He suspects whatever number he proposes will be wrong. 'You'd have the best idea what proportions he'd like, though. Maybe you'd mark them out for me?'

The Prior finds a boulder to set down.

'Around here, perhaps, the southwest corner. This'—a vein zigzagging across his broad, brown forehead as he cradles and sets down a bigger rock—'the northwest.'

Twelve feet by eight, Cormac guesses. 'And how thick the walls?'

A hesitation. 'A handspan? A foot?'

He can't help making a face.

'Thicker, then? A cubit?'

Cormac explains, 'There'll be nothing keeping it together but the rocks' hold on each other. If the walls were more like two feet wide, at least at the base, to make it stable...'

'As you say, Brother.'

'That means there'll be less room inside,' he warns. 'Only about this much.' He holds out his hands to make a span of four feet.

The Prior nods. 'Enough for the three of us to kneel in front of the altar.'

In his day, Cormac has worked with teams of men, and heavy equipment—oak tripods three times his height, compound pulleys to winch up tree trunks or boulders, and log rollers to move them. Here he has only a crowbar, a mason's level, dividers, and an L-shaped square. It'll do; it'll have to.

He fetches the dividers now and uses their pointed wooden feet to measure out the distances. He marks the inner and outer corners of the chapel with pebbles. 'I'd corbel the roof from about here, Father?' He holds his hand just above his head.

'Corbel...'

Cormac hides a smile; he knows one word his master doesn't. 'Set each course of stones a little farther in, so they overlap each other and make a closed vault.'

The Prior nods.

Cormac admits, 'I've never done it, myself, but I've watched it done.' If he can get it right, the stones will kiss, press and hold together. 'It takes two men to snap the lines—to mark out the walls. Father, would you mind helping me with that?'

'Certainly.'

Cormac digs out of a bag the little box in which he keeps the thin cord half buried in chalk. He hands the Prior one end. The Prior holds it firmly to the ground, under the pebble that's marking the inner northwest corner of his imagined church. Cormac stretches the string taut with one hand, all the way over to the inner northeast corner, while with the other he plucks it, twanging an imprint of white onto the rocky ground. It'll have to be redone after every rainfall, of course, but it helps him to picture the whole shape laid out.

The Prior murmurs, as if he already sees the

walls rising in his mind's eye, '*On this rock I will build my church, and the gates of hell will not prevail against it.*' When they've chalked out all the lines, he leaves Cormac to start the building.

First Cormac collects and sorts all the biggest stones he can find—except for round-backed ones, which would be too wobbly to build on. (He wishes he hadn't used up so many good flat ones making the garden wall and the altar.) Usually he'd start by digging a foundation trench and setting the first course into it. But he's working on bedrock here, so that would be backbreaking labour. This chapel will just have to hold itself down by its own weight. All Cormac has is hammer and chisel to make each rock a level place to sit.

He starts the first corner with the biggest, squarest lump he can find, for strength. The stones should be heaviest at the bottom, lightest at the top. Moving along, setting the first course, Cormac places each so its longest length goes into the wall. He's lucky enough to find a couple of through stones that thrust right across the two-foot span, locking it together. But mostly he lines the inner and outer edges of the wall with face stones, leaving a gap in the middle that later he'll fill up with smaller shards and pebbles, the hearting stones.

Whenever he finds a wedge-shaped rock, he sets its thicker end towards the inside of the chapel, so the wall won't bulge outwards over the decades. He's seen a building swell like a woman with a great belly, until it cracks and sheds its load. It occurs to Cormac, too, that each wedge should tilt ever so slightly towards the outside, for the structure to shed rain as beautifully as a duck's feathers. He almost talks to the rocks as he puzzles over them by twos and threes, looking for the angles that tell him which ones will be able to support their neighbours, so this chapel can root itself into the Great Skellig as if it's stood there since time began. So it can last for the ages.

Standing at the stone slab he calls a desk, Trian registers his neck twinging whenever he turns his head to his right to check each run of letters. Five is about as many as he can hold in his mind while he's transcribing. His knife tip stays on the exemplar, pressing down the springy parchment and anchoring his eye to the right spot in the psalm. Imagine if Trian were to skip one of God's words, or a whole line—he remembers a scribe at Cluain Mhic

Nóis who did that, and was given a penance of no meat for a week.

The Prior writes on, with unnerving steadiness, a few feet away.

In recent days, Trian has found his gaze sliding around on the page, so the Prior's made him an eye-guard: a page with a slit cut out of it that reveals no more than one line at a time. The Prior calls it a window into heaven, though to Trian it feels more like a dark cell.

Crisp, clean. Keep the bows plump. Give each finial the same claw. Don't go too fast or the verticals will slope. Don't relax the hand too much, or the headstrokes will be too long.

Yesterday the three of them celebrated Pentecost, which means seven weeks have passed since they set off on their pilgrimage. Pentecost is the day the Holy Spirit came down on Jesus's bereft followers in a strong wind and flames that didn't burn, granting them the ability to speak in unknown tongues and cast out demons in his name. Trian wishes he'd been there; wishes he had such powers. The grace to keep copying for forty days and nights, for instance, like the spellbound novice in Cormac's story on whom the sun never set until his whole book was written.

Ink pools in the base of Trian's letters before it dries; all things incline downwards, from a dropped egg to rain and hail, and he wonders why, but that way lies distraction. He peeks at the sky, because if a shower is threatening, he should put the manuscripts safely away in their chest. Or wind—that's a threat too. Even a kittiwake passing overhead. (The birds have already fouled the cistern once, so Cormac's made a thin slate cover.)

For all Trian's efforts to concentrate while he's copying, doubts swarm about him like biting flies. If he doesn't grasp what an abbreviation mark or suprascript line means, he reproduces it by sight, as best he can. But sometimes he can't tell one word in the Psalter from the next. If only there were marks between words, to keep them apart—dots, or spaces even—those would make the copying so much easier. It shouldn't matter whether Trian knows the word, so long as he copies the letters in the right order. But the downstrokes of *i, u, m,* and *n*—how can he be sure he's not confounding them and making a jumble of holy writ?

Already he has to interrupt the Prior's flow of work at the end of each psalm, to ask him to check Trian's copy before dictating a preamble to the next. Or whenever there's a passage Trian can't puzzle out because of cockling—the wrinkling and pleating of a page, as if a demon's breathed on it in the night. Then occasionally a word will make so little sense to him that he wonders, *What if an error crept into one of the earliest copies of the psalms and has been faithfully reproduced by every scribe (including the Prior) since?* But then, who's a young monk to voice such a suspicion?

Mostly he tries to keep his mind on his pen. So many things blunt a nib; so many times a day that Trian has to sharpen it or cut a new tip. And always he's tormented by the stunted unevenness of his script. Will the perfection of God's meaning be able to shine through this clumsy fence? His left palm cramps and his flexed wrist aches; his right hand feels bruised where he grips the knife handle too hard. *Three fingers write,* the saying goes, *two eyes read, one tongue speaks, the whole body toils.*

When at last he hears the Prior's bell marking the end of the morning, he lets out a grunt of relief, which earns him a sharp look from his master. Head down, Trian puts away the books and writing things in the holy chest.

After psalms, readings, and prayers, it's time to eat. Almost always great auk—Trian catches one every two or three days. (He tries to spare young ones that haven't had the chance to see the wheel of the seasons go all the way round.)

But Cormac does his best to vary the fare. Their little plot's doing remarkably well, a sign of God's favour; it's producing a few green onions already, and saw-toothed seedlings of fat hen, as well as narrow arrows of tangy sorrel. Trian relishes every leaf.

At today's meal, Cormac lets out a satisfied belch. 'How's the scribing?' He must be able to read Trian's face, because he chuckles and quotes the Scripture: *There is no end to the making of books, and much study wearies the flesh.*

Trian mustn't complain, so he changes the subject. 'I see our chapel's rising.'

'Slow work. I'm only on the third course of stones.'

'What matters is the quality of the effort,' the Prior says, 'however long it may take.'

Is their master praising Cormac's stonework, Trian wonders? Or rebuking him for his concern about its pace?

Cormac's eyes are on the translucent flames. 'By the way, Father, we've only bits and pieces of charcoal left.'

Trian's alarmed to hear that, but the Prior chews on.

The tension between his elders sours the last bite in Trian's mouth. He thinks of Abram's plea to Lot: *Let there be no strife between us, for we are brethren.* He jumps up. 'I'll look for something else to burn, then, will I, Father? Driftwood, maybe?'

The Prior eyes him. Trying to decide whether this is some pretext for taking an afternoon away from the copying?

It is, of course. But still, they do need fuel. Trian brushes his greasy hands on his robe. 'I'll go this minute.'

The Prior releases him with a small nod.

For hours Trian scrambles around the edges of the Great Skellig. No driftwood anywhere. He notices that footfall has scored and wrinkled the ground with faint paths wherever he or the Prior has gone exploring. (Cormac, distrusting both his balance and his eyes, stays close to their camp.)

Trian gets down to points on the foreshore he's never visited before. One rock floor has swellings like breasts; many coves he finds choked with rotting tangles of wrack. And after all this exploration, he's managed to gather no more than a handful of waterlogged, splintered sticks.

He's hungry. He finds himself eyeing mussels and limpets on the rocks. *Unclean,* he reminds himself. The Prior knows these things.

Trian's mind is racing through the alternatives to wood. Plants ripped out of the ground?

No, they'd burn up in seconds. He seems to remember his folk throwing dried seaweed on the fire, but even if the monks could sun lengths of the stuff on rocks during a spell of fine weather, they've no building to keep it dry in after.

Bird droppings? No, those sticky white-green spatters are nothing like cow pats, which dry out into grassy discs; even if they weren't too wet to burn, they'd send up a choking smoke.

It has to be wood, but there's none to be had. Trian's mind goes in tired circles. If the Prior's unwilling to leave the Great Skellig even briefly, couldn't he give his monks permission to take the boat off in search of land that has trees to cut down, charcoal or turf to trade for? Can he really think they'd be lured back into the world by a single journey, corrupted as fast as apples in a barrel?

But the point of a rule is to put self aside, Trian reminds himself. To answer, *Your will be done,* as Jesus did when his Father sent him to die on the cross.

Breath harsh in his chest, he sits on a high ledge and shuts his eyes. If he was a piece of timber—a fallen trunk drifting down the great Sionan and out into the sea, or a mast off a wrecked vessel—where would the currents carry him? He pictures the knobbly outline of the Great Skellig, its protrusions and folds.

His eyes pop open. The day they moored, where the flat platform came down to the sea, didn't he glimpse a cave tucked behind? If flotsam happened to drift in there, it might well get stuck. It's worth a look, at least, because Trian can't present himself on the Plateau to chant None with no more than these few wet sticks.

Down at Landing Cove, he cranes around the rock to his right, but can't see a thing from here. He'll have to go in. He lifts off his robe and sets it, with his shoes, high enough to stay dry. He wouldn't chance this on a rough day, when a roller could smash him on the rocks. In nothing but his woollen braies he steps down into the motionless water, his toes feeling for sure footing—but it's all slithery with weed, and he slips, and bangs his elbow, and is in over his head, loose in deep water, splashing to the surface, gasping from the cold.

Trian paddles on the spot till he gets used to it and his breathing steadies. He fixes his gaze on the shadowy space at the back, under that overhang, and he makes his way towards it, into it. Yes, a cave, and choked, clogged with driftwood! Is this the hoard of years of waves carrying snapped branches and lost logs, fallen huts and broken boats to their last rest, tucked under the Great Skellig?

Much later, halfway up the cliff path, snake-haired and salt-crusted, bloody-knuckled, Trian pauses to adjust the long branch resting on his shoulder. Then he carries on dragging it up the hill. The driftwood is walnut-dark, heavier than it looked when he decided to haul it up, but he can't stop now; he wants to present one great log to his master the moment he tells him the news. He heaves hard, and walks on. Tries to remember the name of that good man who carried Jesus's cross for him for a while.

The Wailing Woman faces due west, as if watching for the sunset. Mary, sorrowful mother to them all. Trian stands still long enough to heave a breath, and prays: *We fly to take refuge under your cloak.* He eyes the descending sun, and hurries on.

The Prior's magnificent face broadens into a smile at the sight of the wood. 'Well done, Brother Trian!'

Trian aches with gladness. 'There's lots more,' he says, eyes down so as not to seem boastful. 'Though it'll be too waterlogged to be much good for burning yet.'

After chanting None, the men work together to bring up the driftwood. Cormac attaches ropes to the winch that's been pegged into the rock since the day they made landfall, and positions himself there, on winding duty. Trian follows the Prior down to the platform of rock where he left all the flotsam. Together they rope it in a great dripping bundle, and Trian scurries up the path to help Cormac draw it up the cliff. They set it in a great pile on the Plateau where it will catch sun at almost any hour; the breezes should help dry it out too.

That evening they rest by the fire, where Cormac's already added a few of the sticks to the charcoal. Still aglow with sweat, Trian picks splinters out of his white-sponge fingertips. The flames leap blue and purple, and the wet in the wood hisses fiercely. He smells salt; the smoke catches a little in his throat.

The Prior, dishevelled but magisterial, sits down on his bucket. 'Did I not say God would provide?'

'You did, Father.'

'You did,' Cormac admits.

'I tell you, Brothers, what seems impossible to us is easy to him.'

The hottest day so far, and Artt's temper is rising. Writing outdoors, standing at their rocky desk, means the light is usually wrong—stabbing his eyes or casting heavy shadows—and his back, still so able for hard feats of lifting, responds to standing still all day with a dull ache.

He's groggy from lack of sleep, too. He's woken by the dawn every morning and drags himself off his tick right away. His soles slip on the dew as he makes the circuit of the Great Skellig, walking the pattern, keeping the devil from getting so much as a toehold on their holy mountain. Everything glitters, that early; wet spangles the small leaves and the exposed veins of crystal in the scarp. The relentless beauty exhausts Artt.

Summer's under way; their pile of driftwood is drying fast. All over the island chicks are breaking out of their eggs, shrill little reminders of the passage of time. The copy he's making of the Old Testament is on its third gathering already, but Trian's Psalter limps on, maddeningly slow. Artt has preached to the young monk as eloquently as he can; urged him to run to the Scriptures as a gasping fish returns to the waves. To shelter in these words, cling to them, mount up high on them. Writing, Artt teaches his young follower, is praying with both hands, fighting the devil with pen and knife, each word a deep wound in his side.

Trian does everything he's told, but sluggishly and cack-handedly.

'Excuse me, Father, but would you look at this hole?'

Artt narrows his eyes as he examines the curl of thread from where the parchmenter mended the tick-bite into a pucker, not well enough. 'Did you stretch the scar, or finger it?'

'I did not.' Trian wipes his nervous fingers on his robe. 'I just turned the page and saw where it'd opened up.'

Flaws can creep into vellum at any point: scabs on the living calf, a careless cut during the slaughter or flaying, specks of rot during storage. Much like sin, it strikes Artt: the kind that men are born with, the kind they blunder into in childhood, the kind they walk into as men.

Trian offers, 'I could sew on a little patch, maybe?'

'That won't hold,' he snaps.

'Should I just write around it, then?'

'Pretending it's not there?' Almost a shout. 'No, Brother, an eyesore only gets worse. With handling, this tear will widen and gape like a woman's part until it swallows up holy writ.'

Trian blinks like an idiot.

'Cut out the page,' Artt tells him. 'Bind in a fresh one with no faults.'

He nods miserably. 'Oh, and Father? I'm running out of ink.'

Artt turns a deaf ear to any whining about supplies.

'I was only wondering what I might use for black, instead of charcoal melted with pine pitch.'

He sighs. 'Any soot will do. Char an oily bird—a puffin or shearwater.'

'I will, thank you.' Trian goes back to his text.

But the next time Artt takes his gaze off his own pen and glances to his left, he finds Trian absorbed in watching a great auk shift about on her nest. 'Brother!'

Trian jumps. 'Sorry, Father.'

Artt leans over and raps the paper eye-guard. 'Look here.'

Dark clouds have gathered over the sun, he notices.

'Weather's turning,' Trian murmurs. 'Should I pack up the books just in case?'

'Work on,' Artt barks.

The rain holds off for the rest of the afternoon, but the warm air thickens.

At their evening meal, chewing on roast puffin, Artt registers that the island is oddly silent. 'Have our feathered tormentors given up plaguing us?'

'Storm's coming,' Cormac predicts.

Trian nods. 'They always hunker down in crevices beforehand.'

Sure enough, soon the wind's rising so fast that Cormac has to put the fire out. Artt takes the little bottle of holy water and sprinkles it in all four directions, reciting prayers for calm weather. Trian rushes to move their three lumpen ticks into the shelter behind the hanging sails where the monks' goods and tools are secured, together with the sacks of down and feathers they've been amassing. He runs back and forth to the driftwood pile, collecting armfuls of branches to stash away from the coming rain.

Feeling the first big drops on his face, Artt throws on his cloak. He picks up the holy chest and swaddles it in the cloak like a child. He folds himself into the shelter, picking his way over piled sticks. 'Get in, Brothers.'

Cormac squeezes in behind the flapping hides. 'Brother Trian!'

A faint reply; something about the firewood. 'Get in here!'

Trian appears, lugging a great log.

The three of them huddle together uncomfortably behind the sails like chicks in a too-small nest. Rain is coming in at the bottom, drenching them to the knees already.

'A *wise man built his house on the rock,*'

Artt recites, though he's not sure the other two can make out his words over the rising wind. *'The floods came, and the winds blew and beat against that house, and it did not fall.'* His eyes are watering in the pummelling air. Something out there crashes and whirls by: what's been lost? *Things, only things,* Artt says silently, with a shiver. *Let go of them all. Let the storm rage; let the demons bite.*

He's hit by a memory of sitting in clean linen in the hall at Cluain Mhic Nóis two months ago. A civilised, respected guest, whose name went before him. And now look at Artt: a fishy-smelling vagrant in wet rags. He and his monks like kinless men, outcasts.

But they washed up here by God's design, he reminds himself as the wind screams and the sea batters the cliffs. Castaways by choice, marooned on purpose, gladly imprisoned be-yond the reach of men. This island is a ship to heaven, and they won't founder no matter the weather. *'The Lord is my rock, my fortress, and my deliverer.'* He howls the words with wet lips. *'A shelter from the wind and a refuge from the storm.'*

The night's one long sleepless tempest, to Trian, till just after dawn, when the wind finally drops and their wet sails stop lashing. He seems to remember the Prior chanting Vigil at some point; Trian wasn't able to distinguish the words, but he hummed along—unless he dreamed that?

He staggers out of their cramped shelter, rubbing his eyes.

The wicker creel is gone, and so is all the rest of their precious driftwood, no doubt swept into the ocean or smashed on the rocks below. Trian thinks of how much work it took him to collect it, and sets his jaw so hard a tooth throbs with pain.

As he wanders along the clifftops, his frustration begins to ease. The air smells new, and cool. How well the bird flocks seem to have come through last night's lashing! Some nests must have been blown into the void, but there's no visible gap in the bristling ranks along the cliff ledges. Trian does happen on one kittiwake in the fescue grass, apparently unharmed but stone dead, eyes open, stiff on its back. He picks it up, remembering the Gospel line about sparrows: *Not one of them falls to the ground without your Father knowing.* The kittiwake's shorter than Trian's hand, and as light as a drawing of itself. Was it worn out by the bruising wind, or struck against a rock?

A tiny life, he thinks, lived according to God's instructions. Such poised, still feet. The kittiwake has only three toes instead of the four most birds have, he notices, and they end in tiny sharp claws. Did God give it those for clinging onto its nest? But then...what purpose might the little line of red around its eyes serve? Or the bright drip at the corner of the beak, and the same red on the long tongue-dart inside? Trian can't puzzle out the divine intention behind the painting of these details. Maybe the Creator's fond of variety for its own sake, and takes delight in all the ways his creatures differ from one another?

Best not to eat this bird, Trian supposes, in case it was sick before the wind knocked it down. He goes to set the airy body on Cormac's midden. The decaying stuff hums with the play of insects. He calls, 'What are you doing, Brother?'

'Thinning out the spinach,' Cormac pants, bent over his plants. 'If I keep only the stronger seedlings, a handspan apart, they'll have more of a chance.'

'How're the turnips?'

'Swelling nicely.'

'Any of them ready to eat?'

'Why don't you be the judge?' Cormac rubs the dirt off one the size of a walnut and tosses it to Trian.

He crunches the white flesh between his teeth. He mumbles, 'That's the best turnip I've ever had.'

Cormac chuckles and finds another for himself. He's harvesting leaves of fat hen, Trian sees, and sorrel too. 'At least whatever we grow here is safe from goats and rats and mice. And from men too. Remember the time holy Comgall caught some thieves?'

Trian shakes his head. 'I don't think I ever heard that story.'

'Well, those curs had the cheek to plunder vegetables right out of the saint's plot. So Comgall lifted his holy bell in his left hand and cursed them—asked it as a favour of God, who struck the lot of them stone blind.'

Trian laughs, before it occurs to him that Cormac mightn't find the notion of going blind so funny.

But Cormac doesn't seem offended. 'Though some say, once the thieves begged forgiveness and did penance, Comgall cured them, and even let them join his monastery.'

Repentant sinners could make the best monks, Trian supposes, since they'd be under no illusions about themselves.

He notices that the kelp dressing on the vegetable beds has shrunk right down. 'Would you like more wrack, Brother? A gale often washes up quantities of the stuff.'

'I would—if Father can spare you.'

He goes off to ask.

'Very well,' the Prior says grudgingly, 'but catch a bird for our meal too. And then get back to the copying.'

On the path down to the shore Trian nearly trips over a pair of rainbow-faced puffins. From their burrow he hears a faint cheeping: their egg must have hatched. He goes down on his knees in the mud to peer in, but can't see that far into the dark. Farther down the cliff, though, in a crevice, he glimpses another, grey and fuzzy, looking like no relation to its spectacular parents. Imagine having emerged from your cracked white shelter last night, into such a storm-tossed world.

There's still a heavy swell left over. The waves push into Landing Cove one by one. Like grandparents and then parents and then children, it occurs to Trian, each generation taking its turn. Tangleweed lies thick on the rocks above the tide line, like Joseph's coat-of-many-colours in its intricate luxuriance, tiny insects jumping through the tangle.

He remembers the foreshore in the story

where holy Senán's sister had to be buried because her brother wouldn't allow her any closer, not even when she was cold in death. That was harsh. Do saints have to be so harsh, to be so holy? No, that can't be true. Trian frowns over the stories that give it the lie. Comgall forgave the thieves in the end, didn't he? Cóemgen let a crow nest in his own hand, for forty days, and wouldn't disturb her; Colm Cille spared a whole grove of oaks the axe.

An armoured thing crawls over the pebbles; thin, waving feelers and two huge dark blue claws. *Lobster*—that's the word. Trian remembers them from his childhood. Boiled, they turn red, and you smash them open to get the luscious meat. He never knew it was forbidden.

His stomach growls at the sight of the shellfish clattering down into a rock pool. He wishes he still didn't know it was forbidden; wishes he was innocent and could cram his belly with whatever dirty, delicious stuff he found.

Trian thumps his chest hard, and tells himself to get on with his work.

For lack of a hook or even a rake, all he can do is gather the reeking clumps of seaweed in his arms and wrench them off the rocks. He wishes he had the lost creel, or had thought to bring down one of their sacks, even.

Mounting the cliff, he can't see where he's putting his feet; at one point he trips on a ribbon of kelp and slips onto the pile. He bursts out laughing at the notion that if he's to fall to his death, after months clambering up and down the Great Skellig, it'll be for the sake of some maggoty seaweed.

Craning up, Trian's disturbed by something about the silhouette of the clifftop. Didn't it bulge out before, just there? When he climbs nearer, the hollow is fresh; he realises a whole chunk of the cliff must have been broken off in the storm. Strange to think that a landscape can be transformed, just like a man's face. Are wind and waves and rain God's fingers, then—still tinkering with what he made more than six thousand years ago?

That prompts Trian to gaze over his shoulder at the Saddle, the island's thin waist. Will the Great Skellig itself be eaten away over time till one day it breaks in two? Maybe everything wears down in the end.

As he deposits the seaweed on Cormac's midden, Trian registers the Prior standing at work at their desk in the distance. He hurries off in search of dinner. Many kittiwake and guillemot are still sitting on their eggs, and don't budge even when Trian works his way within arm's reach. It's love that dooms them, he supposes; they won't leave their clutch, not even to save themselves. He takes just one of each kind, today, and tries to break their necks before they know their time's up.

'I only mean one sleeping cell between the three of us,' Cormac pleads. 'Just for bad weather. We saw the other night that the overhang's not half big enough for us and our things.'

The Prior's dry lips purse.

'Now we have less driftwood left to feed the fire at night, it takes days for our robes to dry out, and our mattresses are damp too. We could catch our deaths.'

'*Whoever seeks to save his life will lose it,*' the Prior quotes, '*but he who would lose his life for my sake will save it.*'

Cormac can't argue with the Gospel, but doesn't quite see how it applies to the hut he wants to build.

'All these daily protections we say,' the Prior adds—'why do we snivel so?'

'Snivel?' Cormac repeats.

'What are these poor bodies of ours, that we should expect Christ and his angels to shield them? Why dread sickness and death at all, when we should rather trust God to do with us what he will?'

Cormac never considered it that way; never felt the need to justify his preference for survival. A quick thought flickers: *This is nonsense.* Doesn't every creature on the earth, water, or sky want to stay alive?

But he dips his eyes and makes himself mutter 'Amen.'

The Prior's tone is calmer now, as if he's solved a theological conundrum. 'From this day on, I say we'll beg no further protection, except against the assault of sin.'

Cormac doesn't answer. If their master says it, then that's how it'll be.

But the sleeping hut, that's why Cormac rashly began this conversation. He tries again, going roundabout. 'Really we were lucky we didn't lose more than the creel and half the driftwood, Father, and that was only a summer storm, not a real winter gale. The water that blew in under the sails—what if it had soaked the holy chest, with the books and writing materials inside?'

Is that a shift in the Prior's expression?

'I'm only proposing one little hut to shelter our treasures as well as us. A simple hive shape, to keep it watertight. Aren't bees the most virtuous of insects, always working for the good of their brethren?' Cormac pictures the beautiful curve of the cell—like an egg half-buried in the ground. 'No need for windows—or a smoke hole, even, as we'd keep our fire outside.'

'All right,' the Prior says reluctantly. 'But as soon as this hut's done, you'll return to the greater work of the chapel.'

Hiding his grin. 'Of course.'

'And the hut will be built faster by two of us, so you must teach me.'

Cormac winces. 'Oh, but Father. You're a man of deep inquiry—'

The Prior shakes his head. '*Ora et labora.* Prayer and manual labour are equally noble.'

The man's no mason, that's what Cormac meant. Well, there's no point in arguing.

He chooses a flat spot on the Plateau, on the other side of their fire from the chapel, and uses the dividers to chalk a wide circle, nine feet across. The space inside the round hut will be a square, he decides; he and the Prior snap those four lines.

Next they gather stones, and lay them out according to size. Cormac starts setting the first course, between the outer circle and the inner square.

The Prior lifts a rock and holds it. 'Just here?'

Cormac hesitates.

'Too round? Should I take some off the side with the mallet?'

'Ah...That crack in the middle, see, Father? I fear there's a frailty there.'

The Prior tosses that rock aside.

It feels disrespectful to treat his master like a novice—but it would be disrespectful to the building to use the wrong rocks. 'If we find a long one, like this, we'll use it for a locking stone, to go right across the full width of the wall.' Cormac lugs it into place.

'Excellent. Every stone we add takes us a step closer to heaven,' the Prior says.

Cormac nods. 'And we should try to cover every joint in the first course with a stone in the second, so there's never two joints on top of each other. The rule is, *Every stone must lie on two.*'

The Prior nods. 'Like us.'

'What's that?'

'Three men, Brother. Each one leans on two, and each two on one.'

HARVEST

During Sunday Mass, when Trian receives a piece of the Host on his tongue, it smells and feels and tastes like plain oatcake. He has to gather all his forces to make himself believe that it's truly the body of Christ.

He lives for the Sabbath, but for a shameful reason: because it's the one day in seven when he's freed from the copying. At the week's end, Trian's cramped hands can loosen and uncurl; his neck can straighten. In between the holy hours, he's allowed to go and pray anywhere he likes.

Today after the noon meal he heads straight down to the sea. On the cliff path, puffin chicks cheep from every crevice. Trian does pray as he walks, but with his eyes wide open. *O winds and clouds, bless the Lord. O mountains and hills, bless the Lord.*

In Landing Cove he leans against the boat

that's resting like a gigantic creature's discarded shell. Idly he checks that her joins are still tight and sealed with resin, her greased leather not showing any cracks. Does the Prior mean to leave her here as a sign of their old life, like a curiosity from a past age?

In the rock wall behind, a purple patch has a darker splotch in it. Trian puts his face closer. It looks like a piece of fern caught in the slate, but when he scratches it with one black-rimmed nail, it's hard. How did a leaf get trapped in the rock? Such divine handiwork. The book of the earth has enigmatic passages that Trian can't interpret, but still he loves to read it. It seems to him that nature is God's holiest language. Everything created seems to express its Creator; everything cries out, *You made me.* Trian wonders whether these birds wheeling overhead, even these rocks, might be his sisters and brothers.

He sits down at the waterline, now, dipping his feet in up to the knees. The tingle is delicious. A sleepy afternoon, the water barely lapping. On impulse, Trian pulls off his robe over his head and folds it up. Who's to say a man can't pray in the water?

In up to the neck, gasping from the chill, he holds a big breath and dips his head under, pushing his eyelids open. It's a green, flickering world down here. Two kicks power him off from shore, and the seabed's falling away from him, as if he's gliding like a young eagle over this silent, glowing landscape. The boulders below have turned weird, some coiled like worm casts, others forming columns of mauves and emeralds: *corals*, that's the word. And the bright waving things: anemones? Trian rears up to let out the old breath and take in another. Facedown, he swims faster, farther off. The clarity on every inch of his skin.

O rivers and seas, bless the Lord. O creatures that move in the waters, bless the Lord. So deep now; the floor's shelving sharply to black as he moves farther offshore. Trian kicks his feet and shoots away. The sense of height is dizzying, yet he can't fall. He's floating along on the skin of the water, like a passing cloud.

High on the Plateau, Artt's ringing the holy Hour of None.

No sign of his monks. They're too far off to hear, though they're supposed to stay within range of the bell that keeps them all tied together with its invisible threads. Could they be so deeply immersed in prayer that they don't hear? Artt suspects old Cormac of dozing his Sunday away, and Trian's distracted by every passing bird. So Artt rings again, and keeps ringing, and waiting, and his anger rises. Two such ordinary men, marked out in his dream so he could bring them along to an island at the ends of the earth. But godliness remains impossibly far out of their reach, because they can't be bothered to get on time to the holy service.

Here comes Cormac now, with a strange hopping gait. Artt calls, 'What's the matter?'

'I might have done myself a bit of hurt, Father.'

How, in the middle of a quiet Sabbath afternoon? Cormac's careful to avoid the vertiginous cliffs. 'Did you roll your ankle?'

Shyly he lifts his robe to the knee, revealing a bloody gash like a dog bite. 'I suppose I wasn't looking where I was stepping, and a rock slid and threw me down the slope.'

'Careless! Come, I'll wash and bind it.'

Ill at ease, Cormac waves his master away.

'Sit down,' Artt orders him. He goes to fetch water from the cistern, and the herb box. Once Artt's washed the rock dust out of the cut, Cormac takes the cloth and presses on it to stanch the bleeding.

'Is the bone broken, would you say?' Artt asks.

'No, no. I'll dress it with honey...' Cormac trails off.

Of course, they discarded the jar of honey on the riverbank at Cluain Mhic Nóis.

Cormac scoops a palmful of cobwebs from the box instead, and stuffs the wound with them. He uncorks a tiny flask and shakes some salve into his palm, smears it on. 'Aloe, powerful stuff. This'll heal in no time.'

But he's afraid; Artt can hear it in the tremble of his voice, see it vibrate in his hands. *Timor mortis conturbat me,* the fear of death is racking this old monk. He's survived perils, lived decades longer than anyone would have expected, and still he shakes to see his blood spill. Artt wonders, *Is life so sweet to these men that they want it to last forever? Like tired children after long play, racing away from the arms of the father who's come to fetch them home?*

To bolster him, Artt strikes up a prayer: '*Christ's wounds—*'

'*—heal us,*' Cormac replies, his voice faint.

'*Christ's pangs—*'

'*—ease us.*'

'*Christ's groans—*'

'*—our songs.*'

Here comes Trian, draggle-haired as if he's been in the water. He points at Cormac. 'Your poor leg, Brother!'

'Ah, it's nothing.' Cormac binds the cloth twice around his calf.

Artt calls out, 'You absented yourself from service.'

'I beg pardon, Father.' Flushed, Trian drops prostrate on the ground.

Trian's never tended a sick man before. Cormac keeps insisting it's just a cut, even when—after two days of limping around the chapel site, crouching to fit stones into place—his lower leg swells up and leaks through the bandages. The bruising's an extraordinary purple and yellow. The Prior won't let Cormac stand on that leg anymore; he's ordered Trian to keep the old man on his tick by the fire.

Trian doesn't really know what to do with the bronze probe, but Cormac talks him through each step. 'See, it'll let out the noxious blood. A touch deeper now,' he says through his teeth. 'That's right.'

How can Cormac speak as if it's another man's leg, not his own? Trian wipes away the green seepage. He adds more of the salve, and reaches for a clean cloth. 'You bear it well, Brother.'

A laugh hisses out. 'If you're spared to reach my age, you'll find you're glad of even the hard hours.'

Trian knows that anyone can die of a wound that goes from green to black. Still, at least Cormac has no fever yet. He ties the bandage tight.

'Now, how can I be useful?'

'Your job is to rest,' Trian reminds him.

'I am resting, but I need something to take my mind off this wretched leg.'

'Well...I have been thinking about salt.'

Cormac's wild eyebrows go up.

'We haven't much left in our jar,' Trian points out. He's been worrying about this for some time. *God will provide,* but sometimes isn't it up to the monks to seek out his hidden gifts? 'Down on the shore, I saw a white crust around the edge of a rock pool and tasted it, and it's pure salt, dried up.'

'Did you scrape some out?'

'Just a handful. But I was thinking we could make a lot more.'

'What, by setting out a pot of seawater in the sun?'

Trian shakes his head. 'That'd work only if we had many shallow troughs, and weeks of fine weather. No, I thought we could cook it down, maybe.'

'Well, if you haul the water up from the sea, I can stir the pot.'

Trian grins.

He staggers back up the cliffs with two mostly full buckets, their straps scoring his shoulders through the wool of his robe. He fetches the biggest iron pot and hooks it onto the tripod while Cormac, leaning up on his good knee, builds up the flames.

They boil the water all that day. Cormac leans over at intervals and works it with the big wooden spoon, until the liquid looks thick to Trian. By the time the fire's needed for cooking a pair of puffins for the evening meal, Cormac is stirring the sludge almost continuously so it doesn't stick. 'That should be enough.'

'But it's still wet.' It seems to Trian like waterlogged sand.

'If we keep it over the flames, though, it might scorch.' Cormac lets himself subside on the mattress. 'Sit it out in the sun for a couple of days, stirring it ever so often. That should finish it gently.'

Trian wraps his sleeves over his hands, then lifts the steaming pot and sets it down on the ground. The iron hisses and the low grasses smoke. 'I'm curious how holy Pádraig man-aged for salt, when he was a boy on his lonely hill. Would the pirates have given him any?' He mulls it over. 'To think of their faces when they found he'd slipped his bonds and escaped!'

'Hmm. I never pictured him tied up,' the old monk says. 'A herder needs to roam with his flocks, even if he's a slave, so as I saw it, the pirates just left Pádraig with their sheep and pigs in the wild, and he didn't know where else to go. Until the angel came down and told him about a ship, hundreds of miles from there, that could take him away to freedom.'

Trian's nodding; this story's one of his favourites. 'I've always wondered what form the angel took.'

'Sometimes they're said to appear as bright lights,' Cormac tells him, 'or borrow the shapes of young men like yourself.'

Trian snorts at the idea of such an angel—gawky, with a fiery ponytail. 'Is it true they can come as birds?'

'So I've heard. Whatever their outward forms, they're made of light, and they speak without tongues, shaping the air into words.'

'I'd say Pádraig was glad to get home to Albion, all right.'

'Ah, here's the thing, though.' Cormac holds up a finger. 'No sooner was he back among his kin than didn't he have another vision, instructing him to go back and preach the

Gospel to the Irish—the very people who'd enslaved him?'

Trian shakes his head in puzzlement. Clearly there was no escape, not as long as God had a job for you.

He glances at the pot. Tastes the sludge with one finger. 'We did it, Brother. We made salt.'

He looks over his shoulder at Cormac, who's attempting to smile, his face contorted with fresh pain.

Trian's pulse thumps. He should have insisted on keeping the old man lying down today, as he was told. *No,* he roars silently. *Don't dare die on me, our first season. Don't leave me alone here with a saint.*

When Cormac's leg gets so bad he feels it might burst, he stops speaking. He keeps busy, darning their socks. He wonders how much time will pass before their robes and braies will fall to rags. Maybe the monks will end up in tatters of bird skin and feathers. The thought doesn't horrify him, somehow. After all, these days they're burning twigs of driftwood instead of charcoal, and taking Communion of oatcakes. There seems no limit to what they can do without.

Every morning Cormac urges himself to mend fully, or die, nothing in between; if he winds up with a crippled leg, he'll be a perpetual burden to the other two. He can't decide which is more likely, death or recovery. Cormac's seen sick men writhe and screech as if they're giving birth, and be back on their feet a week later. Or, of course, lie down for a rest and never stir again.

In the meantime, he sets his teeth and never bothers mentioning the pain. His latest task is making soap, so his brethren will be able to wash the fishy stink off themselves in the months to come, whether Cormac's with them or not. Where will they bury his body, he frets, given that there's no soil here more than an inch deep? Really he should be put in the midden, giving back all he's made of, except the Prior would probably call that sacrilege.

Age quod agis, Cormac reminds himself. Keep his mind on the soap. He spoons ash out of the side of the firepit, and puts it in water to boil till the grit settles and the lye rises to the top. For lack of beef tallow, he's collected a bowlful of fat drippings off a roast auk, and he pours in the lye now. He mixes it up, trying to avoid getting any burning splashes on his skin, then puts it aside to set. 'It'll be a bit harsh for a few weeks, before it cures,' he warns Trian.

'Brother, lie down,' Trian pleads, putting the back of his fingers to Cormac's forehead. 'You're burning up again.'

There are dried leaves in the herb box that might help the fever, but Cormac doesn't say so. Better to save the medicine for the other two in times of need, since they likely have so many more years left in them.

Inside his pounding head, Cormac's thinking of all his markings. The cat that was pricked on his back when he was a boy; that tattoo has stretched and faded with his skin, but the pigment's never washed out. The odd shiny pink mark on his hands from cooking, and nicks from chisels. A scar over his lip, where his wife scratched him in a quarrel once, before she was his wife. A bump of lead under the skin of his upper left arm—an inch-long sling bullet he got in a clash between clans, which he's carried ever since. The ugly pair of scars where the javelin went right through his right side in battle, and somehow didn't spill his guts. The little crater above his left ear, where his skull was smashed by a slingstone, then drilled open by deft Brother Fiach—there's nothing shielding Cormac's brains at that spot but red skin. The fact that he's still alive makes no sense; he's a walking miracle. He lives and breathes at his Lord's whim, and he can only say *Deo gratias*.

He knows Trian's working hard to nourish him back to health, cooking up handfuls of turnips, sorrel, the tender top three leaf-pairs of nettle, whole heads of spinach. But Cormac's stomach turns at the food; he shakes his head at the bowl. He's talking again now, because if he can't tell stories, what use is he at all? His gaze falls on the Prior's missing finger. 'The young hero Cú Chulainn,' he begins in a rasping voice, 'he was so favoured by the old gods, he could swim like a fish the day he was born. Small, Cú Chulainn was, but with seven raven-clawed fingers on each hand, seven toes on each foot, and seven pupils in each eye.'

'Favoured?' the Prior queries. 'With such deformities?'

'Well.' Cormac's lost his thread. 'The hero's beauty was legendary all the same—hair of brown, red, and gold, all threaded with gems.'

The Prior shakes his head at the gaudy image.

Cormac's mind slides off down another track. 'Holy Brigit, now, she disfigured herself on purpose, for the love of Christ.'

Trian looks bewildered. 'Why would Christ want that?'

'No, no, listen. Brigit's father was a chieftain

who begot her on a slave woman. He planned to sell the girl off to one man or another,' Cormac wheezes, 'only she'd sucked in the love of God with her mother's milk, and meant to live a consecrated virgin. She tore her face and body so all men would be repelled by her. But once her father let her take her vows, her beauty was restored overnight!'

Cormac's thinking of the round cheeks of his little daughter. She comes back to him more, these fever-muddled days, than she has in twenty years. Sometimes her brothers, too; occasionally their mother. Is this a sign that Cormac's dying? Not that he has the least hope of seeing his family again on the other side. They were pagans, back in that other life. How he wishes he'd heard the Gospel before the plague came, and could have had them baptised too, before he lost them. If only there was a heaven with room for them all.

Artt's tried to stay composed, even on nights when the old monk's been tossing in delirium on the other side of the banked embers. He's kept up the perfect rhythm of the holy hours, dividing the chanting of the psalms between himself and Trian. But slowly, as the wet gash in Cormac's calf dries up and closes over, Artt allows himself to feel relief. No one's dying; not yet. It seems God needs all three of them on his sacred island.

Cormac's soon back on his feet, if hobbling a little. For all his hump, his inflamed knuckles, short sight, and old injuries, the man is invaluable. With Artt at his side hoisting each stone to head height, Cormac has the dome of their beehive cell corbelled tight in a week. They use it as a store for all their possessions now, as Artt sees no need for a roof over their heads at night until autumn.

Now that lesser task is done, the two of them will be able to get back to the greater one—raising the higher, thicker walls of the chapel, God's own house set on the heights of the island.

Tonight Artt watches Cormac roasting them three puffin chicks for dinner—his fingers turning the skewers with snatching movements, to angle the raw sides of the birds down so they sizzle and twitch over the flames.

'We've only a few bits of driftwood left,' Cormac mentions.

'Well, I'm sure Brother Trian will find us some more.'

Trian speaks up glumly. 'I've swum right to

the back of that cave, and gone some way into other openings, south of us and on the north-west side. Not a stick.'

These mopers, Artt thinks—always brooding over what's to become of them next month, next season, next year. Can't they hear the music of eternity?

One of the puffin carcasses rips off its spit and drops into the fire. Cormac reaches for the big knife to skewer the flaming bird.

Something occurs to Artt. 'Wait.'

The meat's flaring up like a great ball of fire. 'But it'll be burnt through—'

'Leave it!' They watch the bird in the ashes burn on greasily, steadily. 'There,' Artt says. 'There's your fuel.'

'A puffin?' Trian asks, bewildered.

'The young ones are so fat, they're balls of grease—why not build a fire of them?'

'To burn? Not to eat?'

'We'll burn some to cook others. These islands are so teeming with birds, I knew there had to be some purpose to their numbers.' Artt laughs. 'See how tenderly the Lord provisions his beloved children?'

These days of high summer, Trian's hands have a lingering reek of blood, even when he's scrubbed them with Cormac's soap. Even when he's bending over the Psalter, forming letter after graceless letter. The Prior releases him from the copying every afternoon, but only for killing the vast numbers of birds they need to stoke their fire.

The rowan has lost her flowers, Trian notices as he's passing, but her first fruits are coming, clusters of green berries that'll soon turn red. He stands stroking her bark with his stinking hands, and watches Cormac and the Prior toil on the chapel. He's only putting off the moment he must begin the slaughter.

His task is to wait on the cliff path for puffin chicks to emerge from their burrows. The fledglings lurch about, trying their flight feathers; ungainly, excited, feet too heavy for their bodies. The adults nudge them from above and call out encouragement from below. Some fledglings fall on the rocks; Trian retrieves them with the noose on his staff, if he can reach. Others he simply snatches off the slope to left and right. He breaks their necks at once, uneasy to be dispatching birds in front of their parents at the very moment when their airborne lives are about to begin. Taking birds in ones and twos to eat, that was one thing.

But scores of young at a time, just to feed the flames...

It takes so little effort, that's another thing that appalls Trian. No snaring necessary, nor feats of skill; no danger. A hard yank on a fledgling's slim neck, then he loops it on his belt. Once the belt's full, he follows the path back up to the camp, their bodies swaying like some ceremonial skirt. He slides them off the rope, dropping them on the waiting pile. No plucking and jointing necessary; all he has to do is keep up the killing. The air stinks of burning feathers and flesh. Their heaven-sent manna turned to greasy cinders.

Cormac wrinkles his nose at the stench of the fire, but says it can't be helped, because they've nothing else to use for fuel. And what are the monks to do for light, in the dark months ahead, he wants to know? They're down to the last two beeswax candles and a stub; what'll they use to see by on long nights, when they get up to chant Nocturns, Vigil, and Terce?

Trian imagines the winter hours the three men will have to spend together in the stuffy stone cell, darkness pressing on their eyes. The puffin bodies in the flames spit oil; the back of his hand stings, and he licks it.

'Like Fionn,' Cormac murmurs.

'What?'

'Fionn Mac Cumhaill, when he was cooking the salmon.'

Trian nods. The king of fish, one drop of whose fat held all the wisdom in the world. He wonders if the poet Finegas ever brought himself to forgive his servant for the accidental theft.

'What about rush lights dipped in bird grease,' Cormac says suddenly, 'as we've no wax? Have you seen any rushes growing?'

Trian tries to recall. 'Mostly toad rush, but it's shorter than my hand, so it'd hardly be worth the trouble.'

That afternoon, down in Seal Cove, at the southwestern end of the island, Trian does find some sea rush—green stalks a good two feet long and sharp-pointed. He brings back a whole armful.

Cormac's been refining his plan. 'Puffins have that little bag of oil in their bellies, that would do for coating the rushes. Easier to drain out than catching the drippings little by little as the birds roast.'

'Shearwaters are bigger, so they might have even more oil. If we caught a whole batch at once...' Trian eyes the clear blue sky. 'We'd have to wait for a cloudy night.'

For now, Cormac shows him how to prepare the rushes, soaking them in a bucket of water for an hour, then stripping them with knives, peeling off the hard green to bare the white pith. 'Leave on just a line of green to stiffen the stem.'

Trian's so grateful this old man didn't die of his infected leg.

Next Cormac teaches him to tie the rushes in handfuls to dry. They make half a dozen bundles in all. 'A stick down the middle of each bundle would stop them from curling up—if we'd any sticks,' Cormac worries.

They have a few branches kept by, for starting fires, as bird corpses are no good for that. Trian tries cutting a slice from a thicker log with the hatchet, then shaving it into thin sticks, but they either snap or curl up. Sometimes living on the Great Skellig is like an elaborate riddle, or one of those dreams in which Trian's charged with sewing nettles to make a shirt, weaving a rope of ashes, carrying water in a sieve.

He makes do without sticks; he binds the bundles tightly at both ends and hopes that the rushes will all incline to curl in different ways, so that in their diverging they'll keep each other true.

The next evening, the warm sky's clouded. Trian tells himself that if the hunt's going to happen, it has to be tonight. Their meal is two puffins, skewered over a fire in which five others are flaming and blackening. As soon as he's eaten, he asks, 'Father, may I go shining?'

'Go what?' the Prior asks.

'Fowling for shearwaters by the shine of a candle, to collect their belly oil for making rush lights.'

The Prior nods. 'That will work. But be careful not to trip, on such a dark night.'

'It's only when there's no moon that they fly in off the sea,' Trian explains. (Could the birds be scared of the moon?) 'But if I may take one of our candles—just the stub—I'll try to bedazzle them with it, see?'

The Prior shrugs. 'Very well.'

'Let me help with the shining, Brother?' Cormac asks.

Even though the old monk's gammy leg might give under him, Trian nods.

'You should wrap your hands in case the shearwaters bite,' the Prior advises.

Trian finds two cloths for each of them to double around their knuckles.

First they recite Nocturns. *'From the rising of the sun to its setting, there is none like you,'* the Prior chants. *'From the great sea to where the sun goes down belongs to you.'* When they've sung the three psalms, heard the readings, and said the prayers, it's dark enough to begin.

Cormac banks the fire, mounding ashes over the blackened bird bones. Trian has the hand net ready, and a short taper; Cormac, a sack and a bucket. Overhead, stars prick out between drifting clouds. Once Trian's eyes adjust, there's enough faint brightness to let him pick his way over to the honeycombed part of the hill. When he steps in a hole, he decides it will be safer to go forward on his knees. Cormac kneels too and fumbles in his wake, dragging the bucket.

Trian listens for the shearwaters coming in off the sea, shrieking to their hungry chicks. He takes out the fire horn and uncorks it. He pushes in the tip of the candle, and moves it about till the wick flares up. 'Here, Brother,' whispering as he hands the candle to Cormac. He stoppers up the horn and puts it in his pouch. 'Hold it up—'

Bird eyes are leaping out already. Pairs of them, framed in dark holes; unable to look away or hide, disoriented by the glory of the light. Trian snatches one shearwater out of its burrow and breaks its neck with a flick of the wrist. Oil dribbles from its beak over his hand, smelling sweet and lightly fishy; precious stuff he mustn't let seep out in the sack. 'Give me the candle, Brother, and you squeeze the oil directly into the bucket, that'll be faster.'

Cormac seems at a loss.

'Turn it upside down and knead the stomach,' Trian orders, handing over the limp shearwater in exchange for the wavering light.

The old monk clutches the bird so hard with both hands, Trian hears oil squirting onto the wood.

Another and another and another. Trian rips the shearwaters out of their burrows and Cormac drains every drop out of them. There are so many fliers drawn to the light, Trian takes up the hand net and makes great swings with it, sieving the air. He reaches into the wriggling, flapping net and shakes the life out of each bird. Grabbing and snatching at the crumbling ground, at the sky, he deals out death like some monster. Down-flecked hands slippery with oil, fingers pecked (he's lost his bandages), painful knees, scraped ankles. The faster Trian kills, the sooner it'll be over.

The hours slither by. The candle burns very low. 'Enough,' Cormac says at last.

'But we need—'

'The bucket's full, Brother.'

They crawl back to the fire, Trian hefting the bucket with great care, a foot at a time, so none of the liquid gold will be spilled; so that no small death will go to waste. Cormac drags the sack of shearwater carcasses behind.

The Prior's awake, lighting a candle, about to ring the bell for Vigil.

Cormac wakes puzzled by the sticky stench of his hands. Then remembers the night.

Trian's crouched over the bucket, examining the oil. He seems limber, as if after a long, unbroken sleep. Cormac tries to remember being that young, as he walks over stiffly to peer into the bucket. The yellowish stuff—some amber and red mixed in—is cool now, forming a wax at the rim. It's separating well, the stomach oil floating above the more watery liquid that's flecked with fish debris.

The bell, again, for Terce, though it seems only a minute since they were chanting Vigil. Cormac hurries to wash his hands, but even with a lot of soft soap the cold water can't shift the grease, and drops race down his skin.

After their prayers, he griddles oatcakes; he's mixed chopped seaweed in to bulk them out. The sack of oats is less than a quarter full, but he doesn't mention it for fear of starting a quarrel. If their master's still dead set against a trading trip this season, he must have some other plan for their future, surely?

'To our book-labour, now,' the Prior tells Trian. 'Be sure to scrub those hands first, so as not to taint the parchment.'

'Will I get on with making the rush lights, then?' Cormac asks.

Trian pleads, 'Father, we've a whole sack of shearwaters that have to be plucked and jointed, or they'll spoil.'

The Prior sighs. 'Time is more valuable than any meat, Brothers, and you spend it like profligates.'

Privately, Cormac can't see why the tasks of chapel-building and book-copying are so much holier than food-preserving. And he's tempted to point out that if you stint men of nourishment, their strength for work will shrink accordingly, and their lives on earth will dwindle. Why can't the Prior see that this bird meat is a bounty of time in concentrated, fleshly form?

But he presses his lips shut. He gave up the right to argue when he vowed obedience. *Monks should be humble as slaves.*

'You may take until noon, just this once,' the Prior tells Trian.

So all morning the two monks work side by side by the fire, while the Prior toils alone at the chapel. The long reeds seem dried stiff enough, or so Cormac hopes. He warms a shallow pan of the bird juice till it liquifies again—without being hot enough to burn his fingers—then undoes a bundle and immerses the naked reeds. He spreads them on a rock to congeal, with another rock resting on top to stop them blowing away. When he's finished the half-dozen bundles, he goes back to the first reeds, which feel firm enough to take another coating. Mutton fat would form harder, Cormac knows, and even a little beeswax would make these rush lights burn so much longer. But this is what God's provided.

Beside him, Trian wrenches feathers and down off the birds.

'You'll be plucking for days. Faster to skin them,' Cormac advises.

Trian nods, and switches to pulling their skins off. Denuded, the lumps of white fat stand out against the pink meat. He uses the big cleaver to chop each shearwater in four. 'We can eat a few today and tomorrow. But I suppose the rest will have to feed the fire,' he says, staring at the pile of limp carcasses. 'Unless there's any way we can save some for winter?'

Cormac mulls it over. 'We could cook them down ever so slowly over a weak flame, all day and all night too.'

'That'll preserve the meat?'

'If we cover it with its own grease in crocks,

sealed tight.' Not that they've many crocks left, after the Prior dropped half of them, but still, it's a start.

'Brother, there's no end to your knowledge.'

'I'm just old,' Cormac says with a chuckle.

Together they joint the birds and layer them with handfuls of salt in the biggest pot.

Brushing stone dust off his hands, the Prior walks over to the fire. 'What success have you had with the lights, Brothers?'

'I'll try one this minute.' Cormac kindles one of the rushes at the fire. The flame shrinks and smokes; that's because the rush is too upright, he realises. They have no iron nips here to hold these lights up slantwise. He tries laying this one flat on a rock, but that makes the flame race along.

'Stand it up in a jar?' the Prior suggests.

Trian fetches one from their stone hut, and Cormac tries that. In the jar, the rush lies diagonally and burns more steadily.

'Not bad at all,' the Prior pronounces.

Cormac's relieved.

The Prior turns to Trian. 'It strikes me that with your young eyes, and these lights, now we have a stone cell to work in, you could keep up the copying after dark.'

The young monk doesn't say a word.

But Cormac can hear Trian's misery, as loud

as a wail. He intervenes: 'Oh, Father, by their nature these rush lights will spit and sputter. Imagine if one dripped on a manuscript, or a bit snapped off and set it on fire.'

The Prior's lips tighten. 'What about oil lamps—would they be safer?'

'Somewhat, but we packed no lamps.' Cormac thinks of those little earthenware ones at Cluain Mhic Nóis.

'Shells,' the Prior says briskly. 'Oyster, or scallop—I'm sure the foreshore's littered with them? You could add little wicks of cord, fill them with this bird fat and let it set. Keep them stacked up and ready.'

Cormac nods. He can tell by Trian's face that the young monk dreads the idea of copying all evening as well as all day, but he has to admit that shell lamps could work.

Trian writes and catches birds, slaughters them and writes. The days are getting shorter but feel endless to him. His fingers are sore from gripping pen and knife, and ripping feathers.

The puffin fledglings are fatter than their parents now. They stagger around the rocks like drunks, trying out their wings, and Trian, watching, seizes and slays them, because those are his orders. He hauls their bodies back by the dozen, to feed the flames. He expected to be used to it by now, but it seems to be getting harder by the day.

The Prior insists it was for this that God established birds on the Skelligs in clamorous crowds when he first created the world. But Trian struggles to believe that such a variety of lightsome and beautiful birds have formed in their translucent ovoid caskets, broken out of them, walked, cried out to their brethren, taken flight, over and over for these thousands of years...all so Trian can now fling them down to flame and char on a cooking fire.

At night he dreams of throttling books in a great feather-storm of flapping pages. He resents the Psalter the Prior made, for its matchless grace that he can never hope to reproduce. But he reserves his real hate for his own grubby copy.

Now that they've made lamps of shells, the Prior insists there need be no slackening with the approach of shorter days. He and Trian should be able to keep at their appointed task all winter in the hut, crouching on their upturned buckets with their manuscripts on their knees. It'll grow cold, of course, he says, but not enough to make their hands seize up.

The prospect of such a winter makes Trian want to run away across the cliffs.

Summer's not over yet, and the aching in his palms is already spreading through his body. Tightness in his knuckles and neck no matter how often he cracks them. He has trouble waking up, whether first thing in the morning or when the bell calls him to prayer in the middle of the short night.

He craves—above all things—his pipe. *Not needed,* the Prior said on the riverbank, but so many of the things they did pack because they thought them needful, and have since been used up or lost, the Prior now deems surplus to requirements, so what was the logic? Trian can't see why the tiniest bit of room couldn't have been made for his instrument. He remembers its light feel in his hands, and the holes, smooth to his fingertips. He shuts his eyes now and whistles, fingers playing the air, trying to conjure up those sweet notes.

It occurs to him that a great auk's wing bone can't be so different from that of a swan. In his next free moment, he sidles off to dig a wing bone out of Cormac's midden and scrub it clean. When he chops off the two ends with the hatchet, he finds the middle almost hollow; he just has to clean out the yellowish sediment with a pointer chisel. Trian grinds the straight mouthpiece smooth on a rock. He recalls, more or less, where Brother Blathmac showed him to put the holes; he drills them gently so the bone won't split, and checks the note by blowing as he goes along. Piercing the first three openings a handspan beneath the mouthpiece, he leaves a little gap, then makes the last two, and finally a V-shaped end to taper the sound as it comes out.

Over their noon meal of oatcakes and blackened puffin meat, Trian lets out a huge yawn.

'Tired from writing?' Cormac asks.

But Trian can't answer that in front of the Prior; it would sound ungrateful, lazy, rebellious.

'I'm put in mind of blessed Ailbe,' Cormac goes on. 'That holy man had so great a soul-friendship for an abbess called Scíath that he lent her his best scribe to make her nuns a copy of the Gospels. But it happened that year, when the scribe had only two of the Gospels written out, he fell ill and went to his rest.' Cormac crosses himself. 'Well, Ailbe, paying the abbess a visit some months on, was mortified to hear this news. He marched to the scribe's grave and ordered him out, setting him to work again till the second half of the task would be done!'

The thought of being exhumed for book-

labour squeezes a terrible honk of laughter out
of Trian.

The Prior glares.

He drops his head and says, 'I beg pardon,
Father.'

Artt finds he's thriving on hard work. Whether
he's hammering stones for the walls of the island's chapel or copying the Greek Testament,
he relishes that sensation of giving everything
in the Lord's service. Squeezing himself out
like a grape.

But after a long morning of pelting rain,
writing in the hut by the faint daylight that
comes through the entrance, jostling elbows
with Trian, even Artt needs air before he can
start again. He sends Trian off to catch them
some fish, as it's a fast-day.

He restores himself by looping the Great
Skellig, pacing out his territory. 'God's eye to
look before me,' he chants. 'God's ear to hear
for me. God's hand to steady me.' Crossing the
Saddle, he lets his hood fall, welcoming the
soft drizzle.

When Artt first registers the notes, he mistakes them for the yip of one of the eagles who

haunt the South Peak. But no, that's a *tune* he's hearing. Could he be imagining it, or is it some trick of the devil's? As he mounts up towards the South Peak, the music gets clearer. He creeps along a ledge and leans around a great boulder.

Trian, cross-legged, piping. He stops and stares guiltily.

Artt walks up to him and holds out his hand.

Trian puts the instrument into it.

It's so well crafted, Artt thinks at first that it's the one from Cluain Mhic Nóis. 'Did you smuggle this in our baggage against my orders?'

'No, Father! I made it, just yesterday. From the wing of a great auk.'

It is a fine instrument, but everything depends on the purity of the intention. In this case, it's rank disobedience. 'So you've defied me by whittling this behind my back.'

'But I couldn't ask—'

'Because you knew the answer,' Artt says. 'You knew you were going astray. You were skulking—ashamed, perhaps, but not truly penitent.'

A sob.

Artt tries to snap the pipe in two, but finds it's too strong. So he lifts one leg and breaks it over his thigh.

Trian lets out a gasp as if he's been stabbed.

Artt tosses the pieces into the void. 'My son,' he says softly, 'a man's life may seem long to you, but it is like the journey of a single day. We are all hurrying towards heaven, and I'm only trying to lighten your load.'

The pale blue eyes are shiny with water.

He makes his voice ring out like a trumpet. 'We can't bring so much as the clothes on our backs with us, not even our own skin or bones—we must leave all that to rot. Each of us will be summoned to the gates at a moment's notice, perhaps many years from now, perhaps today.'

He waits for Trian's acknowledgement. But the young man sits stunned, bereft.

'I'm just trying to keep your gaze fixed above, so you'll be ready, you see? I must part you from everything but God.'

Trian weeps, then, as if finally convinced of his fault.

Artt steps forward to enfold him in a strong and merciful embrace.

THE LAST FIRE

THE GREAT SKELLIG'S emptying. The puffins and guillemots have gone south, disappearing practically overnight; a great exodus, Trian thinks, as when the Israelites were freed from slavery in Egypt. Will the kittiwakes and cormorants be next to head off, he wonders, or might they overwinter here along with the flightless auks?

The birds are spending these last mild days on the water. The sea's their true home, Trian's coming to realise—the island only a precarious, temporary perch where they lay their eggs. Without puffin chicks for fuel, these days, he has to eke out Cormac's cooking fire with the carcasses of great auks, which smoulder more reluctantly. He doesn't hear the shearwaters anymore, on these cooler evenings, and he misses their hullaballoo.

He remembers leaf drop, in the groves of

Cluain Mhic Nóis; the whirling smokes of gold and brown on the autumn winds. Here he has to read the turning of the season in the departure of birds, instead. And in the drying up of the lingering flowers: little pinks of spurrey and white stars of stonecrop, crumpled daisies of mayweed and red-brown pillars of dock, even great purple blooms of tree mallow. Everything's hunkering down, turning back to grey-green.

The one exception is the little rowan tree on the Plateau. Her leaves are red but they cling on with a stubbornness that gladdens Trian, and still she puts out handful after handful of scarlet berries. How she pulls such riches of colour from the dull slabs she's rooted among, he can't tell. He's wedged a few bunches of berries in between the stones of the hut's round roof to dry alongside Cormac's strings of onions. The Prior's decided they should sleep in there now, on cold nights, anyway. They lie wrapped in their cloaks, as close as three bodies in a grave.

Trian sits under the rowan's contorted form, one dank foggy morning, and introduces his arms through her pliable branches. His fingers caress her cracked bark in thanks for her gifts, not only the berries but her persistence, her grace. He needs to learn how she bends and endures.

'Brother, what are you doing?'

He scrambles to his feet. 'Praying, Father.'
It's true, though he couldn't explain it.

'Back to the books now,' the Prior orders.

Trian follows him to the desk in the distance,
already feeling the cramp in his palms.

Cormac has no idea when he and the Prior
will ever finish the chapel. The walls are so
massive, and they've already used all the best
rocks for the altar and the beehive hut. So
he has to pick his way nervously down the
island's steep paths in search of big boulders,
and split them by dropping them. He hammer-
shapes each suitable stone on the spot, and
carries it back onto the Plateau so he or the
Prior can slot it into one of the walls that rise
so unbearably slowly.

His garden is past its best, now, the bloated
turnips gone bland, the bolted spinach bitter,
the great nettles knotty with fibre, but still
he throws everything into the soup. Cormac
never got many leaves of fat hen, but it did
send up a quantity of big brown seeds for
planting next year, as well as tiny black ones
that he grinds by the fistful to improvise a

sort of dark pancake. How he misses leavened bread baked in a pot, the brown crust hiding the pillowy inside.

On Sunday morning, as they eat, the Prior mentions, with a glassy serenity, that there's no more wine for the Mass.

Cormac's eyes meet Trian's in panic.

'Many of the Church Fathers, such as holy Cyprian, rejected the drinking of any intoxicants,' the Prior goes on. 'They offered plain Communions of bread and water, so we will do the same.'

Cormac's head hurts, trying to make sense of this. Oat and wheat are both grains, at least, so in the case of their blackened-oatcake Host, one kind of bread is standing in for another. But wine is the fermented juice of grapes, and water is something else entirely.

The Prior goes on as if he hears Cormac's silent objections. 'The original substance doesn't matter, Brothers. Through the miracle of Consecration, any liquid can be transmuted into the blood of our Lord Jesus Christ.'

Any liquid?

'Amen,' Trian mutters.

Cormac forces himself to echo 'Amen.'

Trian looks around, clearly searching for a new subject. His eyes fall on the unfinished chapel. 'That's coming along,' he remarks.

Cormac thinks of a story. 'I'm put in mind of holy Mochaoi. How he was in the woods cutting timber to build his church, when he heard a gorgeous bright bird singing on a blackthorn nearby, and realised it was talking to him.'

Trian asks, 'What did the bird say?'

Cormac puts on a high nasal tone. '*I am here to tell you your work is good, to encourage you and amuse you for a while with my singing.* So Mochaoi stood there in the wood, entranced and enthralled. It felt to him as if the bird's song lasted one happy hour. The fresh branches he'd gathered didn't wither, and the spiders paused in their spinning. Even the tireless bees left off collecting nectar from the flowers. All creatures were listening to the ravishing music.'

The Prior's eyes have lost focus, as if he's hearing that same song.

'What happened next?' Trian wants to know.

'The bird flew off,' Cormac tells him. 'Only then did the holy man realise it had been an angel in feathered form. So he carried his timber back to the site of the church—and there he found it already built. He didn't know the monks' faces, and none of them recognised his, because not one, not fifty, but a hundred and fifty years had passed.'

Trian marvels at the span of time.

It strikes Cormac now what a sad story this is. To be soothed with music and given a heavenly reward, but in exchange you've lost a century and a half in a blink, and all your friends are dead and buried...If he'd been Mochaoi, he'd have preferred to sweat over every beam of that church than to dream away his whole life in an afternoon. Once childhood is over, don't the years pass too fast already, rolling over a man as fast as waves? But then, the Lord never does stoop to consult his people.

Trian's voice has tightened oddly. 'If the Church teaches that hard labour is so good for the soul, why did the angel entertain Mochaoi with sweet music instead of leaving him to work?'

The question takes Cormac aback. He looks to their master.

'Perhaps to show God's powers,' the Prior says. 'We should never take too much pride in our efforts, since beside his, ours are as feeble as thistledown.' He rises to his feet now and strolls off towards the midden.

Trian says, very low, 'The great auks, Brother. I think they're going.'

This startles Cormac. 'Going where?' He waits. 'They can't be flying south with the others.' Feeling foolish for saying it.

'Going to sea, I suppose. They're fierce swimmers.'

'But they can hardly stay afloat for six months at a time, can they?'

Trian shrugs unhappily.

Because the great auks were already on the island when the boat made landfall, Cormac's been assuming they're year-rounders. How stupid of him not to suspect that the monks' best source of food and fuel might abandon them at the end of summer. 'Have you told the Prior?'

'He'll only say what he always says.'

Cormac nods grimly: '*God will provide.*'

'He broke my pipe.'

Cormac's brow furrows.

'Not God.' Trian nods at the Prior, who's squatting over the midden. 'Him.'

Cormac's never heard this mutinous tone from the young monk. 'No, Brother, we left it behind with my lyre, remember?'

'I made another, and he broke it.'

'Oh.' Cormac's chest hurts to hear that.

They sit in silence, their eyes on the Prior as he straightens and shakes out his robe.

All Cormac can think to say, under his breath, is 'Saints can be hard men.'

The Great Skellig gets quieter by the week—eerily quiet, it seems to Trian.

The day comes when they're gathered at noon, and he has to tell their master that he can't find a single, solitary great auk. 'And I'm having no luck chasing down any other birds.'

The Prior frowns. 'Surely you can make shift to get us other food—fish, say.'

Trian empties his bag on the ground: a slim bream with a bleeding mouth. 'I can, but there's nothing fatty enough to cook it with.' He finds a small, strange pleasure in spelling it out.

In the silence, the Prior nods as if this was all part of his plan; God's plan. 'Well, no more fires, then.'

Cormac gapes. He says it before Trian can: 'What, are we to eat raw stuff?'

A magnificent heave of the shoulders. 'Jesus told his followers to eat *whatever was set before them*,' the Prior quotes. 'Raw is how all nourishment comes, after all. It's only worldly affectation to improve its tenderness and savour by cooking. Our food will be itself now, undisguised.'

Trian looks away to hide his face. He watches the ashes that still glow faintly from last night. He should have paid more attention to fire, while they had it; should have memorised the warmth, the dance of light.

'Let's begin this minute,' the Prior proposes in an almost festive tone. Taking up the big knife, he sets the bream down on the rock and lops off its head; hacks the body into small red chunks. He pops one in his mouth. Chews, removes a bone, chews again. Retches. 'I ate too fast,' he gasps, beckoning for a goatskin.

Cormac passes it to him.

The Prior gulps water. Then he carries on chewing. 'Join me, Brothers.'

Trian's throat locks at the prospect.

Beside him, Cormac gamely tries a piece.

But when Trian does make himself bite into the raw fish, it mostly tastes of the sea: like tears with a trace of blood. He's eating like any bird, now, he tells himself; like all God's other creatures do.

As the autumn winds down, here's the paradox that troubles Cormac. Everything they eat is cold, uncooked and leathery now, from seaweed to the tiny helpings of raw oats soaked overnight in water to the odd fish that Trian manages to catch. But even as Cormac chokes this food down, his mind's whirring with the question of how to save some so that in a few months—by which time it'll taste even worse—it might keep them alive a day longer.

Their larder, a hollow in the rocks, is half a dozen crocks of fatted bird and three of salt-brined fish. They've no containers to store any more than that. Drying's been a failure. Cormac's cut two kittiwake carcasses into pieces and filleted a few large fish, rubbed them all with salt, and hung them up, but they've only attracted flies and gone mouldy. He thinks of all those eggs back in the early summer, beautifully encased in their thin shells; he should have thought to find some way to preserve these in fat or salt. He's heard of burying eggs to keep them, but for that he'd have needed soil more than a fingernail deep.

It's too late in the season to do much about this. The Prior told them to trust in God. Cormac holds to his vow of obedience. But he can't help thinking of the boat, inverted in the cove below; of how the world of men (their fires, their hearths, their fresh-baked bread) is only a few hours' voyage away.

Every day Cormac ducks through the low door in the unfinished chapel's western wall, careful not to clip his head on the huge horizontal lintel. He straightens his back, takes a long breath, and goes to work, raising the walls. Toil is all that keeps his mind off his belly. He works either with the Prior at his side or (when the Prior's copying) on his own. These great hollow walls, why did Cormac decide they had to be two feet wide? They'll eat up every rock on the island and never be filled.

He lived through half a dozen famine seasons before he became a monk. Curiously it's not the worst time that comes to mind, but the one when Cormac was a child. Well, everything's more vivid when you're young. Then again, you snatch at any feeling at all, when you're old, even the aching of hunger, as a sign that you're not dead yet.

He's worried about Trian. Blank-faced, the young monk hunches over his Psalter on the Plateau on milder autumn days, by lamplight in the hut when it's colder. Whenever the Prior releases him, he mopes around the island, looking for bits and pieces for them to eat. Cormac finds him almost impossible to rouse for Vigil at night and Terce in the morning.

The Prior's exasperation is beginning to harden into anger. He orders Trian to skip that day's noon meal as a penance.

Cormac finds a moment to speak in their master's ear, as soothingly as he can. 'Amn't

I right in thinking that scribes are known for depression of spirits, Father?'

'Notorious for it,' the Prior says crisply. 'The gloom goes by many names—*acedia, apathy, melancholia.*'

Cormac nods. It's the repetitiousness, he'd imagine.

'The condition must be subdued through prayer and hard work. If the scribe gives way to his affliction, it becomes a sin, and a great one.'

Cormac sighs. 'Maybe Brother Trian just can't keep going on so little food and sleep?'

The Prior turns away as if he hasn't heard that.

Hunger is a rumble in the concavity between Trian's sharp hips, a high note. He's beset by half-formed, unruly thoughts: *Why did we three come so far to live a cleaner life, to quell all appetites, with the consequence that all we can think about is food?*

Well, all *Trian* can think about, at least. But who knows what goes on behind their leader's broad brow? Cormac is looking gaunt and haggard these days, and Trian imagines he himself wears the same face. But the Prior's perfect features gleam the same as ever.

Today the fishing line, when Trian dangles it from the cliffs, brings up nothing but the occasional sea devil or ray. He knows the Prior won't touch them, but he chews on their raw flesh himself, illicitly. He has trouble believing that these fish could rouse any base desires in someone who longs for nothing so much as a hot stew.

He drags around the Great Skellig whenever the Prior lets him off copying for half an hour, but rarely catches a bird anymore. If he gets near a kittiwake he tries a smooth stone in his braided leather sling: set, whirl, release. But his aim is rusty, and the bird almost always wings away.

As a child Trian used to set snares in loops of twine. It took hours of watching from a hiding place, waiting for a bird to step into the baited loop. He remembers, what were they called, *gorge hooks*? A little bone sharpened at both ends, hidden in a lump of meat, and tied to a long cord weighted down by a nearby boulder; if a bird swallowed the meat, the hook would lodge in its throat. But for bait Trian would need meat, or fish at least, and right now he has nothing. He shouldn't have thrown away the last of that ray. Would a cockle do, or a few limpets? First he'd have to make the bone needle, anyway. And before that, he must catch something for the other men to eat. His mind moves in groggy loops.

The big black cormorants are very few, this late in the season, but there'd be plenty of meat on them, even if it tasted as rank as their eggs. There's a sea stack where a couple of cormorants stand and stretch out their wings to dry. If Trian swam out to it, he supposes the birds would flap away contemptuously long before he got there.

He binds wing feathers together with twine to make a long, pliable rod, and knots his waxed noose to its end. Creeping silently along the cliff, he lowers it down to slip the loop over a cormorant's head. But the bird startles and flaps away, ripping Trian's noose and stick with it.

His attempts get more brutish. With his staff he tries clubbing kittiwakes from the length of a man away; they easily skitter out of range. He lurches around with the hand net, but can't get close enough to bring it down over any bird.

One day Trian spots a cormorant on a ledge above Seal Cove, busy swallowing a fish. His hand net would be useless against such a giant. He crawls up behind the cormorant and hurls himself on it, arms out, hoping to pin its wings with his elbows and wring its neck—

But it snaps out its wings with an outraged honk and shakes him off. He slithers down the rocks, banging his hip.

Trian limps down to the shore at Seal Cove and rips up handfuls of purple and green weed for his bag. Only a couple of limpets on the rocks; he prises them off.

He remembers the rule even as he's breaking it; he gnaws their rubbery flesh and finds he doesn't care that they're forbidden.

What can he eat next? He sees no scallops or cockles or oysters. There's so little eating on a winkle, they're hardly worth it, but still he gathers the sea snails with his blade. He pulls up one tangle of mussels—blues, purples, browns, and blacks together—and sniffs at them.

His attention's caught by the cry of a baby.

He spins around and there, rolling in the surf, making something between a grunt and a groan, is a seal pup. A whitecoat, still young enough to be helpless in the water. Injured, sick? Or just lost? The pup's creamy coat is bedraggled. Hauling itself up the rocks to get away from the punishing waves, it works its flippers exhaustedly. Five claws, Trian counts, more like the paw of a dog, more like a hand.

He wants it: meat, fat, pelt. But those big moist black eyes...

He approaches, and crouches to pick up a boulder. If the pup's lost its herd, it has no chance. To leave it to die would be waste, he reminds himself. To let it die slowly, eyes pecked out by birds, would be cruelty.

But what if its mother were to come back? What if she's out there past the breakers right now, waiting, roaring back at her pup?

The whitecoat gurgles and pants. It's plumped with its mother's milk, brewed from the fish she ate yesterday.

Trian stares into its bottomless eyes. It comes to him that he himself is made of all the birds he's ever caught, which in turn owe their flesh to the fish they've snatched. And the fish are composed of the plants they nibble on, and the plants take nourishment from the sun, which rises at God's command: so he feeds all his creation. Either Trian and the other monks will eat this seal and live another week, or Trian will lie down here on these slick stones and in time his body will feed the seaweed and the fish and the birds and the seals. Everything borrowed has to be returned. The Lord made them all and will swallow them up again. *God gives and God takes, bless his name.*

Trian brings the rock down on the seal's

silky skull, hard enough that one blow should do it.

Artt's not satisfied. No more than a month now until the church year will begin again with Advent. How fast summer has withered into autumn, and how little he and his monks have to show for their months on the Great Skellig. *Man's days are as grass.*

Today Trian has hauled back a gutted seal pup; the dark meat is as dense as venison, lean yet oily, with a wild, gamey taste. The liver in particular—Artt tries not to relish it too much. The problem with hunger is that he can't simply resist it, saying an absolute *no,* once and for all, as he has said to lust. The stomach whines to be fed every few hours, and to ignore it for more than a few days would constitute the grave sin of self-murder; that's why even the desert saints took their locusts and honey. Hunger is a constant argument, and Artt wishes he could be done with it.

The three men eat seal at every meal until, two days on, they can't deny that it's on the turn. Artt supposes it's the oiliness that makes the stuff so quick to spoil. Cormac won't let them eat another bite, in case they make themselves sick, and takes the carcass—still heavy with meat—to the midden.

Late afternoon, and Trian trails up the path from the Saddle, the bag over his shoulder light, holding nothing but seaweed and a few small fish for his brethren. His own belly is full of mussels—dozens of them. Heavy with shame. *Unclean*, and he ate them anyway; stuffed himself with uncleanness.

There's the Prior on the Plateau, kneeling in prayer.

No. Kneeling in a mess of foliage. And where's the rowan?

Trian's mind refuses to accept it.

The discarded hatchet catches the last of the western sun. With his knife, the Prior's slashing off berry bunches and red leaves.

A screech rips Trian's throat.

The Prior turns and calls, 'Brother, see?'

Trian sees. Hears the cuts. Smells rowan juice and tastes the tang. Feels the severing in his own limbs.

The Prior holds up what remains. Racked and twisted, a slanted vertical and two crooked, half-stripped arms springing out. 'A mighty cross to fix to the top of our chapel.'

He roars it: 'She was the only tree on the island!'

'And how favoured, now, to form the holy image of that cross on which Christ won our souls from hell.'

Trian's so close now, within arm's reach of the hatchet. He could snatch it up in half a second.

The Prior's face is shining like an angel's.

Trian shuts his eyes and drops to his knees. But still he sees that triumphant smile, and still he wants to kill the man.

He hits his own chest so hard he winds himself. To long to do murder, to savour it in your heart, that's nearly as bad as to do it. Trian's in mortal sin and he can't escape. He batters himself again and again.

That evening Artt gives his monks—as a concession to their weak understanding—a homily on the rowan. How in the depths of his contemplation, he heard God demand a great cross to affix to the roof of his chapel when it's completed. How their Prior was inspired to shape it from the one thing already growing at the top of the island (by divine plan) in cruciform shape. Could there be any higher use of a plant than this?

Still the two monks remain sullen, especially Trian, who hasn't said a word since he saw the rowan felled. In silence they chew on their raw fish and seaweed, grinding it down. They crouch on their stools around the blackened hollow where their fire used to burn and a rush light now slants in a jar.

Sometimes Artt wishes he'd never set eyes on either of these stupid men; had set out alone in search of his island. Could he have managed the voyage on his own? It might have been better to make the attempt, and die trying.

Time for Nocturns. He stands, rings the bell, and leads the others in the psalms.

Halfway through, Trian breaks off and retches silently behind his hand. Artt ignores him.

But after the final prayer, Trian scrambles away into the twilight and vomits, hard and wetly. Instead of blowing out the rush as a signal to bed down on their ticks in the sleeping cell, Artt moves the light closer to the young monk, scrutinizing him. 'Are you ill, Brother?'

All Trian will say is, 'I beg pardon.'

'You'll feel better now it's out,' Cormac tells him.

But Trian keeps retching. Soon he scuttles away in the dark, in the direction of the midden. Awful sounds of the voiding of bowels.

Afterwards, the young monk throws himself down on the ground outside the hut. He gasps, 'I'll sleep out here tonight, so as not to disturb the pair of you.'

Cormac brings him a beaker of water. Then he goes into the hut to fetch Trian's tick, and his cloak for a blanket.

Hours later, when Artt wakes in the black night for Vigil, he feels around for the fire horn, and kindles a rush in its hoarded embers. Cormac sits up, swaying groggily. Only two of them in here, the huge shadows of their heads wavering on the inside of the dome, and for a moment Artt's confused, before he recalls that Trian's lying outside.

After their psalms and prayers, he stoops over to go out the doorway and check on the young man. The cloak's been cast aside, and Trian—silvery in the starlight—is writhing about on the lumpen mattress.

Cormac's at Artt's side. 'Still not well, Brother?'

A grunt from Trian.

Sometimes the vileness of the body revolts

Artt. Why could men not be composed of air?
Why did God stoop to making a race out of
stinking clay?

'Here's water.' Cormac kneels to put the lip
of the goatskin to Trian's mouth.

A swallow. Another. But a few moments later
Trian jerks his head to the side and spews
again.

Artt leads Cormac back to the cell. Soon the
old man's snoring, but Artt lies staring into
the dark.

The next morning, Trian's worse. He lies limp
and sweating, except when he suddenly curls
up with a groan as if some demon's gnawing
at his vitals.

They ate the same meal yesterday, but Artt
and Cormac have been spared, and Trian's
being punished. For which sin, exactly, Artt
wonders? Why did Trian start beating his
breast like some frenzied druid when he saw
the rowan cut down?

Artt does all he can. He stands over the
young monk and prays for his soul, hour after
hour. He uses their tiny flasks of holy water
and oil to anoint him. He cups water in the
holy bell, for added power, and has Trian
drink from it.

Artt has never been ill, himself, since he did
the impossible and survived the plague. But

his own mother was taken this way, with a flux of the guts that made her bleed at both ends. Artt was five years old; he watched it happen. He's always known how flesh can melt away in days; how no amount of crying will persuade the Lord to change his inscrutable mind. So he whispers: '*Not my will be done but thine.*'

Cormac's no doctor. He can't tell whether it's Trian's black or yellow bile or blood or phlegm that's overbalanced his other humours; he only knows that the young monk seems to be dying.

He tries mashing up vervain and coriander in water, to cool the fever. He gets most of it down Trian's throat, but then it comes back up. Sunken-eyed, shrunken, the young man lies curled up like a baby on a mattress in the stone cell. He has too little control of his limbs even to pick up a waterskin.

Another look in the herb box. Cormac's mind is racing. He could blunt the young man's suffering with henbane and poppy. Some who take those herbs sleep three days and wake up with their fever gone; then again, some don't wake. Trian is already so weak, what if the medicine kills him?

Cormac pleads silently, *Don't abandon us.* The three of them are like one body that needs all its parts. Trian has the most skill and nerve for climbing and fowling and egging and hunting and fishing, shinnying up and down the bony flanks of this island. And other qualities, too: an innocence, a sort of radiance.

Cormac lays a wet cloth over the dark red hairline.

A terrible squirting. Trian moans. 'My fault.'

'Brother! How is sickness your fault?'

'Unclean.'

'Don't fret, I'll mop you up,' Cormac murmurs.

'Ate mussels. Shellfish,' the young man slurs through his teeth.

Cormac understands, and is filled with rage. Not at Trian; at the Prior, and his rules; at all the makers of rules. 'Of course you did. You were hungry, weren't you?'

Tears leak out of Trian's left eye.

Cormac pulls up Trian's damp robe and starts picking at the drawstring of his braies.

Trian's hand flaps in clumsy protest. 'No. Let me—'

But he's as weak as water. 'Come on, I'm not going to leave you lying in your dirt.' Cormac gets the knot undone and pulls the soaked drawers off. With a goatskin of water and a cloth he does his best to mop Trian's buttocks. (Absently wondering how he'll ever get the soaked mattress clean.) Then—

Cormac stares. In the dim of the cell, at first he's not sure quite what he's looking at.

No wonder Trian's parents impressed on him that he was *made for a monk*—not meant for marrying, likely not capable of getting children.

Cormac shakes his head in confusion. As the apostle Paul wrote, *Now we see dimly as if in a mirror.* Cormac can't fathom any of this, but he has to believe that God does.

Moving lightly, he finishes cleaning Trian, whose eyes are shut, as if he's being lifted and dropped on the strong tide of fever. Cormac tugs down the hem of Trian's robe, and looks for the spare pair of braies to put on him.

Nothing more that Cormac can do for now, so he goes out onto the Plateau to soap his reeking hands and rinse them in the pot by the cistern. Where the rowan used to grow, a dead stub. The twisted cross of her trunk and two limbs leans against the unfinished chapel, waiting to crown its roof. The mist's thickening. It strikes Cormac that fog blinds all men equally.

He checks on their meagre plot. Finding a leathery turnip, he shakes the earth off it and gnaws on it. He pulls up the last tough leaves (sorrel, spinach, nettle, and fat hen) for pestling into a sour paste. Nothing else to save. Time to bed the garden down for its long sleep. He starts shovelling their midden over the low wall onto the plot, hoping that by spring the clumped, slimy stuff will have rotted down and built up the soil. As Cormac lifts and spreads one spadeful at a time, they flash out at him, the undecomposed reminders of the past half year: the pig bones, bird skulls, beaks and feet, eggshells, feathers, curls of leathered skin; hard cinders from their fires; dry fragments of onion skin; always the reek of the monks' own excrement.

It occurs to Cormac to take the last of his onion sets out of the herb box. He pushes them right into the stinking matter, in faint hopes of an early-summer crop next year, if by any miracle he and his brethren manage to hold out that long.

OVERWINTERING

NIGHT AND DAY now Cormac tends Trian in the beehive cell, while the Prior sleeps outside. He cleans him as necessary; he never says a word about how Trian's shaped.

On the third morning, Cormac wakes to find the young man sitting up beside him. Trian looks ravaged, befuddled, but alive.

'*Deo gratias!*' Cormac hurries to open one of their crocks and mash up the preserved, cooked bird.

Trian seems to regain strength, spoon by spoon.

That Sunday the Prior offers a special Mass in thanksgiving for the recovery of Brother Trian and the preservation of their fellowship. 'Our faith stands like an island,' he proclaims, 'lashed by a sea of doubt.'

For Communion bread they have a pat of soaked raw oatmeal. And when the oats are gone, as they will be in a week or two, Cormac supposes something else will have to stand in for the Host: a leaf? A piece of seaweed? A bowlful of air?

He's altered, he knows; he's brewing an infection of the spirit. These days, when he goes poking around the Plateau in search of anything remotely edible—the last of the bitter spoonwort, campion, dock, stonecrop, spurrey, tree mallow, even flakes of orange lichen, in hopes their colour might carry some vigour—in the back of his mind, Cormac is picking a fight. As he and the Prior keep adding to the walls of the chapel—almost roof-height now—his fury rises too.

One day he finds himself tracking the Prior up the little slope to the North Peak. Their leader stands staring out past the Lesser Skellig, towards the hills of the mainland. Seven, eight miles away, no distance at all. Cormac squints, wishing his sight was sharp enough to let him spot the smoke of a settlement. 'Father,' he begins, too abrupt. 'Would you think again about one short crossing before winter, just for food and fuel?'

The Prior gives him that stony stare. 'Those whom God loves best keep at a remove from the world of men. Remember holy Cóemgen, who lived off the nuts of the wood and the herbs of the earth.'

'I'd love a good nut!' It bursts out of Cormac. 'There are none on this island, and precious few herbs. Look at us, reduced to the state of beasts, clinging to a cold rock and chewing on raw weeds.'

'God will provide.'

'He has,' Cormac snaps. 'He's provided a boat.'

The Prior pulls himself up to his full height. 'The vessel was the means of our voyage, that's all. We might as well burn it now, if it's a fire you crave to warm your hands.'

Is their master losing his wits? 'You'd do that? You'd trap us here?'

'Trap?' the Prior echoes. 'God gave us this Great Skellig. Why would we spurn his gift?'

'But Father.' How can Cormac wake him from this spell? 'Brother Trian nearly died on us, poisoned by—'

He breaks off so as not to give away the secret of the mussels. 'Half-famished! Don't you care whether we survive?'

He means the question rhetorically. But the Prior puts his head on one side. 'Would it matter so very much, in the final reckoning?'

Cormac blinks.

'After all, it's not as individuals that we have

any importance,' the Prior muses. 'We three were called to found this holy house, and that's what we've done.'

'Found it, but for what?' Cormac demands. 'I thought we were building for the future, maybe for other men who God would guide to sail after us. But now I see you mean this to be our tomb.'

The Prior doesn't deny it. 'God owns our souls, whether they're dressed in feeble flesh or not. What grounds have we for believing that our living pleases him any more than our death?'

Cormac is staggered. He finds himself thinking of austere Comgall, who one night took pity on his shivering companions and lit them a fire with his loving breath. This man is different; his heart is a desert. 'You called us a family, Father. Your family.'

The Prior shrugs. 'I have no other.'

'Then—'

'But I say, with holy Paul, *Christ Jesus is my Lord, for whom I've lost all, and count it as dung.*'

Dung. The word heats Cormac's face, and he stumbles away.

Time is the problem, as Trian sees it. The days are shrinking, and he needs all the remaining light to work on the Psalter, because in their cell in the evenings he can barely see the page by the wavering flicker of the scallop lamp. But he has to steal an hour or two to find the monks something to eat, by fishing from the rocks or scavenging down by the shore. So maybe the real problem is food. If they open too many crocks and devour their stores of bird meat and fish, they'll starve before autumn gives way to winter. But if they don't eat enough now, how will they be able to work long and hard enough to find more to eat? The oats are all used up. The three men have dark circles under their eyes; they're windy and their breath stinks.

When Trian's belly is empty, he can't get to sleep for its grumbling. Cormac has stuffed their hoarded bird-down into their ticks, but the bristly old leaves still scratch. Then again, sleep is little comfort. When it takes Trian half the night to drop off, he dreams of the rowan, wailing and waving her flayed arms. Or of the grey-fleshed dead scribe (the one the saint dragged out of his grave to finish copying the Gospels), scratching page after page to earn entry to heaven, or even just the quiet of death again.

After such dreams, Trian can't rouse himself at the sound of the bell in the darkness, for Vigil, or in the morning, for Terce. If the Prior has to shout in his ear and rip away the sheepskin cloak, Trian throws himself down to ask pardon, and the Prior will order him to get up and make one hundred genuflections. A day that begins that way…the work always goes badly after, because Trian's tired, and loathes himself, and his hands shake.

So the problem is work, really. He can't form his letters well when he's cold all the time and his belly growls and his eyelids drop and he's distracted by the question of what the monks will eat next, because no problem is greater than that. As he writes, his mind roams the island, probing its crevices, vainly grabbing at the last few birds, who flutter out of reach. If Trian's eyes stray, the descenders of this line's letters will entangle the ascenders of the next. Lack of sleep is the problem, he decides. If he could only find the time to get enough sleep and find enough food and do enough work and…

Trian lurches up in the morning, eats what little there is, and toils on. He's so worn out, he can think of no other way, no deviation from this stony track.

Cormac comes up to him outside the hut and takes him by the sleeve. 'Brother.'

Trian raises his sore eyes.

'You understand we're stranded now?'

He can't think of a word to say. He nods.

'Our master won't let us off the island, no matter what happens. Sooner or later, we'll die here.'

Trian is too tired to be shocked by any of this. What's to be done? They are vowed men. He pulls away from Cormac and stumbles on.

In a cold breeze, alone outside the beehive cell the next morning, Trian is making up more ink for decorating the initial capitals when his numb hands fumble the vermilion. The jar drops and cracks like an egg on the rock, spilling its scarlet powder. Trian falls to his knees but already the stuff's smeared on his shoe, blowing across the Plateau, dusting red on a hummock of thrift. He struggles to scoop some up but he's only making the mess worse. The three fragments of the jar are stained with what they used to hold. He fits them back together neatly, emptily.

He goes to wash his hands with the fishy-smelling soap. Then he seeks out the Prior—eventually finding him in prayer, on the North Peak—and kneels to show him the shattered jar.

The Prior speaks with a quiet chill. 'It's not me you've offended by your clumsiness, it's God.'

'I beg pardon. I've heard a sort of purple can be ground from cockles—'

'Get up.' As Trian does, the Prior fingers the shards; examines a trace of red on his own fingertip. 'This vermilion is ground cinnabar, a rare ore dug out of the mountains in Spain.'

The man knows everything.

'It makes its miners so sick,' the Prior tells him, 'they're known for falling down in fits. Men died to gather this precious red, so that you could make God's words glow.'

Trian gnaws his lip.

'So don't talk to me of cockle shells. Have you no red in yourself that will substitute?'

He's bewildered. Then, 'My blood?'

'Just as Christ poured out his for our sins. There are pagan scribes in the Far East who'll use no other ink.'

Trian bends his head and thanks his master.

'Don't cut your fingers,' the Prior warns him, 'or you could smear the copy.'

'Then—'

'Under your tongue.'

Trian hurries back to the hut to make good

his error. In the dim, he lifts his tongue and slips his knife into his mouth. Careful, now, in case he goes too deep and makes a mute of himself. The sting makes his eyes water; under his tongue the hollow fills with a warm trickle. It's salty, metallic, and he has to resist swallowing the delicious, savoury broth. Instead he spits it out into a small bowl.

Trian seizes a clean pen and hurries to begin the inking before the blood can congeal. He places the tiny dots around every curve and sweep of the black initial. All that disappoints him is how quickly the bright red dulls to brown. It seems there's no rare ore in Trian.

He works and waits for the wintry day to be over. The light fades, and it's Vespers again, and a bowl of fish tails to chew with his sore mouth, then Nocturns, the impossibility of falling asleep, and Vigil—the Prior declaiming the Gospel in his ear, '*Why are you sleeping? Get up and pray*'—and sleep so heavy it seems his cloak has turned to lead, and relentless light's return.

The coldest morning so far. Singing Terce in jagged voices, and chewing on seaweed, and here's Trian on his bucket leaning over the Psalter again, pivoting to write in his copy, mouth still tasting like the point of a spear. Swaying, cooped up inside the bounds of an *o* and a *b* and a *p,* caged between the lines, Trian mutters the next words of the psalm as he copies them: *Our souls escape like birds from the fowler's snare.* What he wouldn't give to escape this wearisome labour! To be changed into a bird, now—to wing away over the Skelligs and their sea stacks and little islets. Unknowing, indifferent, freed from duty—from thought itself—needing only the lift of wind.

Trian has made a mark in the margin. Not a blot or a smear but a tiny shape, a round head with a beak. When did he do that—just now? Was he asleep, or in a trance? He can't erase it, so he keeps on drawing, giving it a tiny curved breast and wings and a tail. Feet tucked under because it's in flight.

'What's this?' Massive shoulders in the doorway block out the light, as the Prior leans in to examine the page.

Trian jerks. 'Just a picture.' He struggles for words: 'The psalmist compares the soul to a bird here, and I found myself drawing—'

'You *found yourself* doing it? No one sins by accident.'

Trian sets down the pen on the ground as if it's burning hot.

'Such appalling arrogance, to think the words of God could be improved by your scribble.'

'I'll scratch it out—scrape it off.' Trian has the knife out already.

'You think it won't still show, in the bare margin, the stain of your daubings?' With a lunge, the Prior snatches away Trian's knife by the blade. 'You've spoiled the whole leaf, almost two pages' worth. All that work for nothing.' He folds back and flattens the gathering so the offending leaf of vellum lies on its own on the upturned bucket. He cuts along the spine, which takes him two tries; the knife point protests on the brass edge and rips a jagged piece off the parchment. He grunts in fury.

'Father, shall I—'

'Ruined!' The Prior lurches out of the hut.

Trian dives after him.

'Look what you've done.' The Prior hurls the whole gathering away.

Disbelieving, Trian watches the wind catch the sewn pages and carry them along like some broken-winged, headless bird. He drops to the ground at his master's feet.

'Sloth!' the Prior screams. 'Disrespect for Scripture, pride, disobedience, self-will. You've defaced God's holy work.'

Trian weeps into the turf. 'Let me make satisfaction.'

'It won't undo what you've done.'

'Please, Father! Set me some penance.'

'Go down and stand in cross-vigil in the water, then, until the sun sets.'

Trian runs to the cliff so fast he almost over-shoots the path and slithers down the slope.

Down at Landing Cove, he leaves his shoes above the tide line. He wades into the water in his robe, up to his neck. It bites like ice.

Trian plants his feet on barnacled rocks, widens his stance so he won't be knocked over. He spreads out his arms in cross-vigil and turns his palms up to the sky. Watches the white disc of the cloud-masked sun inch overhead. Water to his chin, gnawing his flesh. He tells himself this is not full winter yet; he's hardly going to freeze by nightfall. The salty swell must hold some memory of the summer warmth, surely.

He's already hurting all over. But pain's only a kind of labour, after all. He can bear it. One long day in the water, that's all, and then his master will forgive him.

Pain strengthens the soul, sharpens the mind, subdues the will.

This is colder than hell.

Trian deserves it.

Pain's a kind of prayer. Doesn't he owe this aching and more to Jesus, who lovingly suffered so much to redeem all mankind? This should work as surely as a wheel moves a cart: confession, contrition, penance, then absolution. God is landing loving blows on his child, that's all; knocking self out of Trian.

Is this how the rowan felt as the hatchet blows rained down on her?

Pain brings wisdom, Trian reminds himself. The longer he stands here, the closer he'll come to being one with the fish, one with the rocks, one with the sea itself—with all that God's made. He can't feel his limbs. Water in his ears, his nose, his throat; he spits and struggles upright. His hair's loose, red weed floating around his face.

Hours.

Trian dozes and dreams that he's become a featherlight copy of himself, like that kittiwake he found after the storm—that his body has shed all its awkward weight and survives only as pure line.

Cormac watches from the cliffs, and keeps watching, even though all he can make out is a blurred shape in the surf.

He mustn't go down to the shore; he mustn't intrude on this awful privacy. If he hauls Trian out of the water, he knows the young monk will only shake him off and wade back in to begin his penance all over again.

No one could accuse Cormac of being soft.

He's seen men writhe in a tangle of their own guts on the battlefield. But he finds he can't stomach this, somehow. Is it maybe because of what he knows—what he saw when he was nursing Trian?

That shouldn't make any difference. So what if the young man's oddly made?

Or part girl, even. Don't women often bear what would break their mates? Cormac's known several who've died with babies halfway out.

Besides, full male or female or somewhere in between, Trian is made of strong stuff. Cormac thinks of the hero Cú Chulainn, with his fourteen sharp fingers and toes and burning pupils; the fierce beauty of his strangeness.

Then again, Trian's been so ill. So close to death from those bad mussels, not long ago.

Still, if he came through that trial, this seapunishment won't kill him, surely?

The shape in the water staggers, lurches.

No, Cormac can't watch in silence any longer; can't stand by. What's choking him is the injustice. Trian's done no harm. For the Prior to lose his temper so savagely and set Trian to use his own blood to replace the red ink dropped by mistake...and then to send him to stand up to his neck in the cold sea all day for a drawing no bigger than his thumb-tip...It's a kind of madness, it seems to Cormac. The man has to be stopped.

He hurries up to the Plateau, soles slipping on the scree. He finds the Prior on his knees by the damaged high cross, murmuring in prayer. He musters all his nerve to interrupt.

'Father.'

The Prior turns his head stiffly.

Cormac tries a soft approach. 'I'm sure Brother Trian's truly sorry for his errors. Can't you forgive him, as God forgives us for His son's sake?'

'Gladly—'

His heart lifts to hear it.

'—once he has made restitution.'

'But Father...' He wavers. Grasps at words. 'Trian's an odd one, but he wants only to please you, and please our Lord. He's not like other young men.'

'How is he not?'

Cormac's desperate. It's a grave matter to tell a secret. And such a secret. But what else can he try? How else can he shake their master out of his hard-hearted certainties? 'There's something about him.'

The Prior snorts. 'What something?'

'A burden. Or—no, more of a mystery.'

'Brother, spit it out.'

Cormac gnaws his lip. He can't think what else to do.

The Prior demands, 'What *mystery*?'

After all, they're all three bound together on this rock for life. Sooner or later, there'll be no more secrets. Hadn't Cormac better risk telling it in his own words now than waiting till the Prior happens to glimpse it for himself?

Faltering, he does his best to describe as much as he knows; uses all his eloquence to make the Prior grasp the uniqueness of Brother Trian.

The Prior's ash-grey eyes reveal nothing. But he says, 'Fetch him out of the water, then.'

'May I?'

'Right this minute.'

As Cormac picks his way down the cliff, grabbing at the ropes, his heart's hammering so hard he forgets to be afraid of the steep descent, the rolling pebbles. Relief and dread wrestle in his chest. Has he managed to persuade their master to be merciful?

'Brother?' he calls, approaching the cove.

Nothing.

'Trian!'

Belatedly the waterlogged figure twitches in the surf, staggers a little, lifts his head.

'You're to come out.'

Trian lifts his red-rimmed eyes.

'Your penance is finished,' Cormac tells him, though the Prior didn't say that. Suddenly Cormac's afraid of what he's done. Is he a blundering tale-bearer? Has he only made things worse?

Trian crawls out of the water, skin bluish with cold, as if he can't feel his feet.

Cormac wishes he'd thought to bring him a dry robe, or a cloak. He leads the way back up. Twice on the way up he waits to catch his own breath, leaning on the rock face. The second time, Trian comes up behind him. The young monk has a better colour now, even though he's still soaked, and he's moving rather faster too.

By the unfinished chapel, Artt readies himself. He's trying to fathom how his dream of half a year ago could have led him so wrong.

Hearing footsteps, his head snaps up. He strides to meet the monks. 'Brother Trian.' He bends down and hauls up the wet robe.

But Trian goes scarlet and pulls away.

'Let down your braies,' Artt orders him.

His arms clamp to his sides. 'I was taught to be modest. Never to let—'

'What I teach is obedience,' Artt growls. 'Bare yourself.'

Cormac hangs back, his face contorted with worry.

Trian stands very still.

Artt prepares to meet a refusal; tightens his fists.

The young monk hoists his robe, undoes his braies, and lowers them.

Artt bends to stare. He's never seen one of these botches that Pliny calls *androgyni*. Not a true male, made in God's image, nor a true female, shaped to bear young. Neither fish nor fowl. It turns his stomach. 'Cover yourself up.'

Trian scrambles to dress.

'Brother—no, I can't call you that anymore,' Artt corrects himself, 'as you're no monk. Unless it's a whole man who vows chastity, the sacrifice is void.'

'I didn't…' Trian gasps: 'I don't know exactly what I am.'

A weed in the flax, that's what; a pebble in the grain; rot in the fruit. It's all quite clear to Artt.

Cormac sputters: 'It can't be the lad's fault, Father. Who but God made him this way?'

Artt speaks as though from a great height. 'Perhaps his mother erred gravely, and the infant was marred as a consequence.' He turns back to Trian: 'Or it could be a mark of some weakness of spirit of your own.'

Trian's face has fallen in on itself.

'Ah, no. Would you look at my hands, for instance?' Cormac spreads them to display the swollen knobs and pearly cysts. 'Misshapen by any measure, but they do their work. How's Brother Trian any different?'

'This case is not alike,' Artt tells him. 'Remember the Scripture: *Male and female he made them.*'

'What if...' Cormac is flailing. 'Could that line include some who are male *and* female, both in one? Mixed, somehow—is that beyond the bounds of possibility?'

This commoner, who's spent most of his life in heathen ignorance, daring to debate theology! Putting his finger in Cormac's wrinkled face, Artt warns, 'That's heresy.'

The old monk astonishes him by persisting. 'His parents must have known he couldn't marry—must have given him to the Church for a safe harbour.'

Artt wheels around, pointing at Trian. 'Then it was a plot. You entered the monastery by stealth, like a thief in the night.'

Barely audible: 'I was only thirteen.'

'And these half-dozen years since, why did

you never own up, even in private Confession? Why keep it from me, your master and soul-friend, this last half year?'

Tears drop like jewels from Trian's jaw.

Artt must have courage enough to banish all monsters. He quotes, '*Who may live on your holy mountain? Only he who walks uprightly.*' He looks at Cormac. 'We can no longer have him—her—this creature—in our fellowship.'

Trian bends over as if he's been punched.

Artt pronounces sentence: 'You must leave us.'

Silence, except for the stir of the wind.

'How on earth can Trian leave us?' Cormac demands.

Artt knows what God requires, but not the details. His mind's whirling. He takes out his knife and sharpens it on the little whetstone from his pouch.

Cormac lets out a moan at the sight of the blade.

The rattleheaded fool must think Artt's about to do some butchery. But Trian doesn't quiver. Does he too believe the knife is for his throat, Artt wonders? Whatever else he is, he's brave. Artt moves close enough to put the blade to Trian's neck, and cuts through the cord until it's weak enough to sever with a tug of his hand. The wooden Greek cross comes away, and he shoves it into his pocket. 'I release you from the vows you had no right to take.'

He can't confiscate the robe, as they have no other clothes. How to remove the tonsure? Artt starts scraping at Trian's skull, to obscure the outlines of the holy triangle. The bare patch widens under his blade; pink-grey scalp spreads like a puddle around the red-brown triangle of skin tanned by the summer. He finds that nothing can erase the mark. As he works, he prays for further instruction. Should he put Trian out to sea in the boat? He's heard of criminals being set adrift that way. But that might amount to murder. What if Artt gave him an oar?

He wipes hair off his knife now, and sheathes it. 'I expel you from our brotherhood.'

'How can he not be one of us,' Cormac wails, 'when we all have to share this Great Skellig?'

Trian still doesn't say a word.

Artt finds he's come to a decision. 'The person will live out his days here, but apart.'

'How, *apart*?' Cormac asks. 'Like a slave or a prisoner, you mean?'

He shakes his head. 'Separately.'

'Eating apart? Sleeping alone? You wouldn't do that to a dog.'

'Brother Cormac,' Artt says, very low, 'hold your tongue.'

Trian finds himself left behind on the Plateau. Salt has dried in stiff tracks down his face, and his cheeks have cooled. Beyond shame, now, it seems. Even beyond grief. He's weak as water; he remembers he hasn't eaten since dawn. He sits down on the rock. He feels very old. There's a psalm he's trying to recall. *For you are God, my only safe haven. Why have you cast me off?*

The Prior is approaching with a bulging sack.

Trian looks up. He doesn't have it in him to kneel, or even rise.

'I've packed you a share of everything we own.' The man's tone is punctilious. 'Food, salt, one of the waterskins, some tools, everything needful.'

The Prior's justifying himself to God. 'Please, Father,' Trian says. 'Any punishment but this.'

His master—his former master—sets down the sack. 'Choose some part of the island for your own.' Then he makes a cross on the air with the bell. For a moment Trian mistakes it for a blessing, till he sees the Prior's used his left hand. The cursing hand.

Artt goes to find the holy chest in the hut, and hangs his white stole around his neck. Outside, he rings the bell, and keeps ringing it until his one recalcitrant monk comes.

Cormac's eyes are puffed with weeping, as if he's lost a child of his flesh.

'I mean to offer a Mass of special intention, now, to rededicate us,' Artt tells him. Adding, for clarity, 'The two of us.'

But Cormac grabs him by the arm. 'I've prayed about it, Father. This banishment is both cruel and stupid. You call this *fellowship*?'

Artt yanks away. 'You misjudge me, Brother. I have no malice in my heart.' And how does the old man dare to judge him? 'I do only what God bids. As must we all.'

Cormac steps back. 'Then I throw in my lot with Trian.'

Artt stares. 'With the freak? This is revolt.'

The word doesn't seem to shake Cormac.

'Must I remind you that the vows you took bound you to me forever?'

'Then release me.'

Artt shakes his head. 'I cannot. You're the same man you were that day on the river-bank.'

Cormac's mouth works. 'I didn't know I was swearing fealty to a lunatic.'

For a moment Artt can't catch his breath.

'I see now you won't rest till you've made this island a hell on earth,' Cormac says. 'I release myself from my vows.'

'That's not possible. You would be an apostate—a foul deserter.'

He roars, 'I'm not your man, but Christ's!'

Artt breaks away, striding towards the unfinished chapel—his church to come, which rises so clear and perfect in his mind's eye, dominating the island with its twisted wooden cross, ruling over the whole ocean. He steps through the entrance and stands in the unroofed centre. Closing his eyes, he stands very still; makes an offering of himself.

Trian is up on the South Peak, lying on the narrow spar that pierces the abyss. The eagles cry overhead. What's Trian now? A ghost wandering between life and death, earth and heaven, belonging nowhere.

All this fuss. Such a small part of his flesh, what is or isn't between his legs. Not spirit but matter, a little bit of matter, so why must it matter so much?

Trian inches forward on the spur till the stone runs out. Moving like a snake, the creature cursed *above all other animals, to crawl on his belly, and eat dust, all the days of his life*. Trian wouldn't jump, he'd never jump, because then the devil would win his soul. But he finds himself wondering, as he hangs his aching head over the gritty end of the spar, if he were to tumble, seized by that invisible power that makes all things in this world plummet, would God see, God who watches the fall of every sparrow? Would he understand that it was none of Trian's doing? Might Trian's soul escape judgement and float free as his body sank under the waves?

No. The knowledge is a yoke dropped on his shoulders. Life is the weightiest of gifts, and there's no giving it back till the end.

Trian starts edging backwards along the spar.

How to live apart, though, as an outcast? To haunt the edge of their monastery, hiding himself. Can Trian hollow out a little rain-hole up here on the South Peak, for water, or will he have to spend his days skulking around the Plateau so he can steal from the cistern without encountering the men who used to call him brother?

He staggers to his feet. He drifts, he climbs, not really seeing, only covering this shrunken territory. At one point his foot slips, throwing him down, and he clutches the ground as if it's precious to him. As if all he wants is not to fall and be killed. Because even this unbearable life is still sweet to him.

Trian's lost track of the time now. He's back at the eastern end of the island without having found anywhere to hide. He sways, looking out at the Lesser Skellig, which like its greater sister has been deserted by almost all its summer birds. Spots appear in his vision and he rubs his eyes to erase them. Two miles away, at most: on a calm day like this, might Trian just be able to swim that far? An absurd idea, but he can't think of another. Even with this wretched sack of necessities tied over one shoulder, dragging him down? Still, it would be worth a try. He'd be truly *apart* then; islanded, isolate. A permanent exile from human company, from human speech. If Trian were to live alone on the Lesser Skellig, waiting for the return of the spring flocks, would he turn half-bird himself?

The vertigo is probably only weakness, he realises. He rummages in the bag for a crock and pulls the stopper out. He pushes his fingers into the thick fat, finds a piece of cooked puffin breast, and wolfs it down.

Cormac is frantic. He's scrambling down to Landing Cove for the second time today, even though the heavy sack he's packed keeps pulling him off balance. He fingers the fissured wall for grip. Every so often he stops to catch a breath and cry out, 'Trian!'

Only a cormorant replies. No glimpse of the young monk anywhere; no trace of his passing.

How did it happen that they came to this place? Was there a different way the currents and breezes could have taken the boat that would have washed them up on another, gentler island, where spring and summer and autumn might have played out differently? Or have the three of them always carried this terrible tale inside themselves?

Down at the water, the boat lies inverted on rocks surf-spittled and slimed green. Cormac bends his shaking legs and crouches beside its shell. He won't give way to despair. He has to find Trian. This island's become a fortress that the two of them must escape.

What makes him look up? Craning his neck back painfully. The figure on the heights above him is indistinct, but unmistakable. What's Trian doing up there?

'Brother!' Cormac's voice cracks.

Is the young man contemplating the most awful sin? A final casting-off, a cutting of all ties. A single thrust, that's all it would take: those long legs would straighten and spring and Trian would be launched into the glittering sky, his speed searing the air as he dived, legs fused, sack pulling him down, arms winging up. Does he remember the pointed rocks under the foam, ready to smash him? Or will he jump far enough out to drop into open water, sew his body cleanly through its hard blue skin, down down down past weed and fish until he's swallowed up in the eternal chill of the deeps, and the sea seals itself up over his head?

'Trian!' Cormac howls. All he's failed to do, the many ways he's let this young man down...when it's for this, it comes to him now, it's for this that he's been allowed to live so inexplicably long: to save Trian.

All Cormac can do now is bear witness. Hold his breath.

High above him, one hand goes up, waving.

Trian picks his way down to the shore, to where Cormac is straining at the upturned hull. Does the old man mean to cast the boat away, set her adrift?

He goes to help. Between the two of them, they manage to turn over the leathern shell and scrape and bump it down the stones. Both are wet to the thighs already. The hull splashes into the foam. Without mast, yard, or sail, it's as bare as a cupped palm.

Cormac drops a half-full sack and a waterskin into the boat. He picks up two of the three oars and sets them in her too. The rope tethering her to a spear of rock slants stiffly. He throws one leg over the side and clambers in.

In misery, Trian asks, 'You're leaving?'

Cormac holds out two hands. 'Not without you.'

Trian twists away with a kind of shyness. The boat rocks between them. He keeps his eyes on the cove's rock walls, their fault lines, the incomprehensible words they spell out.

'What's there to keep you here?' Cormac asks.

My vows. They're broken, but he still feels them like invisible ropes. They've been broken for him, he reminds himself. Trian's cross has been torn off his neck, his tonsure erased, the very name of *monk* stripped away. The only master he knows has disowned him.

Cormac pleads: 'Get in. We may have no sail, but we can row.'

Trian holds onto the gunnel. To set out once more, banished from his only home...

He turns the question over in his mind. Can he let Cormac set off alone, as solitary as a drop of rain on a curling leaf? This man who—Trian knows it now—has been the truest of fathers?

He asks confusedly, 'Would you be our leader?'

The old monk throws up his hands to ward that off. 'You and I will go in true fellowship.'

'Go where, though?' Where on earth can they take refuge?

'We're God's children,' Cormac tells him. 'I suppose we'll end up wherever his breath blows us.'

The boat's tugging at her leash. The tide's on the turn.

Trian takes that as a sign, for lack of any other. He lays his own sack of supplies and tools beside Cormac's. He wades over and unhitches the rope, gathering it into a coil. He gets over the side. Taking up his oar, he shoves them off the rock.

From his high perch, Artt watches the tiny vessel move out of the bay, the pair of sinners rowing. Thieves, turncoats, demons in human form...

And the Lord said, I will wipe man from the face of the earth, and the beasts and the creeping things and the birds, for I repent I ever made them.

Then the fury is over; Artt finds it's blown right through him. They're gone, the two of them, so what do they matter? Unworthy from the start, always chafing against his rule. Clearly Artt misunderstood his dream: the two monks were like the boat or its baggage, nothing more than the means of his pilgrimage.

Well, he need be nobody's Prior anymore. His bonds are broken. No more obligation to teach, guide, direct, and chasten. No human babble to clog up his ears. Artt has this whole island to himself and it's his alone. The steep land will be his pristine page and he'll write on it with every step, every prayer, every breath. A bastion of faith, a sentry post where he will man the outer frontier of Christendom: oh, such a place it'll be now! No one and nothing to bar his way to heaven.

AUTHOR'S NOTE

Off the coast of County Kerry in the south-west of Ireland, two jagged islands rear up. The larger has been called Skellig Michael since sometime before 1044. The first record of monks living there can be found in a compilation of stories of saints written down several centuries earlier, *The Martyrology of Tallaght* (c. 790–830). Archeological evidence of human presence there survives from about a century before that. Tradition holds that the monastery was founded even earlier, around the year 600, at a time when clusters of Irish monks were retreating to remote places, so that's when I've set my entirely fictional story of a first landing party.

Out of the more than two dozen Early Christian monastic sites known in Ireland, this was the most isolated (from the Latin *insulatus*, 'made into an island'). The settlement stayed small, likely never growing to more than seven drystone cells on Skellig Michael and a tiny oratory on Little Skellig. Its monks (more pragmatic than my invented characters) seem to have survived over the long term by keeping sheep, goats, and pigs, and trading with larger communities for firewood, grain, and wine. They may have retreated for winters to the mainland at Ballinskelligs, and in the twelfth or thirteenth century they moved their base there, keeping up the island buildings for use only by hermits and pilgrims.

A UNESCO World Heritage site since 1996, Skellig Michael, like so many other secluded, sacred places, is now at risk from over-tourism. The island has been a magnet for *Star Wars* fans since its use in 2014–15 as the location of Luke Skywalker's hideaway in *The Force Awakens* and *The Last Jedi*. The monastic ruins face another threat at human hands, too—the increase in extreme weather consequent on the climate crisis.

My treasured friends Margaret Lonergan and Susan Coughlan, thanks so much for sparking this novel by bringing me and mine along on a boat trip around the Skelligs in July 2016. Almost four years on, I had researched and planned *Haven* and had managed to secure a booking for a landing on Skellig Michael...when the island was closed due to what the monks would have taken in their stride as the latest pestilence to plague humankind. So I've never been there, except in spirit and imagination—the one form of travel that can't be forbidden.

In writing *Haven* during the on-and-off COVID-19 shutdowns, I've drawn gratefully on the work of too many historians to name. I've guessed when I had to. We know of no manuscripts produced on Skellig Michael, for instance, but copying was a core part of the mission of early Irish monasteries. In the archeological record there's no evidence that the monks ate great auks, but it struck me as likely, given that those huge flightless birds were a mainstay of North Atlantic coastal communities till they were hunted into extinction over the centuries between about 1500 and 1850.

Richard Manning, many thanks for survival tips. My beloved father-in-law, David Roulston, caught most of my boat-related errors. One of my monks is named in homage to Irish booklover and publicist extraordinaire, Cormac Kinsella.

Finally, *Haven* is dedicated to my very

dear friends Anne Schuurman and Zoë Sinel, a medievalist and legal scholar respectively, who've been backers of this project from the first day I mentioned it. May all books have such champions.

ABOUT THE AUTHOR

Born in Dublin in 1969 and now living in Canada, Emma Donoghue writes fiction (novels and short stories, contemporary and historical, most recently *The Pull of the Stars*), as well as drama for screen and stage. *Room* was a *New York Times* Best Book of 2010 and a finalist for the Man Booker, Commonwealth, and Orange Prizes, selling between two and three million copies in forty languages. Donoghue was nominated for an Academy Award for her 2015 adaptation starring Brie Larson. She cowrote the screenplay for the film of her 2016 novel, *The Wonder,* starring Florence Pugh, coming from Netflix in 2022. For more information, visit emmadonoghue.com.